Death on Lovers Lane

Crystal Allison Gore

Copyright © 2023 Crystal Allison Gore

All rights reserved.

DEDICATION

I'd like to dedicate this book to my friends who encourage me in my writing and let me talk their ears off about my latest projects (in no particular order): Sarah Wiese, Emily Terrebonne, Will Marks, Amber Leible. And to my other Dallas friends who help lend to the story, thank you for letting me borrow from your experiences.

Cover Created by:

Matt Everton

Welcome home Marigold Lee Bryant.

Chapter 1

"KTX5 Oldies! It's a sweaty ninety-eight degrees outside in Dallas, so let us play you some Ninety-Eight Degrees."

I flicked the radio off as I watched for my exit. I tuned my arrival into silence; I wasn't sure about being back. It was too soon after everything. Too many memories. But I was out of options.

Donning sunglasses, with the car's visor down, I squinted against the sun's glare to make my turn onto Lovers Lane.

Familiar old addresses greeted me from their white chalked outlines.

12015.

12017.

12019- My old house, a large two-floor colonial with dormer windows poking through the roof, teasing the viewer there was a third level. My heart lurched.

It lurched again as I noticed they painted the eves a garish red. "New money sins," my mother would say whenever I reported back. I didn't want to think of what they'd done to the inside.

My fingers gripped the leather steering wheel, forcing me straight, fighting the natural inclination to turn onto that narrow drive and past the rose bushes my father planted.

But I drove on.

1221, 1223, 1225

1227- My fingers relaxed their grip and allowed the turn. This house was another colonial, slightly larger where the dormer windows were real, and a wide front porch beckoned. The driveway was old red brick, matching the house, and winded deep into the property. I stopped right in front of the garage and looked up at the guest house perched under another set of dormers. My new home.

A bittersweet downgrade.

It would be rude to sneak on up, even though I already had the keys. I was back in the South, now, where manners and sweet tea reined, and I was still my mother's daughter.

One leg reluctantly slunk from the car. Then the other. I breathed in the hot, muggy, pollinated air and allowed the humidity to twist my blonde hair into frizzy curls. Essentially, it was home. Home enough.

The honeysuckles still lined the front porch, the same set of rocking chairs sat next to the entry door. They freshly painted the eves a muted, pearlescent white. Old money.

Wood planks creaked beneath my feet, announcing my arrival before I could ring the bell.

The heavy wood door swung open.

"Marigold! You look even prettier in person!"

I reeled back a step, not meaning to. There was just so, so much.

The woman before me was a shiny, buxom blonde squeezed into a pink velour track suit with an iced coffee in one hand and a white fluffy dog tucked underneath the other.

"Why, you're just as everyone described!" she said, and the dog added an approving bark. "Poe," she introduced the pup.

"It's nice to meet you," I said, hopefully before my long pause became rude, "And Poe, too. He's beautiful. Very-er-very fluffy."

"She."

"Of course."

Regret kicked in. I should have gone up to the guest house and rested, decompressed. It had been a long drive, and I felt like I still smelled like stale coffee and Fritos.

"Well, come on in. I'd love to get acquainted. Lemonade?" she winked. "And don't think I won't add some liquor!"

Half of that sounded good. The alcohol part.

"Sure, I'd love to."

I mean, I had to.

They trapped me.

Via a woman with an overwrought perm.

But I was the guest in need of help, the recipient of her charity, and thus, at her beck and call for social niceties. For she could have easily said no. She could have not wanted the intrusion of my stay and have been totally in the right. Now that I was here, I would have to-I gulped as I followed her in and sat at the kitchen island- I would have to suck up. Get her to like me. So I could cash in on that "she can stay as long as she needs" ticket. Because I had nowhere else to go.

That was the thick of it.

The red-eyed family, they'd built a better life than I.

The woman pouring my drink with that four-carat ring on her finger? She won the game of life.

Me? I'd gotten far, then Chutes & Ladder-ed my way to the bottom.

"So, what brings you here?" She slid over my drink and took a sip of hers. "I mean, I know bits and pieces. But it's always best from the source."

A series of poor decisions?

"An overpriced Beamer from my Dad," and then I flinched. That was a strong pour, perhaps truly befriending this woman was a wise course of action after all. "Sorry. The truth is, the job ended with nothing else coming up. It's all a sensitive subject. But I've got leads here," I shrugged, "So prospects look good." That was as much as I could offer. I was curious at what other bits and pieces she heard. My words were the official family cover story.

"Well, the guest house is fixed up. We renovated it last year. You'll be comfortable. As long as you need. Okay? Find the right job. Not just a job. Not on account of us. Food, dinners out, I don't think you'll have any expenses."

Was she the nicest person ever?

I felt bad now for not bringing her some sort of offering, like a fruit basket. All I could offer her was the storm cloud that enjoyed following me. I couldn't do that to her.

"Thank you, Emma. Your lemonade is delicious."

She poured us another round.

"It's nice to share it with someone," she admitted, her heavy-hooped earrings bobbling along with her movements. "I miss my sisters, Rose and Lauren. We'd sit around kitchen drinking this, catching up. I hope you'll get to meet them while you're here."

"So you mean in this giant house? Feet don't come running down the stairs at the pop of a bottle? Clearly the kids were raised wrong."

The kids were actually full-grown, moved-out adults.

Emma laughed, "Right? Well, the hubs is always working and so is Jake, if he's here. Amy doesn't like me much."

"Evil stepmother syndrome?"

"Fourth evil stepmother."

I'd forgotten how many weddings of Mr. Jameson's that I've attended. I'd skipped, I'm guessing, what would have been the last two.

"Ouch."

"Imagine she's like 'why bother' to get to know me. But I'm here to stay."

I raised an eyebrow.

"Oh, honey," she winked, "I'm here to stay. And so are you. The pre-nup's ironclad."

Huh. There was more to Wife Number Four than all that pink velour.

I raised my drink. "Cheers to that."

Chapter 2

While we imbibed, the gardener and maid unloaded my car and trekked everything up to the guest suite. While most of my belongings were in storage, I crammed that sedan full of everything I could bring with me. Pretty sure I looked like a hoarder on a cross-country road trip.

I wandered into the bathroom, leaned over the sink, and splashed water on my face. Being back was weird. It was like stepping into a heavily edited old photo album. Some people cropped out, some added in, and most retouched. It was the same, but still incredibly different. This guest house above the garage for instance. I used to come up here and play video games with my brother and his best friend, Jake, in the 90s. Every afternoon we'd hide out here amongst the yellow sponge painted walls with daffodil paper trim until our mom called, summoning us home to do our homework. Jake was lucky, Pam (his stepmom at the time) never cared. He could stay up late and play, filling out his homework answers from my brother's papers during lunch the next day. They were a grade above me.

The suite now, though, was clean and modern in that cold, corporate way. My kitchen felt like a break room- a very nice breakroom- that belonged in a corporate high-rise. I wished for that familiar yellow daffodil trim. As if something could stay the same for me.

I splashed more water on my face and applied a fresh coat of makeup and a good dousing of deodorant. Make myself presentable instead of pitiable.

Dinner tonight, a homecoming party for me, was the last thing I wanted. I wanted to slide back into town, slip between the locals like a ghost. Pop in and say "boo" to just a few.

Instead, the spotlight would shine on me. On poor Marigold, who lost her job and her man. Who had to come back home and stay with family friends. Shelley, my best friend, loved her parties, and my arrival was a grand reason to have one.

One more swipe of lip gloss.

A pucker and a blot.

I got this. I could do this.

They were my friends.

"Why do you run from the people that love you?" my ex once said.

Because if they knew me…

No. Do not think like that. I pushed away those sorts of thoughts as I ran anti-frizz serum through my hair. After dinner, I'd get more vodka with my hostess. Get to know her a bit better. That thought would get me through the evening.

… They would run.

Shelley took my coat and hung it up, quick with getting a hand on my shoulder and steering me towards the dining room. I was a flight risk; we both knew it. I'd rather be anywhere else, and my bed and my pajamas were only a few miles away. I *could* run. Leave my car in the drive and face the shame tomorrow. She tightened her grip and added another hand to hold my arm.

"I really am glad you made it. Marigold, the whole gang? How long has it been?"

One year. Four days.

The last time? The audio clip lived in my mind and played itself whenever other volumes were low. When I was in a bath relaxing. Long drives across the states with nothing but grass and cows. At work, waiting for files to load.

"Marigold... I think our relationship has run its course. Don't you? You see, I think I've fallen for someone else. You'd like Megan."

The humiliation burned.

I swallowed and pushed my thoughts to mute and managed a smile. "Shells, I'm happy to see you. I'm sorry I let it be so long. I had to get away. I had to…" Run away.

"I know," she dropped her voice, "But you can't run forever."

So it would seem, as fate betrayed me once again.

We stepped into the formal dining room, a wood floored, white chair-railed sort of place. Made to make one feel warm and cozy. At least it tried.

The cheerful hum of chatter stilled, and all eyes locked on me.

And then at him.

And then back at me.

Shelley squeezed my arm once again and ushered me inward. Bright smiled and bubbly, she ignored the shocked stares and said, "Hey everyone, it's Marigold! She's back in town."

"Marigold," he said, the only *he* in the room that mattered, "It's good to see you. You look great." To those that knew him, he sounded genuine, to those that knew him well, as I once had, he was lying.

"Thanks, Theo. Likewise. It's good to see you," I recited.

The collective room sighed in relief. No shouting, no tears, no drama. No. I was a southern belle. They should have counted on that. The rage was properly internalized.

The dinner party went back to their appetizers and Old Fashioneds. The hum of continued conversations filled the room, and I could let out the breath I did not know I held.

"See? Not that bad. Just a moment of uncomfortableness and then from here on…"

"A 'lil taste of Hell. The entire night. Don't sugar coat it Shelley-belly," a deep, and unfortunately familiar, voice came from behind, "Marigold. It's been a minute. You look much better than the last time I saw you."

He was kind enough not to elaborate. Jake Jameson. I knew I'd run into him; he'd be impossible to avoid. I only hoped that he'd stay away, fill his time with work and ignore my arrival. That was too much to ask for.

So there he was. Not working. Handsome as ever. Studying me with his intelligent brown eyes and fluffy Hugh Grant hair. Knowing I was burning with humiliation at seeing him again.

Great.

Shelley served him a poke on the shoulder. "*Jake.*"

He gestured a surrender and passed us by, heading off to pester another unfortunate guest.

"It'll be fun, Marigold," she said, and frowned at my raised eyebrow. "Okay. Or at least in one evening you can get your awkward hellos all out of the way and then continue the rest of your stay in hiding."

"Let's let that be the plan."

Shelley sighed, her shoulders less square, her perfect curly blonde hair failing to bounce, as she acquiesced, "Let's get some alcohol in our system."

"That's another solid plan."

Once again, by the elbow, she led me towards the bar. I was still a flight risk.

Chapter 3

For the last time that night, I pulled into the driveway and slunk out of the car. The house was still lit up, so I assumed wandering in for a night cap would be encouraged. Contrary to my earlier plans for the homecoming party, I did not get wasted. No. I wanted to keep escape optional.

Shelley was right. It was good to see her and the gang again. Not Theo. Seeing him was like having a bad stomachache and reaching for the hot peppers to finish me off. But that was over with, and some vodka lemonade with Mrs. Jameson would be my bottle of Pepcid. I was curious how much she knew about everything in our lives. And I wanted an update on how the family here was doing and on other big Dallas changes.

As I headed towards the house, the side door flung open and out struggled Mr. Jameson, hauling two bags of trash as he muttered under his breath. The garage door clanged open. With all that noise, I should have easily snuck in the front entrance, but he sensed my presence, and stopped his mutterings, for a brief second appearing sheepish.

"So my new neighbor arrives!" he greeted, dropping the trash and coming my way.

"Mr. Jameson, it's been way too long," I said those words too many times tonight, but right now I meant it. He had always been my father's best friend. They were business partners, owners of a law firm together, Jameson-Bryant Law, and they were inseparable. Our families spent nearly every holiday together; he'd become like a second father. The school system accepted his signature on my permission slips.

He wrapped me up in a big hug, my feet lifting off the ground.

"It's Paul, you know that," he clapped me on the back and stepped away, surveying me, "So the prodigal daughter returns."

"So it seems."

"You okay?"

I nodded.

His mouth set in a firm grim line, knowing I wasn't quite telling the truth. How could I be okay? The good thing about second dads, is that they don't press. They were like grandparents.

"Drop by the office tomorrow and I'll take you out to lunch. I expect a full catch-up on what you've been up to."

"Deal. And… and thank you," I wasn't sure how to express my gratitude, "For letting me…"

"Nonsense, Marigold. Family helps out. Whenever, wherever. Just remember that whenever Jake needs bail money one day, okay?"

I laughed. It wasn't a favor ever to be called upon, given that Paul was a wealthy defense lawyer. Jake, now one himself.

Ugh. Jake had probably grown into a good one, too. He was always tall and had this presence and that rich timber of a voice. Seeing him tonight was not good for me either. Jake was off limits for friendship and anything more.

Off limits.

"Deal. I'm going in for a nightcap with Emma. Are you joining?" I needed a drink. I didn't need to dwell on Jake's success. Or Theo's.

He shook his head, "Got a testimony to mull over."

Words I heard from my Dad all too frequently.

"But thank you. I think Emma gets lonely. The folks here haven't welcomed her with open arms yet."

Silently, he need not add "nor ever would they." I knew what people thought of her before asking. Expendable Wife Number Who-Even-Knew. Gold-digger. Wasn't she from Oak Cliff-nudge-before it became gentrified (that bit was from Shelley)?

"I think I'll enjoy hanging out with her. No favor at all."

Paul smiled, "She's different. She's kind. I think that's what scares them off. I don't deserve her."

"Probably not."

"Well, let's keep that our little secret."

What should have been a quip had us both flinch. We had plenty of secrets. Didn't need more.

"Ah, right," he muttered and picked up the trash bags once again, trying not to stew in the newfound awkwardness, "Get inside. And don't forget lunch tomorrow."

"Forget a free surf'n turf? Never."

I gave the front door a knock, but no one answered.

Since Paul was in the garage, Emma was the only one left to greet me. When I didn't hear her footsteps, I felt it natural to push the door open and step inside.

"Emma? Emma, I'm back from the party," I called, rambling in their foyer. It was a grand foyer. Square and stately with dark woods and a wide staircase that shot straight upwards to the second level catwalk. Many times, I'd stood there, kicking off my shoes, throwing my backpack down and calling out for whomever was home.

"Emma?"

While the house was large, it was cavernous and open, and my voice carried, so to not answer… She'd be in the bathroom or somewhere with the door shut.

The idea to go on home flashed through my mind.

I should have called it a night.

But I was…

Lonely.

Not ready to travel up to bed alone.

Seeing Theo again put me in a state of emergency, where all systems were fully instructed to keep running. Run fast, never slow, out run all thoughts. Out run the memories that charged ahead. The torn emotions raging, threatening a tidal wave.

I needed that drink. There wasn't anything in the guest house yet. Even if she couldn't join, I was fine with drinking solo. When Paul came back inside, he could roam the house and find her for me.

"Emma, I'm busting open more of that lemonade."

And maybe some chips. I was craving something simple and salty after all that fancy party food.

"Hope you..." I timed each word with a step toward the kitchen, "Don't..."

"Hope you don't..." I started again, like a broken record, and grasped for the kitchen counter to keep me upright as my knees locked, "Hope you... Hoooo..."

Oh my goodness.

She was dead.

Chapter 4

She was dead.

As in blood pooling, as in…

I reached the sink just in time.

I filled my mouth with sink water and swished and spat and then did what I should have done before. Screamed bloody murder.

Because that's exactly what happened.

That carving knife sticking out of her chest.

Chapter 5

"You've had a shock. But I have to understand everything that happened tonight."

"R-right, of course."

"So... You..." the police officer tried to lead me, unsuccessfully, "How did you enter?"

"Mm?"

The officer's voice was small and tinny, as if at the other end of a tunnel. Like we were playing telephone. Instead, we were sitting side by side on the couch in the formal living room; he had draped a blue blanket over my knees and given me a bottle of water to sip.

"Your full name again. Let's start at the very beginning," he sighed.

"Marigold Lee Bryant."

"And you're from…"

"Here. Dallas."

"Good. Now… How did you enter?"

"The front door."

His face creased in a frown, "Did Mrs. Jameson greet you at the front door?"

"No."

I took a sip.

"No?"

"I stepped in."

"You entered without permission? Was the door unlocked?"

"I… I…" I took another sip of water. Couldn't he go away?

She had looked so… surprised. Her eyes were still wide open. Her hand on her stomach, her mouth wide as if there was once a scream. Did she fight? Call for help?

And Paul and I were outside chatting. Planning lunch.

"It was unlocked?"

"Ohmygoodness, Paul," I covered my face with my hands, "Someone has to tell him."

Please don't be me.

"He's the one who called us," the officer said. I could hear the concern in his voice. I dropped my hands to my lap again and watched my water tumble to the floor.

Oh? He did? He knew?

"Is he okay? Where is he? He can't be okay; his wife was murdered."

"He's with another officer," he said in that calm "I'm dealing with a crazy woman tone," raising my heckles.

But that was good. Anger instead of shock. My head was clearing. Anger always helped me like that.

"Let's focus on what you remember. Not on Paul."

I frowned. I didn't remember Paul calling. I didn't remember him entering the kitchen. It was just me, screaming.

Another sip of water. Glad it hadn't all spilled out.

"Officer," a stern voice from the doorway interrupted, "That's enough for now."

"Who are you to say so? I'll let you know when I'm done."

"She's my client."

I looked up at my savior to offer a thank-you smile but cringed when I saw it was Jake. Though I was in no state to turn down help. When Jake offered his hand, I took it.

"I'm merely trying to figure out what happened."

"Are you okay? Jake asked me, loudly, but then bent and whispered in my ear, "Tell them nothing."

Of course, I would not tell them anything. It prickled me that he felt a reminder was necessary.

"Questioning her while she's in shock. Considerate," Jake said, already guiding me off the couch, "We'll reach out tomorrow for her statement. I'm curious as to anyone to find out what happened. But pressing a shaking witness? Low."

"Miss, now you stay right here, and we will finish."

"He's my lawyer," I interrupted, finally standing squarely on my own, "We'll be in touch." I sounded strong, much stronger than I was. My father's daughter. The first rule of being a Jameson or a Bryant: Never be deposed when not in top shape. There was too much to lose.

"You okay?" Jake asked, after we drove in silence for a while.

"*You* okay? That's your stepmom. I-I just met her," I asked, deflecting. Even though it was warm out, I tried to keep from shivering by clamping my hands between my thighs. But I was okay- at least I think I was. I was getting better. I was the alive one in this situation. I would get better.

Emma would not be.

Jake gritted his teeth, "We weren't close. At all. I'm upset, but... It's like it happened to Dad's best friend. I'm sad for him, for her, but..."

"Not for you?"

"Maybe I'm still processing?" he threw me a glance, "I called your dad. He's catching the first flight out."

I frowned.

"It's always the husband, Marigold," Jake's voice finally broke, "It's always the husband."

My mouth ran dry. No way. No way. Paul was a kind man.

Unless you weren't family, of course. Emma was family. He was well known for being a shark in the business. Willing to dance with line of legality to free a client. But he was a "protect the family" sort of man. When his cases got rough (or if the client was seedy) we even had bodyguards.

"You don't think?" I ventured.

"No."

"Agreed. Totally agreed. Paul's 'Dad Number Two.' I'd trust him with my life."

"Glad you said that."

"Why?"

"Because it's his life in your hands now. You were the last one to see them both."

I gulped. Ah, that's why he saved me from the police. My testimony had to be gold. Complete and coherent. Of course, Jake would already be in lawyer mode. It was the way he was raised. The robot software installed early in his life.

"It's okay to be upset, you know. It's very human to be. This is a lot," I said.

He sighed, not bothering to give me a proper answer. Instead, he continued his download, "Another Senior Associate is with my Dad right now. I figured someone not in the family would be best."

"Of course. Who needs family at a time like this? Have you even told Amy?"

"Someone should get some sleep," he pulled into the driveway, turned off the car, "I'll tell her tomorrow."

Jake's house was a street over from Shelley's. We were back in the M-Streets of Dallas. Where cottage-core enthusiasts could purchase the 1,500 square foot house of their dreams for over a million dollars. Luckily, the homes were far apart and draped in shrubbery, so we had plenty of privacy as we stalled in the driveway.

"Never took you for an M-Street-er."

"Resale value."

"Wake up Amy. Tell your sister."

He unclipped his seat belt and instead of getting out, sunk down in his seat.

"There was so much blood, that took so much hate," his voice nearly a whisper.

I blinked, trying to get the scene out of my mind-as if I could ever forget. I couldn't let myself fall back into shock, talking to Jake was healing. Getting distance from the scene helped. So was reminding myself I hardly knew her, as crass as that seemed. It was my job to be there for the Jameson family, not the other way around.

"Why aren't you telling your sister? Part of your Dad's defense will be him creating a loving family. They need to see a red-eyed sleep-deprived, tear bubbling sibling duo."

Goodness. That was a shameful thing to say. That software came pre-installed in me as well. At least I fought it. I tried to be more human.

"Amy," he winced, "Amy and her fought a lot. A lot a lot. She called Emma a gold-digger at more than one family dinner."

"So you think..."

"What are the odds both my Dad and sister are innocent?"

We paused on my exhale.

Not good, I wanted to say. Not good at all. None of us were purely innocent. We've made plenty of decisions that chipped at our souls. As the daughter of a defense attorney, I learned to never really trust people. Everyone hides their motives. Shoving away their darkness.

So, *could* it have been Paul? Yes.

But no. Just no.

Amy?

Maybe?

If she hired someone?

I closed my eyes and pinched the bridge of my nose; sleep before I started accusing friends. Everyone and everything seemed spookier at night.

"Let's go inside and get some rest," he suggested, and added, "Okay, and some alcohol first. Then we re-convene in the morning."

It was a good plan. Everything would seem clearer after getting some sleep. We silently each drank a glass of whisky.

Well… Almost silently.

"Are we going to talk about…" I let my words fall away and replaced them with alcohol.

He waved his hand, "No. I think we've got enough on our plate."

I agreed. It was less embarrassing this way.

Our drink was more a pouring down medicine than enjoying a nightcap. I borrowed an extra toothbrush and shirt for the night. I'd go back and pack a bag tomorrow. Tonight, I'd just lie low in bed, contemplating a world where I could have drinks with someone and not find them dead on the floor later.

Despite Jake being Jake, I hoped he'd be alive in the morning.

Chapter 6

Okay. So, the party didn't suck, and the mushroom-bacon kabobs were good, even though it spelled of someone trying too hard. In fact, it would have been a grand party if I wasn't so exhausted and wanted to be there. Shelley disappeared on me to do her hostess-ing circles, but as she said, I was amongst friends.

There I was, on the couch, catching up with Amelia, a friend of mine since high school. She was telling me about her date with a guy named Dave- and honestly his name was all I needed to know on how it went down, when Theo and Megan stopped in front of us. Standing there, throwing a shadow over. Holding hands.

As if they needed to rub it in.

As if they needed to say "this is who he chose."

Not you. To be clear.

Not you at all.

I gulped.

"Theo. Megan," Amelia greeted, "Have you tried the Cosmos?"

Megan was all wide smiles, giggles, pink in her ruffly dress (gross), and blown out blonde hair.

"I haven't!" she laughed, "And I aim to try each type of drink served tonight. The Moscow Mules were delightful."

Ah. I've met "Megan" before. Her type. She was on the Junior League to PTA mom step-ford wife track. A likely former sorority girl. I hated that she looked like me. Like a classier doppelgänger.

She was the popular, well-adjusted version of me.

"Then let me lead the way. I think they're almost out," *Amelia jumped from the couch and tried to lead them away. She shot me a look of sympathy when only the pink princess followed. Stranding me with Theo. Who was seriously named Theodore anymore?*

I looked him over and felt that familiar pang compressing my heart.

"I thought I should say hello. Especially since you're staying at Jake's mom's."

He and Jake used to be good friends, throughout childhood, but our breakup and my brother, who used to hang out with them stopped (he moved beyond the Highway 635 circle), and the closeness fizzled away.

"You hang out at his mom's? That's weird," *as a retort it was weak but I cut myself some flack, this was Theo and my brain was boiling on rage.*

How did I ever like this chad?

Why did I think he was "the one"? Theo stood before me like a Ken doll featured in the "Dallas Dude Starter Pack." Seersucker Easter-egg colored shorts. Check. Polo, check. Sun-shades hanging at the collar and thickly gelled helmet hair completing the look. Great tanned calves, though.

BMW keys jingling in his pocket. No mere 3-Series, mind you.

He frowned, revealing his tanned features were about three years from beginning Botox injections, "The same circles. We all end up having lunch at the country club a lot... Now that you're back I don't want things to be awkward. I want to be friends."

I folded my arms across my chest.

"We were never friends, Theo. We met, we dated, we broke up," *I stood, hoping to edge away. Where was Shelley? Seriously, I was not ready for this.*

"I just don't want..."

"You don't want your brunch to be awkward, right? Well, it's going to be," *I dropped my voice so we wouldn't cause a scene,* "I'm going to sit across from you and order my eggs benedict and hash and bottomless mimosas and stare you down."

"Why-why are you so difficult?" *he stammered.*

"Because my parents raised me right," *I paused,* "And there are consequences to cheating. You can always skip brunch."

"Come on, Theo," *Shelley's voice approached,* "You should have known better than to heavy-pet a rottweiler." *She grasped me by the arm and led me away. Saved.*

"I'm sorry I had to play hostess," *she said ducking her head down so only I could hear her whisper,* " I didn't invite him, they just heard through the grapevine. But Band-Aid's off right? Worst is over?"

"Worst is over."

What a naïve statement that was.

"Good. Come on now, we've all missed you. Let's make the rounds this *time-together."*

I nodded, feeling better. It was Marigold and Shelley against the world. Through fickle friends, horrid men, and other natural and unnatural disasters. For maybe a brief flicker, it was good to be home again.

Chapter 7

Amy didn't know.

I shot Jake a look of hope, but he only shrugged his oversized shoulders. A pair of Ray-Bands clouded his expression.

"You said it was an emergency?" she folded her arms across her chest, as if guarding the threshold to her house. "What's wrong? John said he was coming home early. What's going on?"

"Can't you invite your brother in for tea?"

"Where's John?" I asked, talking over Jake.

Her eyes darted back and forth between us.

"John's at a conference," she spoke slowly, watching us as if we were the suspicious ones, "He called last night and told me he was cutting it short and driving in this morning. So, I repeat, what's going on?"

"No one was with you last night?" I asked.

She narrowed her already thin lips. Amy had that fierce 5'4" schoolteacher look, even in pink cotton pajamas. She was short but mighty, her constant morning power walks made her a significant threat to anything under 5'6". Her dark brunette bob cut so crisply that it curled at her ears, framing her ever present pearl studs. Her eyes, narrow and grey were striking and always studying her surroundings. Anyone that saw her would think her to be a teacher or accountant. Maybe a bank teller. The brand was baked into her looks and mannerisms.

"Tell me. Or leave, because-"

"Our step-mom died," Jake interrupted.

"Emma?" Her question was toneless, but she pushed open the door and allowed us inside. "Finally, someone treats me like an adult and tell me what is going on," and led us into the depths of her home.

Jake sat at the breakfast table, so I followed suit; I'd only been to Amy's twice and didn't know the structure of how she received guests. Amy would have a structure.

"So, no one told me. It happened last night, right? John must have found out. Let me fret all night. Goodness," she pulled out a kettle and started making tea, "He had me thinking it was Dad."

"And you didn't call me?"

She turned to glare at her brother.

"No I didn't call. Neither did you. So, it wasn't health, was it?" Amy left the kettle to boil and sat with us, back to crossing her arms across her chest and leaning away from us in her chair-as if she could separate herself from the bad news flowing her way. She was the sibling from the Jameson clan that was always a little harder to get along with. Amy always had one foot out the door, and wisely so.

She moved out to Flower Mound with her cop husband and into their giant mansion. Not a McMansion. Her home was custom, elegant, sleekly contemporary. White and steel with warm touches of wood and copper. The walls in the breakfast nook displayed how she made her money. Covers of "Sally the Snail" her prolific children's book framed and mounted on the wall. It was always an odd sight, seeing this polished, cold young woman dip her brush into ink and illustrate friendly little garden creatures. It took a while to realize that her hard exo-skeleton was only for show.

She hid the softness within.

The softness that demanded justice and security- so she married an eagle scout police officer and hid herself away in suburbia and PTO meetings for her two kids. A stark contrast from her own family.

But what else was she hiding? She had to be shrewd to step away fully from our family business. Did Emma somehow pose a threat to Amy's carefully crafted lifestyle?

She wasn't acting sad-at all. And there was the lack of an alibi…

"If it was John sort of news…" Amy sighed, "It was legal… And maybe part of me wasn't excited to find out. Emma died. How?"

Finally, she looked sad, tired. As if the mental circles to get there wore her out.

"Amy, she was murdered," I said, doing the hard part for Jake.

To her credit, Amy's eyebrows flew up, but then she said, "Murder? I always thought it would be a butchered boob job. Or drugs."

Jake covered his face with a groan, broadcasting his thoughts to me. I agreed with him-this wasn't going well-at all. But that's what happens when robot children turn into robot adults. Her kids hadn't run away yet, nor her husband, thus I knew somewhere in there was warmth. Wherever "Sally Snail" lived.

On the outside though, she just blinked, watched me, and tucked a hair behind her ear.

"She was stabbed. It was ugly and brutal and bloody," I flinched recalling the scene, hoping to draw out her emotion. It certainly drew out that funny feeling in my stomach that I had all night.

"What she's trying to say," Jake said, emerging from hiding in his hands, "Is show some freaking empathy."

"You mean cry?"

"Yes!" he exclaimed.

"Oh."

We sat there in a stand-off till the whistle of the kettle sounded, making me jump. Only me of course.

"Excuse me, sugar?" Amy asked as she got up to serve tea, as if this was a normal morning.

Jake leaned in, "It's like the evil witch from the North or whatever breathed life into her and she took corporal form."

I wanted to agree… but I was the peacekeeper here. We had an objective. Despite how much flack we gave Amy, she was his sister, and a dear friend of mine.

I called out we would, indeed, take sugar with our tea.

"So once more, with feeling," Jake said, "Our stepmom's been murdered. Stabbed."

She sat and served us our chamomile, "Are we concerned a predator is after our family?" she took a sip, "Then thank you for the delayed news. I'm glad the kids are at sleepovers."

I shivered at the chill in her voice. She wasn't wrong, Jake and I both flinched in guilt. Why did we always forget about her kids?

"I think it's more personal. I don't think we're in danger. But… Dad's the number one suspect just by being the spouse."

"Mmm… It's always the spouse. That's why you're here?

Mounting Dad's defense of the happy family?" She shrugged, "I mean, I'm in. I'll cry on the stand if needed for dear 'ol Dad."

"That's great?" I asked/said. I wasn't quite sure how to interpret her coldness. But at least she was on our team.

Jake rose, "Great. I'll be in contact. For now, we'll leave you to process this clearly shocking news."

"Mmm. Well, welcome back Marigold. We should go walking soon."

"Yeah, sounds great," I lied because I knew I'd give in whenever she'd call. I was better at snacking than cardio.

"Welcome back?" I screeched in the car, is your sister a psychopath?

"She's Amy."

We sat there in the driveway, staring ahead.

"I don't think that'll exonerate her," I said, "Oh, your honor, she's Amy."

"She'll need a good amount of coaching before taking the stand."

"She's going to need a personality transfusion! And... and what if it was her? She was totally alone... Bored and left to her own devices on one fateful evening."

"Yeah," he snorted, "Exactly. It wasn't her."

"Huh?"

"Stabbing's emotional. Passionate. Did you see any of that in Amy's demeanor? Has Amy ever been passionate? About anything?"

"Her family? Her drawings?" I shrugged, searching.

He shook his head, "No. If Amy were to carry out a stabbing, she'd hand you the knife and ask you to do it yourself to be more efficient."

"And then put on a pot of tea."

Jake laughed and ran his fingers through his hair, "This is all messed up I should alert her next of kin, and instead I'm mounting a defense." His exhale slouched his shoulders and I could see in his face finally how little sleep he'd gotten. "On any account, thanks for being here. As much as I hate your company."

"Least I can do, since you didn't make me stay overnight there," I shivered, "Totally creepy."

He started up the engine, "Now what I've been dreading. Let's go pay Dad a visit before the cops do."

I checked the clock: 9:07. We had time. Most warrants here were served at 11:00.

"And then after, I need to pack a bag, so I can stay…"

"Yeah, yeah, you can stay."

Nodding a thanks, I rolled my shoulders. They were stiff and achy from stress.

"You okay?" he asked as he frowned.

"Sore. Stress I'm guessing."

I hated being in his debt, but I hated even more the idea of sleeping right near where a woman got murdered.

Were we in danger? If truly we believed Paul and Amy were innocent, then… I gulped. Then Amy was right. Someone could be out there watching us.

Chapter 8

Dad (my real Dad) swept me up in a hug and pat Jake on the back with a proud sounding thump, "Good to see you, kiddo." He arrived at the hotel late last night, taking over the four-bedroom suite the firm often booked for witnesses and their families. There would be the epicenter of operations. He, Paul, and Mitch (the associate officially defending the case) would stay and likely spend twenty-four hours a day going through the defense.

"Your Mom sends her best," Dad said, plopping down on the couch, "You need to make your way to Florida soon you know."

"Soon. Pool-side margs beckon me."

Jake and I settled at the breakfast table and helped ourselves to the breakfast buffet room service delivered. It had that thirty-dollar bacon and eggs taste and goodness. I think I was drooling. Living on my own, I'd forgotten how good their expensive food melted across the tongue. Jake's eyes rolled to the back of his head.

"Those... Pancakes," he moaned.

"Enjoy them... I don't have the appetite," Paul said, making his entrance. He was the one person in the family that had the right physical and emotional reaction to Emma's death.

Jake choked down his bite, coughing, his food syruped in shame. It wasn't much better over here. I let the melon ball I speared roll off my fork and onto the plate as its mate got spat into a napkin.

Red-faced and grimy with tears, made it clear Paul cried all night. The way he sat down into the armchair, stiff and wobbly like a giant, brittle Jenga tower, Paul appeared to be hardly alive himself. The grim reaper paid a visit, yet only whispered in his ear.

That was love. He clearly loved Emma.

"That's an innocent man," Jake whispered, his face washed over with relief, "No one's that good of an actor."

"Never had a doubt, Jake."

Of course, that wasn't entirely true. Now that the blanket of shock had pulled back, I could think clearly.

Paul was an Oscar caliber performer. We've all seen him at trial. Coaching witnesses. Manipulating the truth and making the lie conform to the physical. Paul wrote the book. He guest-lectured, wrote the book, and taught the class.

But now, I believed him because I wanted to. The alternative would be too painful.

"Well, you're hired now that you've eaten the food," Dad said.

"Excuse me?" I was lost.

"We've discussed it. It's how we protect you and keep you informed on the trial," he darted a glance in his dear friend's direction,

"Should there even be one," he looked back at me, "You're too close to the case to be a star witness. We close ranks. Control the narrative. You need a job anyway."

"An interior design job. If you need an office remodel. I'm not joining to be some intern or a paralegal."

"Sign the documents. They're on the banquet behind you."

I gritted my teeth. This was why I left for so long. Why I rarely visited. I was tired of being controlled. Only out of the city was I a free and independent person.

"Just sign them," Jake sighed under his breath, "We both know what happens if you don't."

It wasn't a threat, his face was marked in defeat-as Paul's child, he understood, thoroughly. If I didn't sign, if I didn't help the family in its time of need, I'd be sent away and disgraced. Sent to Florida with the story of a mental breakdown covering their tracks.

Jake was right.

And I wanted to be clued in on the investigation.

"No need to read it over, right Dad? You have my best interests at heart?" That was half sarcasm.

He rolled his eyes, "Standard by the book employment contract.

Nevertheless, I gave it a quick skim-the salary was amazingly generous-more than I ever made, and if felt a bit like charity. But not enough for a bribe. That eased the tension in my shoulders.

"Alright then," I signed my name with a flourish.

I certainly paid for that breakfast. I felt a little cornered, a little manipulated; that contract being all ready. I'd rather be on their team than against. Certainly, safer that way. Shelley was right in calling me a rottweiler- she should have added well trained and will jump on command

42

given a treat. I came from a family of them.

"Excellent. Now," Dad said, pacing the room, "Marigold, let's go into the study and discuss everything you saw. We'll go from there."

Jake squeezed my hand under the table and handed me a croissant, "Fuel." My stomach did a weird little dance, he could be awfully charming and caring, but luckily my brain was in attendance and shot that stream of thought down. His gift was accepted with a mere nod.

Chapter 9

The suite's furniture had clearly been customized for us. Dad sat behind the desk, his elbows on the table and his hands clasped together. He gestured for me to lie down on the couch as he dimmed the lights. My eyes refocused as much as they could, but only outlines and shadows could be seen.

I closed my eyes, drew a deep breath, and clasped folded arms across my chest-hugging a pillow on top as if that would help.

"We need to go to over last night. In detail. I need time estimations," his voice was low and soothing, as if guiding me into meditation, "Remember you are safe here. It's just a memory. Now... You arrived at their house? What was on the radio?"

Dad always cared about what was on the radio. He said it was grounding. Gave you time and place if you could remember the songs playing.

For a moment I bristled, I wanted a bit of Father-Daughter catch-up time. For him to ask how I was. To hear about Mother's gardening club.

Was that selfish?

I knew we had to hasten to make sure no official charges would be brought against Paul. But...

Five minutes. Five minutes would not have hurt.

"Take me back there. Take me to your frame of mind. You're being taped."

"Okay," I paused a bit, closing my eyes and letting myself slip back into last evening. The last place I wanted to be.

"It was around ten-fifteen when I pulled into the driveway-I stayed a polite amount of time before giving the dinner party the slip. Shelley sent me home with a Tupperware of stuffed mushrooms. I didn't really want them. They would reheat spongy, but I couldn't hurt her feelings, so I was stuck with them. I saw Paul right away. He came out of the side door, with a large bag of trash to put in the garage."

"For the record, how do you access the side door from the interior? You've been inside many times."

"Right, it's a door off the back hallway. The kitchen, mud room and back stairwell all feed into it."

"So, the kitchen isn't the only place he could have come from?"

"Definitely not."

"Alright, continue."

"Anyways, my mind was still focused on the party before. I drank little so I could leave early. See, Theo was there. Shelley said she didn't invite him," I bit my lip, "But that just seems not true. The Shelley I knew would never let him cross her threshold. Instead, I got trapped talking to him and she was more less 'oh well.' So, I was kinda perturbed when I got home. I was looking forward to talking with Emma and sharing another drink with her."

"Another?"

"When I first got there..."

Dad held up his hand, "From the very start then."

I gave him the full recap of my arrival, and then began again, "Paul greeted me, we promised to meet for lunch today. He seemed fine, but I realize he was surprised to see me at first. He looked a little annoyed, but I mean no one enjoys taking out the trash."

"What was he wearing?"

"You mean did I think he was covered in blood splatters? No. He was in jeans and a denim button up. I remember because I wanted to make a joke about denim on denim and how the country club wouldn't let him in if they saw that. But I held my tongue. Don't insult the host you're not paying rent to. Life tip."

Dad rolled his eyes, "Don't put yourself in a position where you have to accept charity. Life tip."

I jerked up-anger flowing through, "Done here?"

"Lay back down, Marigold. You know we are not."

Sitting up straighter, only to annoy him, I continued, because I had to; that I knew. I ran through our quick conversation, "... so I gave him a wave as he struggled to throw trash in the bins. There must have been trash already in them. And I headed towards the front door to let myself in."

"Why didn't you wait for him or go in the side door?"

I bit a nail, ashamed, "I like the way the front porch creaks under my feet. Plus I didn't want to help. Not with trash. I was still in my good clothes and holding mushrooms. I gave the -mess- a wide berth. I figured he'd join us inside later anyways."

"And once you got inside?"

"The door was unlocked. I didn't think it odd, it's a safe

neighborhood, and they were still awake."

I told him about calling for her, and then stepping into the kitchen... My mouth ran dry, and I took a sip of water. I told him of finding her body.

"I-I froze. It was like I stumbled into something that wasn't real. I only realized it was when I saw blood, running in a river along the grout lines of the tile. All I could think was 'not again.' And like, I turned and threw up."

"Stop."

I opened my eyes and shook myself till I was out of the scene and back in the hotel room.

Till I could hear only the whirring of the old-school recorder.

"I'm deleting that last part," Dad said, "None of that 'not again.' You saw blood. You threw up. This was your first dead body."

"Right, right," I wrung my hands, "I'm sorry."

"That's why we are doing this," he clicked the "on" button and gestured for me to begin again.

"... So much blood," I paused, "Sorry, I'm still shaken."

"Normal reaction. Go on."

"I-I turned around and threw up. I was lucky the sink was there. And I remember gripping the countertop so hard. As if I would fall too. And I screamed- her eyes were open, glossy, staring at me..."

Paul came flying in, skidding to a stop. His hand over his chest as if to hold his heart in place.

"What-what," he tried for more words, but nothing came out. I could see him mouth her name. It took several tries till her name was brokenly voiced, "Emmie."

I stood there. Frozen. Unsure of what to do. It was like if I took a step, this was real. If I took a step, the future of this story would play out and Emma's fate sealed.

If I stood still, however, maybe she could get up. The undo button could be clicked. No one hit save.

"Did you- did you do this?"

I looked up, Paul was rounding on me, gripping my shoulders so tightly I could already feel the bruising flowering. Rattling my brain as he shook me.

"Is what they say true about you?" he hollered as he yelled in my face, spittle landing on me in fury.

"P-Paul," I pled. I was innocent.

But it was just so much.

The body. The nausea. The shaking.

"That death follows you. That's what they say!" he roared, "And I let you into my home! You killed my wife!"

"I didn't kill- I've never hurt anyone," I cried.

He let me go, pushing off me. His chest heaving violently, as if trying to swallow down all his anger.

My footing failed. Rattled and shaken.

Equilibrium thrown.

I fell to the floor and closed my eyes. If I ended up on the ground... I'd die like her.

The room fell silent. The whirr of the recording tapes stopped long ago. Dad said beforehand going analog meant going stealth. No scraps of saved files in the cloud.

>Rolling my shoulders, I tugged down my top to reveal the bruises.
>
>Bruises from fingers.
>
>I saw the purple splotches in the shower, unsure of the source.

Dad sucked in a breath.

I explained the pain away with reasons like the seat belt, a heavy purse, too tight of bra straps. Something from traveling. Eating more Fritos than vitamins.

But not from Paul's hands.

My mind was going a hundred miles an hour, but I still didn't know what to think. If he could do that to me, could he have... But he never laid a hand on any of us kids or any of his wives.

Dad coughed, and said in a low, slow voice, "When I start recording again, say you saw the body and screamed and fainted because all the blood. That'll fit the evidence. Don't mention alcohol, you drove that night."

"But Dad," I protested. How could he think we could move past this and go on? I expected flames of anger to swallow me up at any moment, but he cringed. He was wringing his own hands, taking a deep breath, trying to stay calm himself.

"Please," he said, "I'll handle it with him. But for your safety, your best course of action is to be a team player. To appear upset for him."

"Yeah. Okay."

He sagged visibly in relief.

Just in case... just in case Paul was the murderer, he didn't have to know we suspected him. Right now, his daughter's life was in trouble- and that was more important than justice for Emma or a defense for Paul. That idea was enough to douse all my flames, and I was instantly glad to have Dad at my side again. We re-recorded my bit and as it clicked off the final time, the tension in the room felt a little calmer.

"Stick with Jake," he said giving me a parting hug, "He needs a friend."

"And you can't watch me twenty-four seven?"

"Something like that."

"Mmm."

I rolled my eyes at his overprotectiveness, but I couldn't help but admit I was glad for it.

Recalling that night gave me chills.

"You watch yourself, too."

"Never stopped."

He gave me an affectionate peck on the cheek with a whispered, "Be careful."

They were right where we left them. Only now Jake was eating the leftover melon balls on my plate.

"I thought they'd go bad," his expression was as sheepish as it could be with a stuffed mouth.

"I suggested to my son that you two start at the country club. My wife spent most of her time there. And if you could find Poe? Take her to the kennel for boarding or look after him?"

"Her." I corrected.

Paul waved his hand, "The dog was hers. We never bonded. But it should be looked after."

"We'll look after it."

"I'll find a kennel," Jake said, at the same time as my response. Our eyes met, challenging.

We would not let a sad puppy suffer alone.

"Dogs mourn just like people. She should be with family," I implored, feeling a sudden kinship with the pup.

"My house is not dog friendly," he turned to his dad, "We'll deal with it. Are you okay here? Can we bring you anything?"

"No," Paul said, "You kids get out of here. We'll keep you updated," he paused, seeming genuine, "And both of you.... Sincerely. Thank you."

Dad nodded, his hands in his pockets, leaning against the door frame. I knew if he could talk freely, he'd say leave. Leave and get that dog. Even if it's small, it's yappy, and that's something.

Chapter 10

I tugged down the shoulder of my blouse and leaned towards him, "Jake, Jake, look."

If there was anyone in this world to trust, it was him. We'd already failed each other so many times, it could only be up from here.

"What?" he dragged his eyes from the car's info-tainment screen, to my shoulder, and then they lit up.

"I mean, *oh*. Here?" he smiled, "Naughty."

"For goodness sakes Jake! I'm not propositioning you. Look- bruises." They'd faded by now, but still lightly bloomed across my skin.

He scrunched up his face and looked closer, "What did you do?"

"It's what I remembered. In the study, when I was with Dad."

I went through my entire revelation with him, watching his face fall and his body squirm. The intent wasn't to make him feel bad, but only to ensure he was working with the whole truth. Roles reversed; I'd want to know. Right? If there was another reason to suspect my father, I'd need to know. To defend him better.

Jake's face contorted in a way anyone else would think he was struggling to digest dinner.

I wished he would say something. Though silence was better than hearing "He couldn't have done that" or another set of words along those lines. Digesting meant he accepted he had to swallow the uncomfortable truth.

Finally, he spoke, "He's never... never done something like that to you or Amy right? Or any of his wives? It's not something that has been hidden from me, right?"

That was one of my own first thoughts.

"First time for me. I think that's why I'm shocked. Before that it's been only kindness and respect from him. But as for the others... Nothing I know of. But they could be keeping their own secrets. Or it could be a one-time high stress thing."

He looked green and opened the car door for more air.

"I keep thinking, 'when there's smoke, there's fire.' There would be signs right?" Jake wiped the sweat from his forehead.

"Yes. I mean I think so. I think there'd be other signs," I gave him a comforting shoulder rub, "Regardless of the answer, you've been a good son. A good brother and friend."

Shooting me a grateful look and closing the car door he asked, "Well, what does it mean for the investigation? What does it mean for you?"

"It means I don't want to be left in the same room alone with him,"

I admitted, hating my own words, "But I acknowledge shaking me that hard is a far cry from murder. And that he wasn't in his right mind, he just saw his wife on the ground. Yet I can't help but think, what if he was in a terrible state of mind, what if they fought? What if he was caught in a blur of rage or passion?" I paused, "Goodness this car is feeling claustrophobic," I turned the AC down, "I'm after the truth now," I faced Jake eye to eye, "No more he's innocent because he's Paul."

"And if he's guilty?"

That was the rub here, wasn't it? The answer didn't matter. The outcome would be the same. Emma would never get justice. Jake wasn't bullying me with the question. His face read of pain. He wanted me to weigh all the consequences of my actions.

Sadly, for Emma, I was no revolutionary. I wasn't strong enough. Neither were Jake or Amy. Yes, I felt guilty, but I swallowed it down with a pill of "I just met her." My responsibility was towards me and my family, and I'd take care of Poe.

I sighed, defeated, "We all took that oath. The truth will just be for us. Anything less would be mutually assured destruction."

Jake should have looked relieved, but he pinched the bridge of his nose and closed his eyes, "After this," he began, "We'll get away. Disappear and spend our days stretching out on sunny beaches."

"I think I've heard those words before," my gaze dropped from his and onto my clasped hands on my lap.

"I'll make good on it, Marigold."

"Let's focus on getting to the country club."

"I'll make good on it this time. I promise."

We drove the rest of the way in silence.

My mood instantly lifted as soon as we passed through the iron gates of the "Highland Park Diamond Waters Country Club." If confronted, I'd never admit to being the country club sort of girl. Never. But I couldn't deny I had a mean tennis game and absolutely no complaints about laying pool side with a mojito and nibbling on a plate of fries. The country club defined my summer life when I lived in Dallas, and that was about nine months of the year. In the winter months the Diamond stayed relevant by hosting dances and cocktail hours. It was no wonder why Emma would spend most of her time here. Especially if her aim was to make friends. Everyone was in a good mood with a daiquiri in hand.

Hopefully today they were chatty.

The first person I saw was Shelley. She flew into my arms, a blonde blur of teal and Chanel 5, her tennis racket hitting me in the back.

"I've been trying to reach you!"

True. I had about twenty missed texts. And ten missed phone calls needing sorting.

"I'm sorry. I'll catch you up if we can get somewhere private," I said, the middle of the lobby was not the best place for a murder investigation.

"So, the rumors are true?"

"And what are the rumors?" Jake asked, standing behind me this whole time like a silent tower.

Shelley flushed, "That your stepmother's passed on."

I smirked, full well knowing the rumors were not so kindly worded. Jake snorted. Ah, so he knew this as well.

"… I'm so sorry for your loss."

"Yes, of course. Thank you."

"Is the funeral soon?" Shelley asked, going word for word from the etiquette guide we'd been bred into, "I'd like to send flowers."

"Shelley," I interrupted, before she asked what to bring to the wake's potluck, "Go to your tennis lesson, then meet us on the terrace for a drink and we'll give you all the dirty gossip."

Relief washed over her expression so conspicuously, I almost laughed.

"Oh, thank goodness," she gave me a peck on the cheek and scurried off.

Jake watched her getaway, "I know you are best friends, but Shells is an odd one. A pretty one. But odd."

"Around you."

"Oh?" he quirked an eyebrow and leaned ahead to open the door to the terrace for me, "Do tell."

"She hates you out of loyalty to me. But she also knows I send you Birthday gifts. It confuses her. Did you like the sunglasses? You never said."

"Wore them so much they got sat on and broken. Did you like that dress for yours? I thought it looked trendy. So not you, but I tried."

"Mmm. It was so short I could hardly sit. My date loved it."

He frowned as we took a seat at a table, "But you packed it, right?"

"Wore it so much it got lost under some man's bed."

"Cruel woman. Here's the menu. Hasn't changed much."

I scrolled the menu, relieved that something in my life remained the same.

"Fries with mayo and ketchup and the mojito please," I ordered when the server asked us for our requests.

"Club sandwich with extra cheese, I'll take the mojito, too," Jake handed the menus back to the waiter, "Thanks Kent."

"I'll have it right out," he said.

"In a minute, pull up a chair. I have a few questions."

Poor Kent looked as surprised as I was. But I said nothing as the perplexed kid sat down with his notepad and pulled up a chair to sit with us.

"See, Marigold. Kent here's been a summer intern at our office on and off during the past summers. Why not this year, Kent? We've missed you."

The boy's face went red, "A summer off. I needed the outdoors."

"Mmmhmm..." Jake teased with a big smile, "And?"

"And I met the kids' swimming instructor in class last semester. She's... Ah..."

"Hopefully one day the missus?" my eyes flicked up to his nametag, "Mrs. Verner?"

"I was hoping you'd only leave us for a woman," Jake said, "You've been working here long enough to have served Emma, my stepmom, enough times, right?"

Kent paled down to a pink. Poor guy. He was an overstretched teenager, well, okay, probably early twenties, but he did not look it. The gelled-down brown hair and smooth round face shaved off the years. On my side of the table, I was annoyed at myself for not realizing Jake would have seated us in Emma's favorite area. At least I was planning on interviewing her tennis instructor when he was done training Shelley (everyone here had an instructor of some sort). They had tennis rackets in the garage, so I assumed it remained the family sport. I had grand investigative plans as well. I could be helpful.

Kent sighed, as if letting a big secret off his chest, "So it's true? I heard rumors, but I didn't want to bring it up. I'm sorry she died. Emma was always nice to me. She never sent food back, even if I got it wrong and she still always gave a big tip. Decent woman. Working in the service industry, I can always tell. It's a shame."

"Appreciated, Kent. What were the rumors about my stepmother?"

The boy turned red again.

"I'd rather know and be prepared," Jake insisted.

"That she died of a drug overdose and was found sprawled across the kitchen floor," Kent sounded embarrassed just for repeating it, "I didn't believe it till you came here."

"Lovely," I grunted.

Knowing the poor woman five minutes, I knew even a pot brownie never passed through her lips. Jake bit back his own answer; I could tell he felt the same way I did. Why did Shelley guess drugs, too? Did the club have a PTA speed ring I didn't know about? The only things I'd worry about here were moms slipping into their kids' Adderall or passing between them Benzos at brunch.

"Is there a drug problem here?" Jake asked.

"Not that I know of."

But he also looked like a teenager. Who'd offer Mr. Wholesome the powdery sort of Coke? I'd ask Shells later. Even though she didn't do drugs (they caused early signs of aging) the girl could find molly in a library. Accidentally (true story).

"Can you tell me anything you would know? Like whom she dined with, what she did when here? I'm asking everyone," Jake pled, now sounding like a pained and grieving stepson. I wondered how much was an act, versus how much of his earlier emotionlessness was trying to act tough.

"Yeah of course. I'm just a waiter but you get to know the regulars," he scratched his head, "She liked the BLT and the light beers. Her husband would join her, if he didn't, another couple would join, or she'd eat alone. She'd talk about tennis, I think her sessions were in the afternoon," he shrugged, "That's it. Try Evan, he's the afternoon coach."

Another couple-I cringed at that-Megan and Theo-we'd have to talk to them soon. Jake was kind enough not to press for more information on the couple, he knew.

"Thanks man," he slid a twenty into Kent's palm, "We're trying to figure out what happened."

"So that's it?" the kid asked, eager to get away, already half-way out of his chair.

"That's it," I confirmed. We learned enough.

"Great, and I'll try to get your meals on the house. Least we can do. You know, on account of everything."

"Appreciated," I said, noting the kind gesture, even if the law office would have paid.

Once Kent was out of earshot, I leaned into whisper, "So after Shelley, we interview Evan."

"Agreed. Hold on, my phone is buzzing," he dug it out from his pocket. As he read, his shoulders slouched making me cringe.

"What?" We didn't need more bad news.

"It's your Dad," his expression made me nervous. "Showtime," he said as texted back and set his phone on the table. "Amy's husband is Dallas PD, we lucked out. He's pulling some major strings and he and his partner are ready to de-brief you at their house. Don't give me that pout. It's a million times better than being dragged into a police station."

"Okay. That's not horrible news. I'm relieved to not have to go to the station. You can stay here and investigate. I'll Uber home and can get my car. Her husband did us a solid," I paused, "Why the face?"

"Your dad texted, too. He asked me what Dad was wearing," Jake sighed and leaned in on the table, covering his face with his hands, "Marigold, when you first ran into my Dad outside, what was he wearing?"

"Denim on denim."

Jake, still hiding behind his hands, "When the police arrived, apparently he was wearing a Kelly-green Polo shirt."

"Oh."

I sucked in my breath.

"Marigold," he sat up again, looking me dead in the eye, his voice breaking, "Why would my Dad change shirts that night?"

Several reasons. But they felt like lies and died across my tongue.

"We'll figure it out. And if they ask, I won't remember," I reached out and took his hand, "We'll figure this out, okay? I got your back."

Jake nodded, looking weary, like a lost child. That ever-present glint in his eye flickered out, and it killed me. As if that knife was stuck in my chest.

He was imaging his own father killing her. I could see it in his haunted expression. How could the same man who assembled bicycles and play catch in the front yard could do such a thing? Despite everything, we'd always believed our parents were truly good. That we were all good.

But I wasn't so sure now. Because I'd do anything for that snarky gleam to fill Jake's eyes again.

"Do you think that we always see our parents through children's eyes? With rose-colored lenses?" he asked.

"Well, yeah. I push the unpleasant things aside. Try to, life's easier that way."

"But what about your shoulder? What about what happened in Austin? I love my Dad, but after that... He's so cavalier about death. About harming people. Why has he not acknowledged hurting you?" he paused, "And we all ignore it. For peace."

I gulped.

That Austin trip scarred us kids for life.

My stomach wobbled at the fact Paul was not above reasonable doubt. There was no real comfort I could give.

"Jake," I promised, squeezing his hand, "Like I said. We seek the truth and protect our families."

That was the best I could do.

He cast me a look, "No matter what?"

"No matter what."

We had to find that denim shirt.

And burn it.

Chapter 11

It wasn't great of me to leave Jake like that, yet making police officers wait seemed even less wise. As I pulled into traffic on the toll road, I felt less guilty. Shells would be with him soon and so would a mojito. I wasn't leaving him alone to ruminate. He also had to call his mother, his real one, and let her know what happened. And then somehow squeeze into the conversation if she'd been hiding anything about his father's actions during the marriage. Easy.

Didn't envy him.

The time to myself should have been restorative, but I pressed the pedal harder to get there faster and be around people again. My mind kept flooding with what-ifs.

What if Paul wasn't the killer? Then there was a murdering psychopath nearby.

What if I had been close to running into said mad-man (or mad-woman, don't want to be sexist till forensics came back. Women can do anything as well as a man, including murder. Plus, it's been reported that women often chose poison and stabbings as their way of off-ing someone. Soo...)

I turned up the radio. My mind was not a safe place to be.

Funny. Neither was Dallas.

"KTOX5 Oldies! This is your Premier DFW Radio Station! For traffic on the hour-every hour. And don't forget our daily drawing to payyy off your billsss! Call 555-2540 and be the 39th caller. Now to your local traffic update! A crash on I-75 will make that 20 min afternoon commute a little over three hours…"

Amy sat me down at the breakfast table again, with the same mug of tea along with the pleasant addition of a trim, diagonally cut chicken salad sandwich with a handful of Ruffles on the side.

"Jake called, said he was eating your lunch too and that you'd be hungry."

"Thank you."

More like "wow" on both their accounts. I dove in, starving.

"So, uh," Amy paused, wringing her hands, so I knew this was bad, "My husband and his partner are in the study. They're asking about Scott. The rumors."

Ah. I put my sandwich down. That's why I got Ruffles too. Part of me was expecting this, since I found the body. Even Paul mentioned death followed me. Word gets around.

"I'm ready for it," it was a half-lie. Because how ready could I really be? Dredging up my fondest memories for strangers. Fun.

Amy shot me an accusatory glance.

"Really, I am. I did therapy."

For about a week.

"Sure. My advice? Get in, get out. Tell them what you know. If it lasts longer than an hour, I'll go in and break it up."

"How are you going to break up a police interview?"

She shrugged, "I have an hour to think."

My eyebrows shot up. She was serious. Setting this up, lunch, a planned rescue... This was a lot from Amy.

"You're helping us out," I whispered.

"I want this over with."

I mouthed her a thank you.

"If I'm the daughter of a convicted murderer, do you think my snail books would sell?" Her words were still at full volume.

Ah. And that explained the sandwich. Because, no, after the initial rush to buy the books by psychologists, no, I did not think her books would sell.

"Even so," I continued whispering, I didn't want the police to how know I felt, "Thank you."

The interrogation went as I expected. John, Amy's husband, asking me the predictable questions of that evening. The only hiccup-it was brief- was my distraction of his partner, Everett James, looking like a Brad Pitt clone that mixed it up with Santa Claus. He had a thick southern accent that really wasn't heard in the city, and I couldn't push down the small smile tattling on me. I was imagining him in a mall-Santa movie; it was perfect. He'd be that rough and slimy Santa taking smoke breaks in front of the children until he found the meaning of Christmas through a sweet love story, meeting the future Mrs. Clause and then becoming a quality Mall-Santa. He could lure in an attractive love interest with those snappy blue eyes.

So that was the minor hiccup. Them asking me about a murder, and me, smiling and laughing and explaining my movie pitch. The idea was met with two scowls that read of not thinking my idea was original,

DEATH ON LOVERS LANE

and that they've probably heard it before. Or C: this was a murder investigation.

But that was the only bump. My recital was seamless and the same as what we recorded. Only now I got to end it with, "I think you know-especially since I was to stay at their guest house-I'm a family friend. And I've been put in the employ of my father, who is Paul's defense attorney. So, me, coming here today is out of the desire to punish whoever really killed Emma and show the defense team is cooperative and after the truth as well."

While I didn't see their eye-roll, oh I could feel it.

"Her father's daughter," John shrugged to his partner.

There was a clear hierarchy here. The bearded Brad Pitt impersonator sat behind the desk, while John and I sat in the two "client" chairs. John could not save me from what was coming, only cast me sympathetic expressions. Great.

In Everett's mind I've already been declared naughty.

"This isn't the first-time death has happened in your presence," Everett drawled, "Odd, isn't it? Strange that on the first night of your arrival someone ends up dead."

That's the angle he wanted to play? I sat a little straighter. "Command the room" my Dad always demanded.

"I'm well acquainted with the legal world. If I was going to commit a crime, do you really think it would have been on the night of my arrival? I think I'd like to make it at least a challenge for the detectives involved."

"She's not wrong, Everett. Marigold is incredibly bright. This is way too obvious."

Everett frowned and stroked his salt and pepper beard

dramatically. Hopefully he was thinking and not in the practice of giving out canned judgements. I also found myself wishing I'd already changed into something smart looking and not ripped jeans with a graphic T-shirt from an arbor day volunteer event. At least my hair served as a bright, frizzy halo.

"Then for your sake, Marigold, I'm listening. I need to know what the actual story of Scott White is. Because all I've been fed are the rumors. And they don't look good for you."

Ah. So, he was at least thinking.

"Tell him the entire story," John said, dropping his voice, his eyes not meeting mine. He knew. He was family. He was a great help settling down the paperwork. "From your lips. Not mine. The truth is more effective that way."

I stretched out my limbs and took a steeling breath. And a long, slow exhale. I was ready for this. When everyone made such a big deal about me not being dragged into the station, this was why. Their kindness was my warning. They were right, a more comfortable setting was reassuring, that for me, at least, in the end, things would work out. I was okay. Even if he was not. Scott would never be okay.

"Scott White saved my life. And I ended his."

Chapter 12

I was in that pit. Without a latter or anyway upwards. Sunlight on a hot day could not reach me. Nor could any kind words or soothing phrases from loved ones. My heart was broken. Thoroughly. In the worst of ways. I felt my remains were shattered across the floor. It angered me that I let a man break my spirit. But in getting to know him, I had finally let down all my walls. Theo had gotten to know all of me and kissed away my vulnerabilities. Smiled away my insecurities. Being around him, my cheeks flushed, and I liked myself even more. Being with him was the only sort of legal high. For me, it was true love. For him... I was not enough. Perhaps he enjoyed my company. Liked the ego boost of adoration.

I didn't know it at the time, but in the end, he drained me, as if he were a wraith, leaving me a hapless shell.

My days after Theo were spent at work, then in bed, crying over the future lost and lies of love. Eventually Mom shipped me off to Pittsburg. A friend of hers was renovating an old opera house and needed an interior designer.

Dallas was suffocating. Planning my schedule to never run into Theo was exhausting and hard to perfect. It was easy to convince me to pack up and leave.

"We don't need the complete love story. People break up all the time," Everett complained.

"But you do. Unfortunately, it's a part of me and part of this story, So…"

"I packed my bags and found a small place in the 'Pitt.' With no friends or family around, I could go to bars and drink and make out with random handsome and not so handsome men. As long as I showed up for work without a hangover, no one would know. I was free and alone. In the worst of ways.

I was free of the confines of the myth of love and could just enjoy a man's arm around me with none of the expectations. See, I figured I didn't deserve love, or to be treated well by men. Not anymore. Theo broke me. He gave me real-world expectations. Jake did his damage before, teaching me that men could declare their love and then reel it back in.

To make things worse, Theo started posted photos of him kissing his new girl. Jake, posting his own smug dating photos. True love couldn't exist in that same world they created. Instead, I found happiness where I could.

And then, one night, it all changed. A tall man with dark hair and chocolate-brown eyes and a jawline that could sculpt glass strode into the dimly lit bar and bought me a drink. A Coke. At first, I scoffed.

"Where's the whiskey? Is that extra?"

Meaning, would things finally get good for me if I let you stick your tongue down my throat? Instead of responding, he ordered himself a Coke and us a chocolate cake with two forks.

"I'm Scott," he said, handing me a fork, "And I'm going to treat you differently than your other guys."

"That's what they all say." I was starting to get bored with him already, he could go eat milk and cookies with another girl, but I noticed freckles dotting across his nose. Perfectly placed. And that convinced my buzzed self to stay.

"But is it what they all do?" he asked.

I took a small bite of confused cake, "No." my voice a whisper, "Far from it."

I continued with my take of meeting Scott. Of how Paul wasn't wrong about me. Of how Scott's mom still calls me, blaming me for the loss of her son. At first there were long, horrid voicemails. Their lawyers. My lawyers (family). And now, a few months later, it has dwindled down to just breathing. Just a silent phone call, never letting me forget him.

As if I could.

Now my phone lived on mute.

"Can I go? Now that I've picked that scab open for you?"

Everett grunted.

"Of course," John said, "I think you've given enough today. Get some rest."

Chapter 13

Only I wasn't really done. The scab was freshly bleeding. But Running from my emotions seemed like the wisest course of action, so I met Jake back at the house of horror. Poe needed rescuing, and I wanted something to cuddle. The dog. Not Jake.

As soon as I arrived, I noted the cop cars in the driveway. The yellow crime scene tape blocking my entry as it stretched across the pavement. I ducked under and made my way to the front door, ready to feed the guard a half-true story about living there and needing things, but Jake popped his head out and did a quick "she's with me," allowing me to bounce past the guard with a smile.

"I'm a paralegal, see," I told the officer, "With a passion for paisley and Pantone."

Jake grabbed my arm and dragged me in before anything else could be said by either party.

"Really, Marigold?" Jake hissed as he led the way upstairs.

"Trying to add a bit of my emotional instability to the evening.

It's not every day a girl gets to revisit the crime scene she stumbled upon."

He paused mid-way up and twisted back at me, "Are you okay? I know your interview had to be rough."

"No. Are you?"

"No."

"But we keep going right?" I asked, knowing if he said, "No, we can stop and drive away and never come back," that I'd be right behind him.

"Right," though he sounded unsure. Still, he continued upwards, "I got here ten minutes ago and have the dog cornered in my old room. I remember he hates strangers and apparently, I'm still one. Or he recalls me all too well and is calling me out on it."

We stood facing opposite end of the closed bedroom door as if we were poised for an FBI take down.

"I'll go in if you cover me," I teased.

"You joke, but he's going to come running out all teethy and slip out and down the hall and we'll have to chase him."

" 'All teethy?' What is with you and Poe?"

"We have beef."

I pressed my palm against the door, holding it shut for a moment, "Now I've got to know. What beef do you have with a seven-pound dog?"

"Now?" he rolled his eyes, "Fine. Poe ate my class ring. I had to feed him laxatives and chase him around. He's not so fond of me either. Can you just get him now? I don't enjoy being here either."

Aggies and their class rings…

"You traumatized Poe! Your anti-dog energy is very unattractive."

"Oh, no, he'll never eat gold again," he waved his arms, "Just…"

he gestured towards the door, "Do your magic."

All it took was me opening the door and calling out to Poe, for the dog to sprint right up to me and lick my arms; I scooped her up.

"Good. We can go," Jake rushed.

Oh, but no. Not when I had the opportunity to walk into the glory of the Shrine of Jake. His bedroom remained untouched from his teen years. Soccer trophies lined his dresser and windowsills. Fast cars and faster women posters lined his walls. The poor dog had been trapped in a room decorated by Pottery Barn's 1999 catalogue page called "Young Testosterone."

"Remember last time we were in here?" My focus was on his bed and the non-descript dark blue comforter. We'd been on summer break in college. Young and dumb. What I'd mistaken for as true love was, instead, familiarity. Laziness. Jake was Jake, and he was… comfortable. Safe. The early college years were tough for me. Visiting him always returned the feelings of high school glory, and at the time I'd been worried I peaked too soon. Whenever he was around, I felt more myself.

Now at least I had the surety of my identity to help resist him: an unemployed designer. And I now knew for a fact that I had indeed peaked too soon. With all this newfound confidence, he didn't stand a chance of me falling back into his arms and into old habits.

His nostrils flared, "I don't think I could forget. Remember that one time both our families were downstairs getting ready for a game night?"

"Do you think they knew?"

Suddenly, I was horrified. Twenty-year-old me thought she was sneaky and clever.

"You wore your 4th of July T-shirt inside out."

"You didn't tell me?" I raised the dog in my hands up to his face, "Get him, Poe. Avenge my honor!"

At least the dog gave a yip.

"What could I have said to not embarrass you? Clothes always tell the truth, don't they?"

I gulped.

That they did.

The mood shifted.

Memory lane shriveled up, and we were right back in the present where smells of Clorox hit my nose and low hums of police voices filled my ears.

"Don't they?" his voice hoarse.

Our minds, in sync, locked on why his Dad had changed shirts that fateful night.

"Come on," he closed the door behind us as we left, "I want to see if there's anything amiss in their room."

The master bedroom was straight down the hall, sealed closed by a set of double doors.

"Not that I've been in here recently," he threw the doors open, "But every stone and whatnot."

He ventured in.

I remained in the doorway, "Yeah, this is weird."

This was majorly privacy invading. My innards cringed at the thought of someone going through my room-trying to learn about me.

"The police have already combed through and catalogued. That's the only reason we are allowed up here. My Dad's a murder suspect," he shrugged as his eyes dragged along the dresser, "There's no such thing as privacy. Not for him," he met my flinch with a frown, "And after what you told me about your interview, not for us."

"They didn't call you in."

"They did."

"Oh?" I set the dog down, he was getting squirmy and needed to run about, "Don't worry I know it's on me to scoop him up again."

"They did, but I explained the conflict of interest and gave them the briefest and vaguest account of what I remembered."

"Lucky," I threw open the closet looking for- I didn't know what. All I could tell was she had a love of bold colors and way too many coats for a Texan. Maybe Emma was an optimist. That thought hit my stomach like a raw egg. I slammed the door shut, "What do you expect to find? Your Dad has too many Hawaiian shirts for a man outside of Hawaii?"

"Something out of place?" he stepped over the dog, giving me a look, and circled the room, "A diary or a ledger? A day planner. We have their phone data-or at least we will have it soonish. But I want something that tells me the story of their lives before she got stabbed. Something the prosecutor won't know."

"Okay," I paused and scanned the room in a more observatory way, "Like it's a stage with its props and we have to figure out the story- the story that's already been played out."

Jake smiled, "Exactly."

"What do you see?" I asked.

"At first I'm seeing a glass of water and Tums and a book by his bed. And a lamp. He was probably reading and fell asleep. A nighttime routine. Her side doesn't have a lamp, but there is a charging station and some loose jewelry. She probably played on her phone and went to bed."

"Their closet is huge and organized," I shrugged, "They cared about cleanliness. Organization. Equally."

"Dad could never live with a slob. Growing up our spice rack was alphabetized," he paused, "The question is, were they in love?"

The room seemed lived in, calmly decorated in neutral greens and tans, in a style that was neither masculine nor feminine. Tidied by a maid. Untouched by any personality.

"There's nothing special or heartfelt. No pictures, other than you and Amy on the dresser," I observed, "So they slept here. Got ready for the day here, but not living."

"Was there... love in here?" he asked, "They always seemed happy."

"That, I can answer for you."

His expression went skeptical.

"Just you wait."

And I tugged open her nightstand, "You get his."

"Oh-no-no-no-no."

"Grow up." Aha... "Non-dusty sex accoutrements. My diagnosis: a healthy and thoughtful sex life."

"And booking myself for therapy later," he got his drawer open, "Same. Heathy sex life." And slammed the drawer shut.

"Puritan," I teased.

"I'd say my reaction is normal. But this is good? Active, happy marriage. One less reason to kill."

"And I found a spicy book," I teased as I held up a day planner, "It was in the second drawer."

Sadly, my discovery faded the blush across his cheeks as he became all business again. But at least, Jake seemed intrigued.

"And so, it begins... Take photos of the days around her death. Do the whole month before too and then put it back? They'll search us on the way out and if this is still here, they didn't find it. Let's keep this to ourselves."

Clever. But there was no reason to tell him that.

"And now the hard part," he said as our eyes locked, making me gulp. I did not like that expression on his face. Some mix of sadness and pity.

To the kitchen. I scooped up Poe and led the way. The quicker I faced the scene, the faster I got out of there and ultimately the faster we found out what happened that night. My foot hit the last step on the staircase with a pause. Jake nearly bumping into me. We were in the back stairwell; the one Paul would have used that evening. Was it really all just last night? Had I just arrived back? This entire ordeal felt like a nightmare that didn't fit in time.

I couldn't be stomping around a house that was as familiar as my own, standing over a blood stain, being handed gloves by a police officer. I took a deep breath and rooted myself, falling apart was unacceptable. Be present-be prepared-a family mantra.

"Not much looks different," I don't think my voice shook. "Our drink cups from earlier in the day were in the sink." Now they had a tag on them with a number that would match it to a numbered photograph. "The mushrooms across the floor. I brought those in. Forgot I dropped them."

Mushrooms were number twelve.

"Number 13, the glass, with the light pink lipstick. That's mine. The other one was hers; she wore a darker shade."

"That's great," Jake said, his hand setting itself comfortably on the small of my back, "Why don't you sit outside? I'll get pictures for us. The police have fine combed everything, I don't think putting you through this is necessary."

"But if we miss something because I…"

My voice shook.

Being back was harder than I thought. Seeing a life reduced to a chalk outline and a number. Number Four.

1. Her pink jogging top on the floor with only droplets of blood.
2. Her oversized bag spilled across the floor. Each item in there had a sub number (2a, 2b…)
3. The knife. The real one went with the body. A replica for investigators lay in its place.
4. The body. Now just a chalk outline.

"Who knows the house better than me? Hmm?" he guided me towards the hallway that led to the backdoor. To the stair and the laundry and the pantry and the garage. Paul's steps that night. "Get some fresh air and sunlight and a moment away from this case. I'll wrap things up."

I nodded. I didn't need to see 5,6,7,8,9,10,11… again.

Hugging Poe for some love, I headed outside. I meant to go outside. But I turneds toward the laundry room and remained in its doorway. The maid came every Tuesday and Thursday. I poked my head in the washer and dryer and the hamper, dug through the dirty laundry in the hamper. No denim shirt.

Not sure how I felt about that.

"… So you're living with me now, 'lil Poe. I am sorry," I scratched his ears, and he yipped, "But I'll give you a good home and I promise to only put you in sweaters on Halloween, okay? We'll find out your favorite foods and get you some new toys. And if you want to chew on something now, well there's always Jake."

"Funny."

I'd heard him approach. Poe and I had been sitting at the edge of the driveway, where it met the sidewalk, as far from the house as possible, past the crime tape and all the commotion. The last time I sat here it was with Amy as we talked about boys and watched my brother and Jake kick a ball around in the yard. Another lifetime. Now Jake cleared past the 6-foot-tall mark and loomed over me like an oak tree. He held out his hand to help me up. I took it and he hauled me with a loud, fake grunt with a fake back stretch.

"Oh shut-up Jake."

"Even if I have good news?"

I eyed him, "You better not hold back good news." There was certainly a dearth of it around here.

"When Shelley joined me at the club, we shared an awkward drink and she invited herself over tonight for a girl's night."

"A girl's night? What about you?"

"I think she's kicked me out? I'll go spend time with our dads and let you two catch up. You did just get into town. It shouldn't be all about Emma. As bad it sounds, your return should be celebrated."

Putting my hands on my hips I frowned, "You're not like 'looking after me' or anything are you? Because if you are I don't want it."

"Not at all."

"Good."

"Good," he nodded towards the car, "So, supermarket, liquor store?"

"Duh, it's a girl's night." I said, passing him up and leading the way towards the car. Getting as far away as possible from that house and trying to remember my favorite margarita recipe and if Jake's house had enough salt and limes. Mentally, I was done with all this. And privately, I didn't care that Jake was going to likely keep investigating while I wound down. Why? Because I was an interior designer. I stepped out of this life, away from being a future defense attorney, and then, of course its ends up being me who finds the dead body. I deserved a break and a drink.

Because there was, apparently, no true escape.

Chapter 14

"I'm exhausted, Shells. Not sure how much fun I'm going to be tonight," I said, throwing my feet up on the coffee table, on top of some worn Architectural Digest magazines, "But thanks for coming over. A girl's night was a marvelous idea."

"And the house plant? Did you like it? I wasn't sure what to get you. There hasn't been precedent for this…"

"No," I took a long sip of wine. Margaritas were too much work. "I suppose not. I like my houseplant. And so does Jake."

Two fern-looking plants sat in the middle of the coffee table. Knowing Jake and I, they would end up on the back patio left to fend for themselves. Jake always said that if he wanted to take care of a living thing in his free time, he'd at least get a fish. I was worried about killing everything under my care. We were all a little worried about poor Poe.

"Are you, okay? You went somewhere just now. Your expression."

Shells was my best friend for a reason.

"I'm sorry for the big party," she continued, "I know you probably wanted it to be just us. But I was so excited I wanted something grand, and it got out of control. And I keep thinking if I didn't throw that party would Emma have been killed?"

"I don't think I can even be slightly upset about you wanting to throw me a welcome party. It's a sweet thought. Though an evening like tonight is all I probably needed-so, I'm glad we're doing it now," I paused, reflecting on how genuinely glad I was. I came back to town for friends and familiarity. "And you can't think like that. Maybe you saved my life, hmm? I wasn't there, so I wasn't in danger."

"Or maybe he'd have heard voices and run away. She wasn't an easy target with company."

"Only to come back later. Maybe it was inevitable."

I shivered, imagining a man at the window peeping in, planning death.

"Let's talk about something else," Shells said, leaning over the couch to pour me some more wine and top off her glass, "Something else, but something related. What are you going to do now? About your living situation? Can't stay with Jake forever."

Frowning, "I hadn't thought that far ahead. I don't think he has yet either. But you're not wrong."

"How long were you planning to stay in the guest house till... everything happened?"

Indefinitely? Till I figured out my life and got a job and bought a plan. Till my mother harkened me back to Florida?

"Not sure. Till it felt right to move?"

She pouted, "So you're not here to stay? I missed you! I want our lunches and our shopping trips back. Double dates. Everything!"

"I'm back," I began cautiously, "With no plans to leave nor stay."

Rolling her eyes, Shelley took a big drink and huffed, "You need deep roots. And your roots are here. In Dallas. Its time to stop being melodramatic."

I smiled over at her, feeling happily buzzed. "Or maybe I'm happy being nomadic?"

"No. You're happy floating over life, drifting away from problems. I'm going to find you a nice little house and tap into your trust fund," she huffed with determination, "We're going to get you a job and renew your country club membership."

"Lifetime member."

"Well cheers! One item off the list."

"And I have a job," I added just to be sassy.

"And you've been withholding this why?"

I shrugged, "Not a job I want? I'm working at the parents' law firm again as an investigator to help Jake with all this... With the event." I took in her frown. She didn't understand how it wasn't a choice, but that was not something I could fully explain to her. "It's better than being left in the dark. And it gives me cash flow. I think it's more their charity till I find something I actually want to do."

"Are you sure?" she dropped her voice, "Working for them? After what happened when you were in the hill country as a kid?"

"Better work with than against. And I don't want to leave Jake alone in this."

"What about Amy?"

"Amy is Amy. She'll help when directly needed. No more, no less."

Shelley hugged a pillow to her chest and agreed. She opened her mouth to say something else, probably about a townhouse on the market near her or something to change the subject, but she snapped it shut at Poe's barking. We shared a worried look. Maybe it was all this talk, that had us on edge, but Poe had been quiet all evening, curled up on a new dog bed from Costco and full of puppy chow.

"Let me, let me go check," I uncurled off the couch, letting my socked feet tip-toe across the wood floor.

"Should you?" she hissed, but did nothing to stop me, "I have my phone on speed-dial."

Shelley seemed to have better survival instincts as she slipped deeper into the couch, pulling the blanket over her till only her wide eyes peeped out.

Should I?

Well, that I didn't know.

I tiptoed towards the kitchen and the barking Poe. He was focusing on the bay window in the breakfast nook, barking at the backyard.

Why were backyards so creepy? So dark and green and shaded by trees. Pleasant in the day, but at night it was easy to imagine anything jumping the fence and peering in. I regretted pushing Jake out the door so fast, telling him we were fine and that he needed time with his Dad. That we were safe. Because we weren't. There was clearly a man out there that killed young women with small dogs in kitchens.

I mean we both had blonde hair. Large purses. Alcohol in our systems. Both stood about 5'6, 5'8" on a good shoe/hair day.

Is that where the similarities ended? Was there something special about Emma that he had to kill? Did their stories intertwine, and it was all planned? Was it random? A stalker focusing on her... and now me?

Poe gave a bark.

I jumped.

"Shh Poe, someone's out there."

The window gave me more a reflection of myself and the kitchen than a view of the outdoors. Geez. I did not want to get closer, but… Better than opening the door? I pressed my nose up to the glass and squinted my eyes to survey the patio. Nothing. Just dark tree limbs swaying overhead and casting unnecessary shadows.

"I think we're okay," I called out to my scared friend, but my eyes traced movement. Of a man. Definitely not a shadow.

Tall. Male. Lean.

Not someone I'd swipe right on.

Not that I could detect features, just that from here, I could tell his shoulders weren't that broad, and…

What was I doing? There was a man out there and I was busy mentally rambling to myself.

"Shells! Shells! Someone's out there!" Poe barked along with me. I swept around the kitchen turning on all the lights. Letting the intruder know his secret was out. We knew he was here and his element of surprise was gone. Hopefully he'd run away.

Because he feared light? Or buzzed women?

Well, hopefully he ran away because this was a spying mission and a not a murdery one.

"I'm calling 911!" I could hear her call as I made a phone call to Jake myself and running to dive back into the couch with Shelley. Two under a blanket had to be safer than one. The doors were locked, we'd been careful about that since arriving at his house. My ears strained for the crash of breaking glass-that was my true fear-that he'd break a window to get in.

"Jake! Jake! Get here," I cried, sounding embarrassingly scared, "Someone's in the backyard. I mean I think he left. He's not in the house, but he could have been watching us!"

"Take a breath, did ya'll call the police?" Jake asked, his voice low and concerned.

"We did. Shells is on the line with them."

"They're on the way," she cut in.

"They're coming," I relayed, "Jake, Poe was barking. He warned us."

"He probably scared them off. I'm on my way, okay? I'll be right there. I have my key," I heard the chime of an elevator, "Do you want me to stay on the line?"

Yes.

"No. You'll be faster. Hurry, okay?"

"Got it. lie low. Stay on with the police."

He hung up, and I felt like the room got ten degrees colder in the click of a button.

Originally, I appreciated Jake's open floor plan, but now I felt exposed. A step up led to a small foyer, where there was the front door. Solid Oak. So that was good. The windows along that wall had thick wood blinds. But the rest of the space was open, the kitchen visible from the sectional couch. Blindless. Just large windows. He'd assumed the fenced in back yard offered privacy. Outside was a covered patio, and a large shed and trees that offered hiding spots to an intruder.

I shivered and was about to say something about being spooked, till I saw Shelley's eyes were still wide. We huddled close under the blanket, and I could feel her shiver back.

"Hey it'll be okay," I lied. Trying to summon some strength for the both of us. Though I was about mentally shattered by now. I wanted to cry and be useless and drink.

But that's not what needed to happen.

"Yeah, yeah, I know," she said, not sounding convincing, "911 and all they're coming."

"We'll make it okay? If he breaks in the back, we go right out the front. Hop in your car- it's at the end of the drive-and I'm sober enough to get us crashed into the nearest mailbox and we'll cause a ruckus. All our neighbors will come running out to save us."

She offered me a small smile, "I'll honk the horn the whole way. Set off the car alarm."

"And Jake's HOA fees will skyrocket," I smiled at her giggle. Better. "And the wine bottles, right? If he gets to us, you distract him, and I'll hit him over the head."

I was about to say more, but the wail of distant sirens froze my lips. Saved. I wouldn't have to worry anymore if hitting someone over the head with an empty wine bottle would be as effective as if it were full.

I mean, it would be close right? Glass shards were always unpleasant.

The wails became louder, and I closed my eyes in relief. We were okay.

"Is that it? Are we done here?" I asked Detective Everett as he kept questioning me about our evening. It was a simple girl's night.

John was doing the same with Shelley at the kitchen table.

Jake and another cop were standing at the back door, looking outside where the intruder had been. I wanted to shimmy up behind them and eavesdrop. Maybe I wanted to be discovered eavesdropping, too. Get another one of those hugs that lifted me off my feet and made my heart pound in a different way.

"We'll have a cruiser come by twice an hour tonight to make sure he's not in the area again," Everett said, "I suggest you three stick together tonight or find somewhere else to stay."

"Staying? Are you kidding me? There was someone outside-looking in," Shelley said, approaching us, "Why don't you come stay with me? I don't live far at all. I'd feel a lot better if you did."

Of course, Shelley would offer her place. She had a big heart, but that was why I had to say no. What if trouble continued to follow me? I couldn't put her in danger.

"Jake and I are holding ground here," I decided for the both of us, "I can't keep running from home to home. He'll show up at your place, too, if I'm the new target."

Shelley paled, "No... You aren't the new target. There's no *new* target."

"You're both pretty convinced that was Emma's murderer out there, aren't you?" Everett asked.

"Well of course!" I huffed, pointing to the darkness outside, "Lurking around kitchens seems to be his MO."

He sighed and folded shut his notebook and tucked away his pen. I'd classify his expression as "not another hysterical woman".

"Ladies," his voice went sarcastically soft, "We're trying to take prints outside, but I think the rain will wash any tracks away. But odds are what you saw, likely an oversized tree branch hitting the shed. Right? It's windy outside."

Oh. Oh. Oh.

He did not.

I swallowed back my rage. Windy? He attributed our panic to *wind*? At first, I thought he was nice acting concerned, but *oh*... Anger dissolved away any coherent thought left, and I bit my lip to hold back any sort of feral growling.

Jake shot me a look to stay quiet. He recognized the expression.

"A fair amount of alcohol was involved this evening," he continued, "And of course given the scare brought on by a recent murder of someone close to you was added to the mix. For that reason, we'll have that cruiser run checks to make you feel safe and not consider this a prank call."

A prank call?

Oh... My lip was bleeding now.

"Officer," my voice, calm, as if I did not want to tackle him and take scissors to that Santa beard, "Someone was outside. I know it. I saw it."

"I'll keep watch," Jake said, "We'll call if we hear anything."

I wanted to scoff at how calm he sounded. Rude. He wasn't there, he didn't know how scary a peeping tom was right after a stabbing.

"Alright then," Everett nodded. It looked like an "atta boy" nod.

"Can I get a ride home?" Shelley asked, "I don't think I can drive yet, and I'm certainly not staying here. No offence, Jake."

"None taken. Only relief."

She rolled her eyes, "But only if I can get a ride in the front seat. Neighbors talk."

"I'm in a fleet sedan. But of course, front seat. Worst they will think is a blue collar man drove you home."

"That's certainly something new."

Somehow, from her mouth that sounded flirty and not condescending. If Everett wore a hat, he would have tipped it.

He did smile, though, and that was something new. I'd have to give her trouble later for never being able to turn it off.

Shells and I hugged goodbye, and Jake and I walked them out. Everett gave us a last "keep an eye out." And we locked the door behind them.

"How are you feeling?" Jake asked.

I wanted to say something silly like "better now that you're here."

Because there was someone out there, right?

"Better," I settled for, stepping down into the living room, "That sobered me up quick."

"So do you think it was alcohol or…" his voice squeaked out, rightfully afraid of my anger.

"No, Jake. I know what I saw. A person, out there, looking in."

"Okay," he held up his hands surrendering, "Then I'll sleep on the couch tonight. No one will bother us. The cops are circulating, and every light is on in this place."

"Every light? All night?"

"Yup, I'll need a loan to cover my electric bill."

"Good." No dark corners.

He took a step down to be level with me, but then placed us, accidentally, in that awkward aspic bubble we always trap ourselves in. The dynamic that molded us- friends/lovers/soulmates/enemies. Which were we today?

We needed to talk.

It seemed so frivolous, addressing matters of the heart while his dad was accused of murdering his wife. While, if he didn't (which is what happened), then that wasn't a gust of wind outside, but… a probable killer.

I shivered.

Jake placed a gentle hand on my shoulder. Squeezed.

"Go to bed," he gestured to down the hall, "Get some rest. You're safe."

Friend? Lover?

I gave him a weak smile and hugged him lightly.

"Alright. Night."

And I turned down the hall. No voice calling after.

Friend.

Chapter 15

"I did a bad thing."

That was Shelley, sounding muffled and sheepish. I shouldn't have answered the call, given the early morning hour, but given what happened last night… There was no way I wouldn't sacrifice sleep to make sure she was okay. "What bad thing did you do?"

"I did a bad thing," she repeated.

At seven am there were very few opportunities to do a bad thing. The only things open that early were bakeries and coffee shops. Unless she had stayed in. And judging by the muffled-ness from her end, she was talking to me from under the covers, hiding from the world from her own shame of…

"You didn't," I groaned.

"It's the two-thousand twenties! You can't judge me!"

"Shells," my words came out as a sigh, "What happened?" When she left here, she was back to being about 95% sober. The sort of sober where

I wasn't sure if she should drive home in the rain (grateful for the cop car taking her), but I'd be okay with leaving her alone with her credit card and cell phone.

"Well, I mean, he was super nice giving me a ride. And then when I got home, he insisted on coming inside and making sure I was safe. Someone is killing hot blonde women, and that's me. So, it was only natural that I offered him some coffee. And one thing led to another."

I groaned, "Coffee should only lead to crumb cake. He took advantage of you! You were scared and vulnerable and he took advantage of his position. I could have his badge for this. I *will* have his badge for this!"

"Oh, don't. I didn't make it easy on him to be the good guy and walk out. I wanted company last night."

Apparently, I could have trusted her with a credit card, but not with a man. Knowing her, she probably made it nearly impossible for him to leave.

"I should have come over. I'm so sorry. I thought you'd be safer," I slid down under my own covers in shame. Did I stay because I wanted to be closer to Jake? Or did I really think Shelley was safer on her own, in her big, empty house?

Well. Clearly, she had enough life skills to make sure she wouldn't be alone.

I was always protective of her. She didn't have that aloof outer shell that Amy had.

But maybe I had to give her props, for finding her own way in the middle of a crisis. Sleeping with the detective was a sure-fire way to not have to rely on the shoddy twice-an-hour cruiser drive-by protection.

I was a poor best friend.

As I didn't deserve daylight, I threw the covers completely over my head. She was better staying away from me and the investigation and the peeping tom. Letting her loose like that, back out into the night, *I* didn't do my part to make her feel any safer.

"I'm sorry," I said again, my voice now muffled like hers, "Can I still get his badge for you?"

"Don't you dare make a fuss. He's out getting me donuts and already suggested dinner plans tomorrow."

Okay. Well done, Shelley. I felt relieved that through this investigation someone would be looking out after her, since I dragged her into this mess. What if the peeping tom liked the look of her? Started watching her in her kitchen? I'd let Everett keep his badge- for now. But I would chew him out later. On principle.

"He looks like Santa, is that what you really want?" I teased, letting her know I was done with worried-lecture mode.

"Isn't that something just to scratch off my list? Sexy Santa Brad Pitt look-a-like?"

I sighed, keeping up with her was going to kill me one day. But for now, she was good.

"Don't pretend that's not on your list. What is it after? Something weird I remember... Medieval Times Knight?" she teased, "Was that before or after-"

Ugh. Sometimes best friends know too much.

"Ok," I interrupted. This conversation was done, "Have fun. Stay safe- in like all ways."

"Bye Mom."

She ended the call.

I muttered curses into my pillow.

Was this another complication, or a good thing?

If she was sleeping with the detective, maybe he'd take last night more seriously? Be kinder and more open minded in the whole murder investigation?

Realize that if someone was out there lurking, then the culprit couldn't be Paul, because he was almost a hostage in that hotel room. This was a good thing. Someone else on our side. Or at least, I could get Shelley to keep in-tune with Everett's investigation.

"Everything okay?"

I popped my head out from under the covers and saw Jake in the doorway, already freshly dressed and with coffee in hand.

"There's crumb cake, store bought granted, in the kitchen," he added, watching me with amusement. "Did you get any rest?"

Meanwhile he stood there stretching and popping his back, so clearly his night on the couch was as good as expected.

"I did, actually. Even with the light on. I think I was so tired and had some alcohol in my system," I yawned, "Yeah, I was totally out."

"Good? And the pillow scream?" he asked between sips of his coffee.

"Guilt. I should have insisted Shelley stay over. She slept with that detective."

"Everett?"

I nodded.

"Good for her. Good-looking guy for his age. Maybe we can use that," he thumped on the door, "Don't forget, cake." And he disappeared, I assumed toward the cake.

Sometimes I admired his simplicity.

Cake.

He was right. Focus on the good things. I swung my legs out of bed and padded to the bathroom to freshen up before joining him.

I slept surprisingly well last night. Leaving the lights on gave me that false security where I felt nothing could sneak up on me-even if my eyes were closed. And Jake being on the couch meant anyone would have to sneak past him to get to me. Looking over at Jake, my gut went all mushy. He'd never let that happen. We cared deeply for each other. It was sick, and our on again-off again love story could only end in heartbreak. We both knew it.

But our hearts teased us.

As if we could work.

That this, sharing a breakfast with him was as cozy and homey as wearing a well-worn pair of jeans. That one favorite pair…

But our hearts liked to tease.

While the brain screamed reason "Get your distance."

I was like a lactose intolerant lapping up ice cream, watching as he slid up his sleeves revealing those forearms.

Forearms! At the table? Did he mean to be so indecent before I finished a cup of coffee?

Distance! My brain screamed.

"Thanks for the coffee," I said, a neutral, boring topic.

"Of course, I'd never let guests starve."

I frowned, "I have to figure out…"

"You're staying here," he cut me off, "After last night especially."

Distance! But now it was more a whisper.

The heart answered, "Thank you. I couldn't imagine staying anywhere else."

"I thought I'd have to fight you on it."

"I'm agreeable sometimes," I smiled with a sly look and twirled my fork as it dove for more cake, "Just don't let people know. There's a reputation to protect."

"I almost want to continue our 'lil breakfast and not tell you my plans for the day. I feel I have to drag you along now, after last night. I was planning on sparing you."

He was frowning.

Wait, a minute. This was premeditated cake. When he bought it, he wouldn't have known about the lurker in the back yard. I stopped chewing and set my fork down.

"What is it?" he asked, concerned.

I gulped down the rest of my bite; it wasn't frosting's fault.

"What is it?" I asked, suspicious.

"Wouldn't it be nice if my answer would be brunch plans and a mini golf date?"

"That's not our world."

"Not yet," he threw up his hands in surrender at my eyebrow raise, "Okay-okay. We need to go interview Meg and Theo-your least favorite people on earth. And given last night, I'm not letting you out of my sight."

"Well, we *are* forgetting option two. Just let the intruder kill me."

I did not want to see them again. It was too soon. Theo's face reminded me of too many cozy dinners. Of too many fights. Of…

That look… telling me I wasn't good enough. I wasn't the one. Compared to Meg, her bright and glowing face, the definition of what was enough. Of what was loved.

My heart still hurt. Coming back to Dallas, it was too soon. But if I didn't come back, Shelley would miss me, and Jake would be dealing with this all alone. He didn't deserve that.

I didn't deserve this, yet I'd go. If only for the reason to prove to myself that I was strong enough.

Jake's look of pity sent me cringing. How many years, what would I have to achieve, for those looks of pity to stop?

"Theo's a fool, Marigold. Anyone can see that."

"No. He's not. He found his perfect Stepford wife."

He leaned in, elbows on the table, in my face as much as he could with a breakfast table between us, "Is that what you want to be? Meg's place is his agreeable trophy-wife that does yoga all day and drinks green-juice. If she gains five pounds, he'd probably divorce her. Is that the life you want? He probably never listens to her or takes her seriously. You weren't made for that."

"It seems easier... Than being alone. Flailing."

"No. I think she ends up even more alone. I think you were born to be someone's thorn in their side."

I laughed. His eyes twinkled at me.

"I'm personally glad you and Theo are kaput. Just saying."

My heart pounded.

My brain screamed for help.

"Let's get this over with," I pushed away from the table, "Give me ten and I'll be ready."

"I'll give you thirty. Let's show Theo what he's missing."

Ha. Not a bad idea.

They lived off Royal Lane, near the Tollway, so it took a bit of time to get there, but it was an easy enough ride that I finished my mascara and lip application.

"I hate it when you do that," Jake said, watching me as I stowed my items in his glove compartment. At least he didn't mention my overreach of using his storage space.

"What if we got in a wreck or I brake hard, and you poke out an eye?"

"Then drive carefully," I said, getting out of the car before he could grunt something back. As if I didn't know the dangers. I needed a moment of silence for my heart as I stood in the driveway of 1402 Castle Court. It was a sprawling mid-century modern ranch-style house. Most homes around here were. The founders of Dallas were clearly scared of stairs. The roof pitched right above the doorway, accenting the recessing entry of a stone wall and three floor-to-ceiling narrow-paned windows. This must be Meg's taste. Theo was all concrete and metal.

Circle pebble pavers defined the walkway to the front door to the driveway, allowing us a neat trip through the planter, filled with little yellow flowers.

I swallowed down my gag-reflex, this was definitely more Meg.

Why was I here? In what way was this normal? Going to your ex's girlfriend's house? Just-no! There should be laws against such things because this heart was preparing to take a beating, and this face was preparing to lie. The fake smile and light-happy eyes were all ready and queued up.

"You ready?" Jake's finger hovered over the doorbell.

To flee? My mind briefly imagined waiting in the car, like I was too cool to go inside. Sunshades on, feet on the dash, attending to an important design emergency text message.

Which would be? Even when working the biggest emergency was an intern huffing too much rubber cement and slitting his finger on the X-Acto knife.

"Marigold? You there?"

Trying not to be.

"Unfortunately."

I looked over my shoulder as he rang the doorbell. Being paranoid was a good mental switch from wondering if this could have been my house if Theo and I stayed together.

"No one followed us," Jake reassured.

"How can you be sure?"

"Because I kept looking myself the whole time over."

"And you're sure?" I still wasn't facing the front door. Instead, I was watching the very quiet street. Only three cars parked alongside the sidewalk and road, and they were here before us, so maybe he was right. "Do you think last night's visitor got what he wanted? Was it just to scare us?"

"I told your dad," He admitted.

I gasped, finally turning to glare at the front door and him, "You did not! Now he's just going to worry." Sure enough, my phone's screen revealed ten missed messages from him, I slid it back into my pocket, that would be dealt with later. "I can't believe you…"

"Told him about the development in the case?" he shot an annoyed look down at me, "Police were called. There was no *not* telling him."

"And it looks good, right?" I asked.

The front door swung open, framing Meg. Perfect Meg. Resentment hit me in the gut like a mule kick. Of course she had short bouncy blond curls, big brown Disney eyes and a mouth full of pearly white teeth that never saw a cavity. Today she was dressed in a lavender sheath dress with a simple grey belt and Kendra Scott drusy studs. Understated elegance. No one blamed Theo for ditching me for this upgrade. But standing next to her… It hurt. I was in jeans and a plain green t-shirt with a small shamrock on the shoulder. Were we anywhere near St. Patrick's Day? No.

At least I spent time on my make-up and did a killer smokey eye.

To frame my glare better.

And I had my bright red lips going for me, so he could better see my scowl.

She paused, nervous for a moment, I was, after all, the angry and embittered jilted ex. At her very doorstep! Lucky girl.

"Come on in," she recovered, darting her eyes between the two of us. I liked to think we made a pair of intimidating specimens. "We're in the living room. I've got some snacks. If that's appropriate for this sort of thing?"

"Snacks are always appropriate, Meg. Thanks for seeing us." Jake said as he followed her lead inside, dragging me by the wrist as he noticed my hesitancy.

But can one blame me?

It was like entering a snapshot of what my life would have been like if I was a little (okay a lot) more together. If Theo loved me.

If I was enough.

Oooh, this was not healthy. I kept chanting "for Emma's murder" in my mind to keep from dwelling on the past as we settled onto the couch. How calming statements have changed.

I was a wreck. A frayed wreck. And did I really owe her this much? I just met the victim for drinks.

Jake sat next to me on the couch, our knees clacking together as we settled in. There wasn't kidding anyone, I was here for him. He didn't deserve to do this alone, proving his father innocent. And Emma, maybe I owed her this, she was willing to let me stay in her home, for as long as I needed. Few people were that kind. There were a lot of reasons to be here, in this living room, accepting a sugar cookie and a glass of tea from my ex's new girlfriend.

Let me make a correction.

Fiancé.

Oh. I swallowed a lump of tasteless cookie and tried not to choke.

That was some sparkly ring.

"I see congratulations are in order," Jake said, he squeezed my knee as I choked.

"Yes, congratulations," I managed, recovering with sips of tea to get the sugar dust out of my throat. Theo always told me he wasn't sure he ever wanted to get married, always citing divorce statistics. Glad math didn't matter to him anymore.

"Why thank you," his voice came from the doorway, pausing, simpering, as he strolled in and settled in the couch across from us, "We're quite excited." Through every movement of his, as he poured himself a glass, stole a cookie from the tray, Theo's eyes locked on my face as if to catch me looking upset. He wanted confirmation that he won. That he crushed me and moved on and found someone else-someone better. And he wanted me to know it. "I'm a lucky guy. I don't think I've ever been in love till I met Meg here."

He never looked away.

I didn't crack. I slipped into Southern Belle Mode, let the filter wash over me, and only offered a small smile. It was a hard, cold exoskeleton that took years to cultivate, but could ensure survival in any situation.

"Bless your heart," I said, "We're sorry to have to interrupt your celebrations with going over such an unpleasant topic."

He flinched but recovered quickly to smile at Megan. He knew when he was up against a Belle.

"Just a few questions," Jake nodded, "I admit, Emma and I were never very close. So I need to fill in some gaps."

"Of course," Meg said wide eyed, "Did you know Emma and I recently started being doubles partners? She's very good at...," she flinched, "She was... sorry... She had a great serve."

"How did you two meet?" I asked. Not like they were the same age and ran in the same social circles.

"We shared the same instructor. He suggested the pairing. Both of us wanted to finally start playing and not just training," she nibbled at her own cookie, dusting crumbs off her clothes, proving her humanity, "We'd grab a meal or snack on the patio after our matches. Talked about our game, what we'd do better next time. We're both solidly intermediate. I'm sorry, I'm talking like she's still here."

"It's okay, Bae, it's been a shock," Theo said in a comforting tone, one I remember him using on me when he used to care. Odd how tones and caring can be transferred to another individual. I swallowed the lump in my throat and wiggled in my seat a bit as if having to physically shake out that thought.

"I mess up, too," I encouraged, "Go on. What sort of other things did ya'll talk about?"

"I'm guessing you're wanting to know if she confided in me, if there was anything wrong in the marriage. Or if... not that I think her husband. I'm sorry. Of course, my first thought was that he did it. Right? It's always the husband. Who else was at home? Who else would have felt that passionately to kill her?" Megan raised her own hand to stop herself, "I'm sorry, that's all conjecture. And I've only met Paul once, and he seemed very nice. He brought Emma her wallet at lunch when she forgot it and they had a laugh, we said hello, and he went to go golf. He seemed very nice. But if there were problems, we weren't confidants. Our conversations were light."

"My Love listens to a lot of true crime podcasts," Theo clarified.

"Your opinion is noted, Megan. Don't feel bad at all for it," Jake said rather smoothly considering we were talking about his own father. "What else did ya'll talk about?"

"Oh... Um... Well, she was very excited about you coming to town, Marigold. I think she was kind of lonely. I noticed she probably brunched with me because no one else would. Everyone talks highly of you, and I think she thought if she got close to you, well, then she'd have it made friend-wise."

I nodded. I hated the thought of Emma being lonely. In that large house. With stepfamily, but not real family. Jake stared at the carpet between his two feet, scratching at the back of his neck, receiving the sting of guilt. To the town, to Jake, Emma was another stepmother coming through and likely on the way out. Why get to know her? Gossip put her as a social climber and a gold digger. Why befriend that and risk your own social demise? Or even the risk of being used yourself.

"Thanks Megan," Jake said, finally looking up, "For befriending her. I should have stepped up to that a long time ago but..." he sighed, "I built up this wall against my Dad's wives and girlfriends. They were only passing through and I didn't want to get attached. I'm realizing with this... I didn't treat them as individual people."

"How could you have known?" she soothed. "Finding her justice, locking up whoever did this, will help her and you. Don't carry that guilt. We all could have been better. And speaking of locks," she handed me a small gold key from her pocket with a pink pom-pom at the end. It screamed "Emma."

"It's her locker key, she was always leaving it at home, so she made me keep her spare. Locker 73 in the main lady's lounge. I hope this helps."

I did not want to like her. I didn't. I wanted to walk out of here saying she was snobby vain, shallow, an airhead. I couldn't. The more I talked to Megan and listened, the more respect I had, and the more that turned my gut. Theo really found an upgrade. Any guy would-and should-break my heart to get to land a girl like her.

"Thanks Megan. This helps. A lot. If there's anything else we'll call," I managed. Well, Jake would call. I snapped the key to my own key ring and the pom-pom livened up my very plain key set.

"Oh of course," She stood to guide us out, "And I'd love to hang out some time now that you're back in town. I need some more girlfriends. All I get is Theo and your brother and Jake and I'm tired of fishing stories."

"Sounds great," I lied, as I waved, what would I hoped to be a very permanent goodbye.

"We'd love that," Theo lied, waving back from the threshold, his lips stretched thin against his teeth. "So much. Better get moving. It looks like rain."

Chapter 16

Rain poured. Even to my sixteen-year-old self, that description rang trite. Water fell in biblical proportions and the Land Rover sluiced through it like Noah's Ark. Instead of going two by two, I was smashed in the back seat between my mouth-breathing brother and Jake. Never letting a stolen moment go to waste, the smashing was angled far more in Jake's direction. Knees and thighs pressing into each other, elbows and arms brushing. I hoped God was looking away, helping us through the storm, instead of witnessing this barrage of hormones.

My brother was busy with his hand-held video game, his mind lost between the headphones.

Jake busied himself curling a finger through my hair, smirking down at me. Sneaking his other hand on my knee. That teenager had the confidence of a college boy, and I was in love. Remembering how his lips pressed again mine... I was scheming to make that happen again.

Jake smirked. He knew my thoughts because they were his.

"Stop it," I hissed, my face red.

"You'll miss me," he whispered, pressing his lips against my ear.

I gulped. I would. But I also wouldn't tell. He was seventeen, but somehow he had packed a lot of life in that one extra year. It was intimidating and sexy and wrong that I knew he wanted to put that hand on my knee and slowly slide north.

"Go to Hell," *I said, my favorite and most unoriginal retort.*

"Kids! Stop it, I need to concentrate," *Paul roared from the driver's seat.*

He thought we were fighting.

Oh, Mr. Paul, we've moved on from being children.

Jake and I shared small smiles, privately celebrating our secret graduation.

Though I couldn't blame him, the rain was getting disconcerting. We should have left earlier when it was sprinkling. Our vacation in the Hill Country was turning sour. Every summer we'd jaunt down to Fredericksburg and let the adults scratch their vineyard itch. Texas vineyard after vineyard. As us kids got whinier and whinier. Occasionally, we'd be allowed our sip of wine, but mostly the under twenty-one-year olds were regulated to the clubhouses. My brother, Jake and I would play board games while Amy curled up in a corner with her sketchbook. This year, Richard and his wife Carmen joined. He was a new associate at their firm, and I supposed this trip was to integrate them. They were in their 40s (old) and perfect candidates to drag to wine tastings.

But this time… instead of taking the group to a fancy cheese-plate, dime-sized portioned restaurant, Richard said, "Why don't we do something kid friendly?" *he looked down at our bored faces as we sat in another clubhouse. Our plate of dry crackers and cheese left untouched. The kids' meal.*

Rain tapped lightly against the window, saying hello, introducing its trouble.

Still, Mom and Dad and Paul and Pam (Wife #3) looked unconvinced. Carmen nodded along enthusiastically, "They've been so good. Why don't we go to Tony's? It's right down the road, it's just like a Chili's but with a little more local flavor-oh- the fried pickle chips are to-die-for."

Dad relented, sealing our fates, "Better than finding the next vineyard, it looks off the main highway. I'm in. A beer after all this wine might be a welcome thing after all."

Maybe things would have been different if there wasn't a sports game on TV. If the beers weren't poured and the stacks of refillable pickle chips devoured and devoured again. For the first time the entire weekend, us kids, nay-teenagers, were smiling.

My avocado ranch cheeseburger, dripping with condiments fulfilled my spirit and oozed down my fingers. Last night dinner was blackened salmon and a cold cucumber salad... About three bites worth.

No one wanted to leave that table. Not even as the weather worsened, especially as.

Until Mom yawned. Then Paul. Then all the adults, coming down from their alcohol high.

"I'm hitting a wall," Paul said. They all agreed.

"It's a tropical wave out there. You should see how bad Houston got it. It's not going to get any better," Dad said.

We were hustled out into the rain, piling into whatever car was closest- we were all heading to the same hotel anyhow. Jake grabbed my hand and pulled me into the backseat, fluttering my heart that he wanted me so close. My car, Paul was driving with Richard in front with him.

The other car was behind us. I could tell Dad was driving, with

Mom in front. Amy and Pam and Carmen were smushed in the back. It was an odd arrangement, but we just landed where we landed, there were not enough umbrellas with us.

It happened right after Jake turned to me and said, "When we get back, let's try and get a movie to watch."

Richard turned, facing us, just as it happened in fact, "Have you guys seen..."

That was all he got out.

The car jerked forward, skidded. I closed my eyes tight; cars shouldn't feel like a turbulent airplane. Jake and my brother lurched forward themselves but managed to hold me back between the two of them. As the car stopped, I peeped open an eye to see if it was safe-or if we were only in the eye of the storm.

It was... relatively... we were pulled alongside the highway. The other Land Rover in the party stopped behind us, its headlights illuminating the scene. The highway cut through ranches and farms, but offered no sign of the civilized, just lush greenery bending to the onslaught of water.

"It was a deer... a deer, I swear..." Paul panted from the driver's seat, "I swear."

I looked out, no trees nearby.

Just a dog- a large one. Watching us by the side of the road, its tongue hanging out. Was that the deer he braked so hard for?

The dog barked, as if to say, "Yes. It's me." All eyes and heads shifted towards it.

"A deer..."

I looked toward Richard to get his read on what he saw from the front. But what looked back at me-rather more towards the roof of the car, *was a pair of lifeless eyes.*

I froze. Immovable and inoperable. My mind failed to function. It was trying to put the puzzle together. Replaying those last few moments from the lurch.

Blood ran rivers across the dashboard. He took off his seatbelt to talk to us.

The back of his head... He must have flown forward and then backwards...

"Don't look," someone hissed.

But I was still broken.

A hand clamped across my eyes, sending me back into darkness. More hands pulled me from the car and back into the rain.

"I got you," Jake said, hugging me close, "just don't look."

I opened my eyes, seeing only the thready blues from his shirt. That was safe. I let my senses be overrun by blue.

My brother joined us, a grip on my shoulder, not letting go, and the cessation of rain-he found an umbrella. Amy piled onto our hug, small and shivering.

"No. Don't look. I'll tell you when it's safe. You too Amy," Jake said as I attempted to twist.

"Well, what's going on?" I asked, glad to note I was coming out of shock. Though I was scared to think what I would see when opening my eyes.

What I could hear though... Sobbing.

Accompanied by a stew of hushed adult voices.

"... get away from here."

"... A deer..."

"We've all been drinking."

"Richard!"

"There's a body."

"A body? He has a name."

"Oh Richard!"

More threads of exclamations to weave the quilt.

"... Too drunk to drive."

"We all were."

"Well, what now?"

"... Call 911?"

"Why, he's dead?"

"... Police..."

"None of us could pass a breathalyzer."

"I could."

"We need two, two cars..."

The voices continued. Accusations. Sobbing. Fear. Words leading nowhere. Till one cut through. I pushed off Jake so that I could turn and watch. He let me, both feeling this was something momentous, something not to miss.

"If there's nothing to find, then there's not a crime." Paul.

A sharp gasp from the newly minted window. Her hand flew to her chest as if she were shot. The bullet, Paul's callousness.

"What would me going to jail accomplish, Carmen? It won't bring him back. I am sorry," his voice dropped, "Truly, sorry. And our firm will care for you the rest of your days, okay? You're not alone. But we can only do that if we have the resources. If this got out, our firm dies too. What were you before Richard? A substitute teacher? Do you want to go back to that?"

"Ohmigosh, my hus-husband is dead and..." Carmen began

sobbing again. Mom rushed over to give her a hug, sending a glare over the widow's shoulder to pierce Paul.

He shrugged, "Nothing I said was a lie. He wasn't wearing his seatbelt. This gets to court-we get it to be a tragic accident, she gets nothing. We get bad PR."

"That's enough, Paul," Dad growled, "But there is no bringing him back. It was a tragic accident."

"One that could bring us all down," Pam pitched in, "Could we actually get in trouble, too? And if Paul gets charged…"

"Then what?" Mom fired, still hugging Carmen, "You have to go back to substitute teaching, too? A man died! And we are just standing here."

"You're right. A car could stop," Paul said.

"Not what I meant."

"But all the same. We bury him. Get the Rover cleaned," he nodded towards Carmen, "You and the ladies go to Europe for a month. We'll set you up, wherever you want. Not Dallas of course. Richard's parents have passed on. Anyone else that would report him missing? We may have him getting 'sick' in Europe with you. Details for later. Thoughts?"

A pause.

"It's the only way. We don't have time for a plan b," Dad said, looking at the ground.

"You can't be serious!" Mom exclaimed.

"It could bring us all down. The police investigating us. Clients would lose trust."

As if Mom couldn't agree while holding Carmen, she stepped back, saying sorry with her eyes and vocally a weak, "Okay."

"Whatever we need to do," Pam added.

Lighting didn't crack across the sky. The earth didn't shake. Only Carmen wailed, falling to her knees.

"You can't do this. You killed him."

"He was drinking, too."

"No seat belt."

"A freak accident."

"We can't change what happened."

More phrases to act as a balm to the burning consciences. And then silence, as if guilt ran dry.

"Alright. We bury the body," Dad said, "Let's get this over with."

"Let's get the kids in the car, they're watching," Mom sighed, "Scar them a little less."

It ended up that Amy, Pam, Carmen, Mom, and I won the privilege of keeping warm and dry by the virtue of our gender and climbed in the clean SUV. Heat was turned on full blast and the car's emergency blanket stretched across Amy and I.

"Are you warm girls?" Mom rubbed my arm, "We're all going to get sick."

"Better than dead," Amy hissed. Carmen sniffed, but she kept her head down, her grief to herself. My heart pulled for her. I think Mom's did too, her face was tight, weary. But she was in control-a true matriarch and kept us from falling apart.

"Girls," she began, drawing Amy and I to her in the back seat, "Carry this with you. Marigold's father and I have a deal, that he'll retire young, and we'll get out of here and we will move far-far away. From all of this. Marigold, Amy, I want that for you. As soon as you can. Get out of

Dallas, marry outside our circle. Who you marry determines your whole life. Go to college, move away. Don't major in law. Nothing close to it. Nothing we could use to keep you here."

Her eyes bore into mine. I gulped.

The weight of her words fell on me.

"If you stay," she nodded towards the window, "This'll all be your life."

My eyes were saucer-wide, as were Amy's.

Was my mother happy in her life?

Had she witnessed Dad bury another body before?

I dropped my jaw to ask, but she held me silent with one look.

"Let questions remain questions."

The car fell silent as we realized the consequences of answers.

Huddled together, we watched the men in our lives dig.

Chapter 17

Beef tenderloin, loaded mashed potatoes, grilled asparagus and French bread. Jake's mouth was already stuffed with food, but I'd only gotten some wine down. My fork poked at the pink meat... I'd get to that later, I knew I had to eat, the appetite wasn't there yet.

We'd been called in for a status report. But what were we supposed to say? Well, we think you might be guilty, but as we all know, turning you in is a total bust. So-shoulder shrug- pass the A1 Sauce?

"I know the circumstances are crummy," I said, buttering my roll, "but it's great to see you, Dad. I'm grateful for the time we're getting to spend together, though Florida looks good on you." There- a safe topic that won't get us killed.

"Your mother would love to see you sometime down there, too."

Ah, well, only slightly attacked via guilt.

"Yeah, yeah. I'll make it down there. Soon."

"Jake, that invitation extends to you as well."

"I'd-wuff-to," his mouth was full of potato.

"Really, Jake? You have cheese dripping on your chin," I said with an eye-roll. Though it was nice to see that somethings never changed. The things that annoyed me, would always stay the same. Oddly, it was comforting.

He swallowed, "I'm only complementing the chef."

"Who is not here."

"Then to whomever is footing the bill," he smiled up to his father, "It's delicious."

It was so natural, for Jake to slip into the son mode. Being a son was a role from birth, but also a habit. How would one shake that off? Did he want to? His father was a (likely) killer. Once again not behind bars. Now we had to play our roles with him as if nothing happened.

Again.

I took a stab at my steak. I wasn't sure I could. I dreamt of the dog from the Austin trip last night, and couldn't shake it. He kept barking. Saying "don't forget me."

Do that again, that is. All the secrets. Was that what Dad was hinting? That I'd be safe in Florida? That he kept Mom safe by not bringing her here. Because he knew before even stepping on the plane who was guilty. Now I was next, to be brought home and protected. I hated the idea of leaving, fleeing to them. I just got here.

I hated the idea of leaving Shelley and Jake, even Amy.

But... the lies, the blackmail... all starting over again.

Clearly, Jake could stay and do it. He was already back to smirking at his dad. Jake was safer, however, since he was the son-the legacy.

"Florida sounds nice, Dad. Actually. I do miss Mom."

"I have to warn you, she'll try and keep you."

Translation: Pack for a long time.

"That's sweet."

Translation: I'll bring 2-3 large suitcases plus my carry-on.

"Where are you staying these days?" Paul asked.

"With me." Jake's voice was firm, protective, building a house around me, using his son-status superpowers.

"You know you're welcome back to the guest house. I hear all the police tape has been removed. I think only the kitchen's roped off now. But you have a nice kitchenette up there."

To think I'd ever want to enter that home again... And to sleep there? I held back my shiver to not insult him.

"I-I don't think I could. But thank you for the offer, Paul."

"Of course not," he frowned, "A sensitive soul like yours. Have to admit though, I liked the idea of someone being on property."

Is that what he thought? That one had to be sensitive in order not to be comfortable sleeping next to a crime scene? Was it weak in his eyes for possessing humanity?

"She's welcome to stay with me as long as needed."

"I'm sure she is," Paul scoffed.

"He's set me up in the guest room. And it's really nice. We don't even have to share a bathroom."

"Well thank you, Jake. I don't like the idea of Marigold staying somewhere alone," Dad said, "Not till we are sure everyone is safe. But did you upgrade your alarm system? I don't like the idea of someone sneaking around the backyard."

"I got Mike working on it."

This was new, my eyes darted between Dad and Jake. Mike was

the handyman our families used throughout the ages. Part of me bristled at the overprotectiveness, yet I was also grateful. There was a murderer and a lurker out there. The more overbearing and overprotective they became, stopping discussing their plans with me, the smaller and helpless I felt. Like maybe Poe and I really couldn't fend for ourselves.

It wasn't a good feeling. Vulnerability.

"We have increased surveillance, cops, driving by at night now," Jake assured.

"I'm so glad that Amy's husband is a police officer. She's safe," Paul added.

Safe from who? You? Does the fact that she's your biological daughter keep her safe? It wasn't too far off thinking he would hire someone to lurk around and scare me. I'm sure he's done it to the jurors.

I poked at my dinner and swallowed some meat down to distract myself. To convince them that the lone lady at the table was not a damsel in distress but was a (pink) red-meat machine. Tough and macho and to be respected. I shoved some potatoes down for good measure.

We had a busy day ahead, and I needed to figure out how to take down the man across from me. No, I wasn't a damsel. I was a threat and my shoulder still hurt, and that made me angry.

And that potato was a bit too hot. I spat it back out into my napkin.

"Getting back to business," Dad said, "I've texted you Pamala's address. Go get a statement from her. We need to gauge her temperature."

"It was a mutual split," Paul clarified, "Shouldn't be too bad."

"Yes, well, we know the investigators will be talking to her. We need to know what they know. She's expecting you this afternoon. Her home's in Rockwall now."

"We're on it," Jake said, like the dutiful son he was.

I just ate more potatoes.

"How did the interview with the tennis instructor go?" Dad asked, "Anything from the datebook?"

Jake slumped, "Dead ends. Date book only had the normal tennis lessons and birthdays and telephone numbers of family. It was more an address book log for Christmas cards."

"And Evan? The tennis instructor?" Paul asked, "She was dedicated to the sport. Maybe he developed a fascination with her?"

"Unlikely. According to Evan she was a middling to average player, and he prefers men. He's married to the guy who runs the spa," Jake said. "It's looking more and more like a crime of passion. Unplanned. Sudden. Domestic stabbings often are."

The table fell silent.

Only the scraping of silverware could be heard.

Husbands were passionate.

"We'll find something," Dad said, "You two focus on Pam."

"Got it." Jake said. Less than thrilled.

Seeing Pam, again… This would be interesting.

Eventually, the evening conversation drifted towards sports, signaling the end of dinner. It was always their last topic to cover. Work, news, sports. If someone suggested drinks during sports, then I was never getting out of there.

I stood, yawned, exaggerating my tiredness, cluing Jake in that we would leave soon.

"Where's the bathroom?" I asked, already knowing the answer.

Always best before hitting Dallas traffic.

As soon as I had finished my business and started reapplying my lipstick, someone began knocking on the door.

"Almost done," I called, giving my lips a blot.

"It's all yours," I said, swinging the door open, and right into Paul.

I gulped. I thought it was going to my father since I'd used the one off his office.

"You seem jumpy. Are you okay?" Paul asked, "You were quieter than normal tonight."

"Lots to think about." I managed to smile.

Why had I never noticed how intimating the man was? He was large in breadth and height and presence.

"If this gets too much for you, I want you to come to me," he said, "You can stop investigating anytime. Let the professionals handle that. I completely understand if you want to spend your time catching up with friends instead. You just got here."

He clapped a hand, hard, on my shoulder and gave it a squeeze. Burning the healing bruise.

I clenched my teeth and breathed through the pain.

Did he know?

Of course he didn't know. Right? He wouldn't remember hurting me?

His expression was one of concern.

But I didn't know if he could actually kill his wife. Till I knew, I did not want to be left alone with him, and I couldn't be sure if he was threatening me or not.

"Let's... Let's join the others. And don't worry about me, Paul. I'm good. Glad to be back."

"Yes. I'm glad you're back, too, Dear."

He smiled.

But something was wrong with that smile.

"Marigold!" Jake yelled from the living room, "Let's get going!" His very welcome face appeared in the door. Frowning.

"All done here," I said, trying not to show my relief.

Saved.

Pam was never problematic. She was a schoolteacher, when Paul met her; she was Jake's English teacher to be exact. Early on she liked kids, but then she began to like handbags and yoga and travel more than tending to her new step-children. She was never cruel or neglectful-maybe more distant and cold. Like she'd make the after-school snack, and then walk away, to the den and drink a glass of wine by herself as she watched TV. Pam quit teaching the second that ring slid onto her finger.

"I wonder how Pam turned out after the divorce and everything," Jake mused as he turned down the volume on the radio, practically voicing my own thoughts. It was an expensive divorce because they were together for a long while and because she knew about Austin. As divorces went, though, it was a friendly one. More a growing apart, like a business relationship reaching the end of a contract and both decided not to renew. But these were our childhood memories. The truth could have been shaded by the adults in the room.

"How are you? Seeing Pam again?" I asked.

"It's weird."

"Any elaboration?"

"I mean," he gripped the steering wheel harder, "She was my stepmom for like ten years. More than that. After the divorce, she met us kids for lunch once. Essentially, she divorced us, too."

"That had to hurt."

I couldn't imagine.

"How can someone care about you and disappear? Or maybe she never did? Maybe none of them cared at all. Katrina lived with us for five years. Same. After the divorce she was gone. No lunch even. Are all women this cold? Or just the ones Dad liked?" He exhaled, shaking out his white-knuckled hands one by one, "Sorry."

"No, it's okay. I want to know what's in your head," I paused, "And at least you know your real mom loves you a ton. She's always mailing cards and gifts."

"Loves me a ton from Germany with her new, what's-his-name husband. Yup. A whole-lotta healthy in there," he said, pointing to his head before falling silent.

My brain couldn't come up with anything helpful to say. No words could act like a balm to that wounded inner wounded child. Only action. Only showing him that at least he always had me as a friend. Hopefully meeting Pam again would show him they had to cut Paul out of their lives for safety and sanity, and unfortunately that would be stepping away from the kids as well. They were never leaving *him*. A concept difficult for a teenager to understand.

Looking over at Jake, his shoulders slumped and that death grip on the wheel, my heart broke. I couldn't imagine having that many Birthdays and Christmases with someone and then poof-stepmom disappears like she never cared or ever wanted to be there.

"They stayed away because of Paul, Jake. Not you."

He nodded. I couldn't really press either, traffic was picking up as we began crossing the bridges. It always surprised me how big the lake was between Rockwall and the DFW mainland. Haze settled over the water and fogged up the red-tile-roofed homes along the water. The map app said she'd likely live in one of those lake houses on the banks. A good settlement for a teacher. Out here on the water, those houses were in the millions. In the suburbs money went a longer way, so it would be a nice, large and spacious home. I was looking forward to a tour and seeing how she decorated.

"Least it's not too foggy. I've passed over here when it's been much worse," I chimed.

He nodded again.

Okay... I turned up the radio, taking the hint and helped the phone in my lap track our path. He'd never been to his ex-stepmother's house. No wonder he refused to get close to Emma. I wondered if I was the last woman he let in, in any significant sort of way.

As I guessed, the house was large, Mediterranean styled, with a green lawn and two gigantic trees at either side of the drive. However, none of that mattered.

There was a minivan in the driveway.

It was a Honda minivan parked next to a sleek, black Volvo. Both had that "my kid is an honor-roll suck up student" decal on their bumpers.

Jake's face paled as he parked behind the van. He turned off the car and sat there, not bothering to unbuckle his belt. It was like he'd been physically slapped and still reeling from shock. That van... It meant she was capable of caring, of loving, just not him.

"I can go in alone," I offered.

In response, he stared at the bike with ribbon tassels in the yard.

"What are we doing, Marigold? Why are you staying with me?" he said with a sigh and finally faced me.

I jerked back against the door, feeling slapped myself. Did not expect that.

"Are you staying with me because your Dad told you to?"

"Jake, I do very few things my Dad tells me to do. I'm a grown-up woman."

"You could stay at Shelley's or a hotel."

I pulled my eyebrows into a frown, "Are you kicking me out? I guess I could go to a hotel for a bit. You know Shelley and I failed at being roommates-we nearly killed each other. Our friendship couldn't survive. Is that what you're saying? Our friendship won't survive?"

"You know how I feel about you. Are you going to stay for a bit and leave? Like everyone else? If you love me, then," he unclicked his seat belt, "Then you should just leave now. I can solve my Dad's case myself. I don't need anyone else. Never have."

I exhaled. Not this. Not now. It was like talking to teenage Jake. We were cruising towards a talk like this, but I wasn't ready, and he was clearly an emotional mess.

"Jake…"

"No. Don't sigh my name. I need answers."

His eyes flashed with intensity. I gulped.

Fine.

Darn that minivan in the driveway. Representing love and family and everything we shouldn't/couldn't have.

"Every time I've given you my heart you have broken it to pieces. *Every time*. Now after you, Theo, Scott, it's finally getting whole again. Please don't mess with that."

"I love you, Marigold. I've grown up. I've changed. You can see that I'm ready."

I could.

This car was getting too small.

"So you've said before."

"It wasn't our time yet, before; I wasn't ready. I love you, and I'm ready, now."

I shook my head. No. I didn't want that.

"Marigold..." he reached for me, but I squished away.

"No. I trust you with my life, Jake. But not my heart. Never again will I trust you with my heart."

I turned and got out of the car. I did not want to see his expression. I didn't want him to see me mop up tears. Because he knew, I knew, that I still loved him. But there was nothing more pointless or scary than to love a man who'd only ever crushed your heart. It wasn't fair, either, that he thought everything happened on his terms. I was almost "okay" and didn't want my wholeness to be taken away from me again.

"Do I need to move out?" I called, still hiding on my side of the car.

"No. Stay as long as you need," his voice, disembodied. Surprisingly warm. He probably saw my tears and realized I wasn't using him. Realizing that not everything could be on his timetable.

"Oh hi there!" a familiar voice cut through the awkwardness, "I heard you drive up." It was Pam, framed in the doorway of her Mediterranean home.

"Pam," I greeted with a smile, and a bit of an oof as she gave me a hug.

"Why it's just been too long! And Jake! Are you taller? You are indeed taller, if that's possible."

Jake was a good sport and allowed himself to be squished.

"Hi, Pam, it's good to see you," his voice ran flat.

"But under such circumstances," she shivered.

"It's tragic," I agreed.

"We've got a lot to go over," he stated.

"Of course, of course. Let's go in the backyard? It's such a nice day that I'm clipping thorns off the roses. My youngest fell into them last year and ever since I've kept the stems smooth. I've set out knee pads for us," Jake's shoulders stiffened at the mention of the youngest, so I took over and agreed for us, "That sounds lovely. Thanks again for seeing us on such a short notice."

I was a little sad, though, to be guided straight outdoors and not having time to be nosy inside.

Pam gave me a winning smile.

She had always been pretty in the classic blue-eyed blonde sort of way, but she was now aging gracefully. If not suspiciously. When we were younger, she had the big-blonde poof, but now, her hair was straight and sleek and pulled back into a ponytail accenting her narrow face and high cheekbones. Facelift? Botox? Lip filler? As we followed behind her, I glanced up at Jake, expecting him to meet my eyes and know what I was thinking. Instead, his gaze remained straight ahead, a man on a mission. That's what I hoped at least. I worried that me not telling him I loved him back meant I was no longer privy to his inner thoughts. That he severed our connection. It was lonely, being the only one in my head.

"I should get right to the point, shouldn't I? I see Jake's expression," Pam said as she sat on her knees and reached to clip a thorn. She passed us each clippers, and while we both took a knee, Jake refused the gardening tool.

I wanted to be a little helpful for allowing us to dig into her past.

"We have a lot on our schedule," he said, trying to appear rude.

"I'd still love to catch up," Pam said, "It's been too long. Too, too long."

"That's just the problem."

Pam flinched. I found no soothing words of my own because he was not wrong. I took my anger out on the thorns. Clip. Clip. Clip. Jake shouldn't have to be dealing with all of this.

"What were you wanting to ask?" her voice slightly colder now. Her clippers working faster.

"How things were with Paul. Why you left. I'm trying to get a clearer picture of my father."

"Emma, right? It was in the news. 'Wife of Dallas Socialite Brutally Slain.' Stabbed. Tragic, completely tragic."

"Do… do you think Dad could have done that?"

Pam melted a bit. I could see the warmth flow back into her. His tone was of a scared, little boy, pleading that his Dad was not a monster. My heart fell a little, right into my stomach, twisting up my gut.

"Your father was a terrific man to date. Trips, gifts, jewelers… He knew all the right things to say and do. And I fell hard for it. To marry, however," she sighed, and gave a thorn a good clip. "Not great. He'd be distant, always working. Always secretive about work. Saying 'it's for your own protection.' There were still lavish gifts, but, no heart. It was like he had won the prize and had no interest in keeping it. A man who only cared about the chase. I didn't like who I became with him-a shallow socialite that went to the club, starving for some sort of acceptance from someone. It wasn't till what happened in Austin where I saw his brutal side. He bought me a gigantic diamond, and that was it-we never talked about it again. But I saw it. The lack of remorse, how easy it was for him to kill someone-Accidentally- and sleep perfectly fine at night," she shivered, "I was too dependent on him to leave. So, I started selling some jewelry and giving cash to my family to hold for me. Got the divorce attorney. Paul only shrugged when I told him I wanted out. Shrugged. Said we'd run our course," she paused, shaking her head, and clipping another thorn away, "Ten years together he never raised a hand to me. Never fought for me or against me. We were essentially roommates towards the end. Do I think he could have killed Emma? Yes."

I sucked in a breath between my teeth.

"But only because of what I saw in Austin. Maybe if she nosed around on his business and he felt cornered? Do I think that's what happened here? No. Paul was old school, you don't mess with women and children. It's a rule, and I think he followed it. Unless she somehow jeopardized his business."

"They had a pre-nup that leaned heavily in her favor," I suggested, impressed at the amount of truth she was willing to spill and hoping for more.

Pam smirked, "The chase. Winning the prize. That's the phase where he was weak. He'd have found a way to make her leave. Isolation. It's brutal. But murder? No way. In his own home? Stupid. That's only for passionate, obsessive people. He's too methodical and robotic."

I nodded, "Would you testify any of this?"

Pam's eyebrows flew sky-ward, "It's my impression Paul likes his privacy. We had a friendly settlement."

"He bought your silence," Jake said flatly, "Nice house."

She didn't take offence, and gestured towards the lake and her pier, "I was just a teacher... So, it's up to Paul. I'll help however."

"I see," Jake said, "And you stayed away? Why? You were my stepmom for ten years."

"Oh, Jake. It's not like I haven't missed you and your sister..."

"Pam." He cut off her apology.

Her mouth dropped open, but she recovered, "Well, he told me to stay away. He said it was best ya'll all moved on together and without me. He was very clear. I was to be the one to walk away since I wanted the divorce. I had to be the bad guy. So I agreed. You don't disagree with someone after you watch them bury a body like that. You just don't. And that's not something I'll tell any jury, don't worry."

We drove back to the city in silence. Digesting. As we left, Pam expressed her love for Jake and Amy, but it fell on deaf ears. Too, little, too late. Though, it was understandable-she was scared. It also meant however, that Pam didn't love the kids enough to fight to see them and give up any of that settlement money. She let them go.

I wanted to ask Jake how he felt, but that wall was up. I could feel it, like a cold, stone, physical barrier between us.

It wasn't until we were seated in a booth with coffee and pie, did I ask, "Well? Where are your thoughts?"

He'd brought a box of evidence with him and set it on the floor, trying to be business minded. Move forward, move forward, I could almost read his mind through the tough set of his jaw.

We were settled in at Lucky's. It was a good choice on his part-he drove us silently there and parked and I followed behind, never asking where we were headed. Lucky's was a 50s style café, and they made fresh pie every day. Today couldn't end any other way than eating dessert. Maybe getting some meatloaf to go. I should have known this would be his destination of choice.

"That we'd get the same answer. If we asked Mom or Pam, or any other women that married or dated Dad. That they'll all help Paul if he asks and meaning our fathers will write their testimony for them. All the divorces were publicly friendly," he said, voicing his thoughts mid-way through them, "Never heard of any problems with girlfriends."

"Are you relieved that," I paused, searching for the right words to dance near an uncomfortable topic, "He wasn't physically abusive, at least? That you didn't miss any hints?"

Had to say "physically" because I was quite sure there had to be some emotional abuse to make Pam feel that isolated. And that was the same road Emma's marriage was on.

"That my Pops passed as basic human? Yeah, a little relieved," he said, spinning his straw around in his drink, "And I'm sorry. Dumping the whole 'I love you' at a time like this. In the middle of everything and you just got back into town. I'm embarrassed," He gave the straw one more spin before he could meet my eyes with a shy smile, "Really sorry."

"No apologies necessary," I sighed, relieved, I was happy to have that smile back. A few stones of that wall removed. It was still up, but at least I could see him now.

"I wasn't-I'm not-in the best place," he admitted, "But whenever you are ready. Those words, they're yours."

I nodded, focusing on my hands that were folded tightly in my lap, "Hold on to them for me."

It was nice to be loved.

For a beat he played with the straw wrapper, and I wrung my hands, neither of us knowing where to look or what to say.

"So the box of locker contents," now that I was switching subjects to save ourselves, I could look him right in the eye like interior designer/sleuth that I was, "ready?"

We had the club unload her locker and box it up for us, and all we had to do was swing by their front desk on the way to Rockwall. It was a little frustrating we didn't even need the key, but very interesting the police hadn't gotten to it first. They were not bothering to investigate. Not good.

Jake swung it onto the table.

There were the standard items: change of gym clothes, a racket, a tube of yellow balls, a coin purse with small bills and coins, a half-full water bottle. Of all things, that's what made my hands shake. A true memento mori, Emma expected to come back to the locker and finish that water. Emma thought she had tomorrow.

"Check this out."

I snapped back and put down the water. He held up a black jewelry box revealing diamond studs, about 2 carats and gave a low whistle.

"Talk about an 'I love you, here's something to keep you around gift,'" he said.

"I forgot Valentines…"

"Sorry about your Birthday…"

"You're right. Those are missed Birthday or forgotten anniversary caliber," I said, snatching them away and playing with the box to make the studs shimmer. "Paul will want these back."

That thought made me sad. The gems would be sold or stored away forever and be forgotten. Maybe Amy would get them, that wouldn't be as horrible. She was married though, maybe John already forgot an important day, so she already had a pair. Amy didn't really need them.

"Am I going to have to wrestle you to get those back?"

"You'd like that," I scoffed. Still not handing them over.

"I would," and that smirky, smile was back. Good. Now so were my pink cheeks.

"Me too." I had to add to the pinkness of his cheeks, only fair.

He coughed.

"Really, we should keep this all together, right? It's evidence. In case someone thinks to ask for it?" he held out his hand for me to place the diamonds in.

"Oh, fine, fine, fine." And I did so. Reluctantly. We'd bonded.

"I promise to forget your Birthday one day," he quipped, as I watched my new friends being tucked away, buried under a Nike sweatshirt.

Goodbye.

"You better," I huffed, "Make me really mad one day."

He crossed his heart, "I promise."

The server came by and refilled our coffees and waters and asked if we needed more pie-sadly that had to be a no. But the coffee was good and hot. It knew what it was: nothing fancy. A rare trait in Dallas, and I respected that.

Still added sugar. But with respect.

"Your Dad texted me," Jake said, staring down at his phone.

"And not me?"

"Really?" he looked over at me quizzically from his mug, "Check your phone."

Four missed phone calls-from unknown. One from Dad. Three texts from him, too.

Two online clothing store notifications for ten percent off.

Jake grabbed my phone from my hands, as sudden as I had snatched those diamonds away.

"It's been since this morning since I've checked it," I muttered, somehow thinking that was some sort of defense.

Holding the screen up as if I hadn't seen it, he commented, "Four calls? Are they still just heavy breathing? This needs to stop. You can't live your life on silent and keep running away. Turn her in for harassment. Talk to John or Everett," he ran his hand through his hair, "I'm surprised no one has already. And now we've got a killer out there. What if we called to warn you? What if someone needed your help, and it was on silent? Do you know we all just accept that we can't get ahold of you?"

I had to flinch at that last one.

"You can have a point," I conceded.

"But do I have an effect?" he slid the phone across the table, and I snatched my baby back and sealed it away in my purse, last time I rested it on a table. "You know," Jake began, "I can see why you can't say you love me, yet. Theo broke your heart. Scott, in a different way, broke your heart. I did and deserve all the eternal punishment for doing such. You're still healing. Love to you has only been painful. I hope one day to redeem myself, and prove to you it's not," he said, sounding awfully full of himself after flipping out over a van earlier.

"Thanks for spelling it out so plainly. Putting it all out there..." I hid behind a menu, "Maybe let's get some fries. Do you like any sort of other food or conversation topic?"

Because, yes, you have an effect.

But the guilt outweighs it. Scott's Mom was harassing me, but some small measure felt like I deserved it. I got to live. I got to run away and rebuild my life. If I told John or Everett, then my punishment would end.

"You're going to that dark place," Jake said, frowning.

I snapped back, "Dark place?"

Don't read me, I wanted to say. It was scary when someone knew me that well.

"It's like your face goes blank and for a moment, you're not here. Where do you go?"

"Nowhere good."

"I can't reach you when you space out like that," Jake said so low I strained my ears to hear.

"Far from it. You always bring me back."

That was truer than I wanted it to be.

"If you ever want to talk…" his voice faded off.

"I know," I shifted in my seat, uncomfortable. I never enjoyed the spotlight, "Dad's text? The whole reason for the rabbit hole we're going down? What did it say?"

He gave me a side-long glance, as if to say "I see what you're doing here." Instead of making me more uncomfortable, however, he picked back up his phone and read, "Forensics were completely inconclusive. They can't even deem the gender or the height of the assailant from the stab wound. No DNA. Lucky break for us."

I gulped and swallowed the words that I wanted to say and then chased them farther down with a swig of coffee.

"Soo…" Jake started.

Our eyes locked. He was going to say it? Maybe he had to say it. It was his father, after all.

"Who do you think got paid off to scrub evidence that well?"

My shoulders relaxed; glad he was the one to break the ice on that.

"*How many* people got paid off?" I asked, "Do you remember the time he took all of us to the Police and Firefighter's Ball? He said it was important to make contacts."

Jake bit his lip, "Do you think?" he bit again, slowing his verbal thought process, "Do you think this makes him more guilty"

"To us. But to the law... Is he a suspect still?"

"There can't be a legal case," he took a sip of his own coffee and his mug banged on the table as he set it down, "I'm half-relieved, half horrified. I don't know what to think. Why did I think I'd hear something different? We're never going to know what happened. The case will go cold and I'll never know if my father was *that* man. Amy won't know if her kids are safe with him. Emma's sisters won't get closure. They want closure. They approved a full autopsy. Now they have to bury her after all that, and without any answers."

"Hey," I whispered, leaning across the table grasping his hand, "We'll find answers. Definitive ones to put your mind at rest. Okay? We won't let it go cold."

He closed his eyes and pinched the bridge of his nose, "I'm guessing the funeral's tomorrow now that the body's released. We can talk to Emma's sisters. Dad has offered to put them up in a hotel, but they refused. They're staying on their own dime- didn't say where."

"So, they suspect him?"

"That or it's just dislike. But likely."

I gave his hand a last squeeze before letting it go, "Can't wait to find out."

"And you need to call Amy back. My sister's pestering me with texts trying to get ahold of you."

"I wonder what she wants," I mused.

"Hopefully an update, if she has a heart. Do me a favor. Let's hear what she has to say, keep our thoughts vague. I don't want to influence her testimony."

Not yet at least.

Chapter 18

Luckily the rain continued to pour. Making the digging harder for the men, but preventing other travelers from driving down the road. Even more luck, Pam was a gardener and had two shovels in the trunk and some other flower-tending gear.

Lucky. That's what Mom said as my quivering lip tried to hold back tears. More of us could have been hurt. She gave me a hug, thanking God for our seatbelts and lives. With her words and warmth I could feel myself calming. Finally feeling the heat of the car's system.

That was until I saw Dad's face in the window. He looked grim and dirty, wild. I was used to seeing him in tidy polos, long khaki shorts, and clean brown loafers. Normal Dad had dark brown hair that was always gelled neatly down-he looked like a professor accessorized with round circle glasses and a briefcase. Always smart and clean.

DEATH ON LOVERS LANE

I recoiled from his taping at the window. Wild Dad was not someone I was ready to deal with; his clothes were plastered in mud, his eyes red, and dirt clung to his face and hair. Spit flew from his mouth as he yelled, "Time to join us ladies!"

Mom reached over me to roll down the window, "I've just gotten the girls warm and Carmen's calming."

"I know, I know but Paul's worried."

"Worried? Now? About what?" *she asked.*

"Future liabilities."

"Ah," *and her face went pale with understanding. Even if I didn't. I knew it was bad when news stole the rosiness from her cheeks.*

"Mom? What is he talking about? I don't want to go out there." *I was warm and dry like she said, and like I didn't want to say I was still wearisome of Dad. He looked more a monster than a man. Like a monster made of mud-pies.*

"Never become a liability, Marigold. Never," *she said, never taking her eyes off Dad's.* "We've been lucky to stay warm this long. It's time for us to do our part."

"Thank you, Love," *Dad whispered, squeezing Mom's hand as she stepped from the car,* "I don't think we have a choice."

I hardly heard him, as I was scrambling out of the car myself, scooting out behind Amy. When adults got this serious, there was no questioning them. And when they dropped their voices and tried to communicate via expressions more than words, that sent my eavesdropping senses into high alert. I caught him mouthing "Florida" to my mother and her timid smile as she mouthed it back.

In the midst of all the sadness and chaos, their secret whispered promise gave me the security I needed to slide from the car and grab Amy's hand. I could be strong like my mother. I was one of them. And the mud-monster man was still Dad. He was our monster.

My parents led the way. Hand in hand. A united front. Amy and I next; her face was pink and splotchy from tears and her body still trembling. I gave her hand a squeeze, "Hey, we've got you."

"A-a man died," she stuttered, "And no one's going to know. Are we all that expendable? If I slip and fall and die, will it be covered up?"

"You can't think like that," I tried to modulate my voice to sound like my parents' even tone.

"Think like what?" she hissed, "That my Dad's drunk driving just killed a man? And there are no consequences? My Dad killed a man- and he doesn't seem to care. That's not natural, right?"

It wasn't. If I accidentally ended someone's life, I don't think there'd be an end to my vomiting. Or crying.

I looked at Pam dragging Carmen along a good eight feet away, they couldn't hear us.

"Nothing that's happening tonight is natural," I agreed, "But maybe it is- in the more animalistic sense."

Amy gave me a look.

"Hear me out. Your father's most basic instinct is survival of himself and his family. He's slipped into primordial roots to protect what's his. Going to prison doesn't fit that agenda. My parents are reacting the same way, taking Paul's lead."

"Do you hear yourself? Are you justifying covering a crime?"

"I'm justifying watching out for family and friends. Your tribe. It's only natural. I made an A in psychology the last six-weeks. I know."

"Your Mom may be wrong you know. It's too late for you. I'm getting outta this family as soon as I can. But you? You're staying. You've drunk the Kool-Aid."

I flinched, "You're wrong."

I only wanted our parents, our families, to be good people. I loved them. This couldn't define us.

But it would.

Our voices fell to a hush as we gathered around the make-shift grave. A coat of dirt already coating the body so that we could not see what death looked like-again. Only the fibers of colorful clothes contrasted with the mud.

Paul and Jake also looked like wild mud men, matted with dirt and soil and rain. If they scrubbed, they'd still never feel clean again. I hoped that wasn't the case; I tried to catch Jake's eyes, but his gaze never left the mire.

"Richard was a good man," Paul began, "He deserves more than this. We can all agree on that. God rest his soul." He closed his eyes, "We will take care of your family. That I promise you." Paul scooped up a wad of clayey mud and threw it down to cover the body. "Now each of you are to do the same." This time, he was addressing us with his large, reddened eyes.

My father stepped forward first and tossed in his own handful of dirt, "To a good rest."

As Jake bent to pick up soil, Mom interrupted the ceremony, "Come now? Even the kids?"

Paul nodded, "We're all here. All guilty of covering this body, a death. No one ten years from now could take a polygraph and fake his or her innocence and make a deal. Tonight stays between us. For the construction and protection of our families' futures. Throw it in, Jake."

I gulped. Watching Jake, then Pam, Mom, Amy (she closed her

eyes). Then it was my turn, the wad of mud oozing cold and bloody between my fingers.

"You were nice," I said, closing my eyes and launching my contribution into the grave.

Then Carmen, who stood next to me. She dropped in a wildflower. Covering her mouth to cover the sobs.

"I'm sorry, My Love," she said loudly as the flower fluttered down, dropping her voice so only Richard and I could hear, "I'm sorry, but you left me amongst wolves."

After that my heart pounded in my chest, it was all I could hear. We were the wolves.

We watched a man die.

We covered it up. To protect our own.

Amy was right, it was too late. I looked down at my muddied hand, only she was wrong, it was too late for her as well.

Chapter 19

The ride to the hotel was silent. We had a row of rooms, Amy and I sharing; I knew Mom and Dad were next to us and Jake and my brother across.

"I get first shower." Was all Amy said before she disappeared into the bathroom.

"Yeah, sure," I responded to pretend I had any sort of control.

I stripped down to my underwear and turned the heater on and... wasn't sure where to land, so I stood in place, between the beds, hugging my arms around me to keep warm. Mud and rain still clung to me like a second skin. Hair matted against the sides of my face, all caked and stringy.

I wanted to cry; my mud-brown eyes turned a watery red, as they tried to hold it all in.

I could see Richard talking... and then not... and blood... It was a video clip playing on repeat.

"I'm out," Amy announced, "I hurried for you."

She was fresh and clean and clad in simple navy-blue pajamas. As if nothing happened. I wanted to look that way, even if it was a lie.

"Thank you." I flew past her, eager to feel clean again. Warm again. If that was possible.

"You need to hurry, too. Your mom wanted all us kids to meet up in her room."

"I know!" I shouted over the rush of the shower. The bathroom filled with steam, it felt luxurious, and I breathed in, hungry for any form of antidote.

Not much later, true to my word, we were gathered in my parents' room. Mom and Dad made us tea and laid out small bags of chips and candy from vending. Then they left to visit with the other adults.

"How are you?" my brother asked, draining his mug of tea in two sips. The four us sat at the room's breakfast table, save for Amy. She was spilled out on the bed with a pile of magazines and notebooks.

"You'd think I'd qualify for an actual beer and not chamomile?" he continued before I could answer, "I think I should be in there with the adults. Not at the kids' table."

I flushed. My brother was always trying to act more adult than he was. This time though, he may have been right. Being left alone with offerings of tea and candy seemed pedantic. Like we weren't part of the team. And, I mean, we weren't. We were teenagers. They had experience with-hopefully not this-but with legal stuff and making hard decisions.

"We're not kids," I agreed. We were somewhere in between. "I hate being left out, too."

"I didn't see you leave the car to help."

I flinched at his words. Because he was right.

"Forget it," he grumbled, picking up his iPad, "I'm going to go chill for a bit."

He took over the desk chairs, his feet up on the desk and earphones shoved into his ears. That was my brother-he bonded with music more than people. I hoped he found his comfort there...

I leaned on people. Probably too much.

I looked up at Jake, wanting warm smiles and comforting words from him at least. Though my brother was wrong, this tea was helping. I yawned.

"You drank it?" Jake asked.

I looked over at his filled mug, "You didn't?"

"I think I'm with your brother on this one."

"When alcohol caused all this?" I slammed my hand over my mouth, "Jake, I didn't mean to say..."

"What? The truth? My Dad killed someone and didn't care?"

"Jake... I..." my words fell away. There wasn't a thing I could say that would make anything better.

"You know I'm going to Texas A&M in the fall, right?" he looked at me with hard eyes.

"Yes," I couldn't read his expression. "That's not for a while still."

"It's also not that far off. Which is why we need to cool it for a bit."

My heart fell into my stomach. This wasn't Jake.

We'd already agreed when he went to college, we'd just be friends again. Accepted our families' lives were so intertwined that if we were meant to be, then in time we would be. If we weren't, well, we'd given each other space to evolve and find love.

Then we'd always be in each other's lives.

But now his eyes wouldn't reach mine.

He strayed from our breakup plan.

Our last date was to be eating cake, listing out for each other top three and top worst three things about ourselves. We had a plan to avoid heartbreak. Had to, we had to share turkey day and Christmas afternoons.

"Jake... The plan." I whispered.

"Please. Why don't you go hang out with Amy?"

"No. We had a plan." I banged my fist on the table. Neither Amy nor my brother bothered to look up.

Finally, Jake met my eyes. They were darker than normal, from milk chocolate to dark. Lidded and haunted, as if he had attended another sort of graduation I was not privy to.

"I buried a man," his voice broke, "Dug his grave in the middle of the wilderness. Have you considered I'm no longer worthy of your plan?"

My mouth fell open. Not worthy. Those words stole my breath.

Vigorously, I shook my head, "No. I was there, too."

"It's different. You saw my father. I saw the monster I turn into."

"Jake..." my love and pity for him bled into his name and he winced, but his shoulders remained resolute. He'd decided. We were over. For good.

"I'm going to major in law, go to law school with your brother, and we're taking over the family business. That's the plan. It's the way it will be. This was my first shovel. Not my last. Run Marigold. Because I can't."

Chapter 20

I wasn't sure how to get us out of this mental quagmire.

I needed a cold, emotionless thinker.

Jake was wrong on this account, we needed his sister.

"Thanks for answering," I said, as Amy picked up. And before she could respond, I went straight into updating her on every conversation Jake and I have had. "What do we do?"

"Mmm..." she mused, I could hear tea being boiled in the background, "I believe I can help you."

Even through the phone, I could sense that smile of secrets, knowledge, and calm coolness. There was a scary amount of Paul in her.

Chapter 21

Loving a man is the most foolish thing this woman could do.

Completely foolish.

Worst of all was when thoughts of him swirled around my mind, tying it into a knot, so I could never let him go.

Foolish. Because those knots got tied around my heart.

I couldn't get Jake out of my mind.

Every boy I talked to, I compared. And they never measured up. No one was as funny, as sweet, as kind. No one lit up at my jokes like he did, and no one had those dimples that revealed themselves whenever I walked into a room. It was love. We'd started out as puppy love in high school, and I was crushed when he broke up with me. Back then I had the resiliency of youth and a football team at my disposal to bounce back with. In college there were cute study partners to free my mind with.

But then... that one Christmas break. I mean, I thought he was handsome in the summer, and at Thanksgiving... But maybe he needed three more weeks to grow into a man. Maybe the stress of finals filled out his form.

The way he looked at me, when I walked through that front door, holding the fudge I'd made for the Christmas party, it fully collapsed my lungs.

He'd seen me. For the first time, as a woman.

Maybe I also needed that extra three weeks for full maturity to kick in. Maybe wearing a turkey sweater and sweatpants at Thanksgiving was not the way to go.

For Christmas, though, I wore a short, red sequence dress, and my blonde hair cascaded down in curls. I felt pretty. He offered to take the baked goods off my hands, and one thing led to another, we were upstairs, making out in his bedroom from that one gentlemanly act and the mischievous spark in his eye.

"The party," I kissed him back, "Everyone's downstairs."

"They can wait," he groaned, cupping the back of my neck and pulling me closer. "I have a lock on my door now."

I wasn't sure in what world that statement was romantic, as my mind filled with all the reasons and other women that he'd need a lock on his door for.

"Wait," I pushed away. "We're doing this again. We always make out, split up, rinse and repeat. Aren't you tired of it? I mean are you seeing anyone right now?"

"No. I'm pre-law. I don't have time to date. Are you seeing someone?" He may have sat back, but his fingers were still dancing across my shoulder.

"Not currently. I mean I've gone out with a few guys, but nothing serious."

"Then what's the harm of making out a bit with my future wife?"

"You're what?" I snorted, "I think you are really, really presumptuous here."

My scoff was an act. To not scare him away. Wife? Since when was that a word he played with? I was the childhood girlfriend. Holiday make-out buddy. But wife? My mind went dizzy, and I tried to hold on to reality and not daydreams. The hold he had on my never fully dissipated, even with time.

"Everyone knows it. Why do you think no one's come up here to check on us? It's the plan."

"It's the plan?" my voice got squeaky, "I have an arranged marriage? Well no. That is stupid." I rolled away and off the bed and put my hands on my hips. It wasn't the most authoritative look, a dress half zipped and mussed hair. "Be honest, Jake, do you love me?" I pasted the top of my dress against my body with my hand, "Do you? I don't want someone to marry me that doesn't love me."

Marrying me for duty? That would crush my heart.

"I... I feel like in this moment, it may be unwise to answer."

I pointed to his open shirt, "Yeah, button yourself up, then"

But he didn't.

He swung his long legs off the bed and stood in front of me, running his hands up and down my shoulders. Removing my hand that plastered the fabric to my skin and then placing it in his.

"What if I told you," he whispered, "That you are gorgeous? That I'm studying hard so that one day I will be worthy to call you my wife? Because that's my plan?" he paused, "What if I'm planning a romantic proposal?

Something special like making you dinner and spelling out 'Marry Me' in cheese?"

I giggled. He knew my love of food.

"What would you say then?" his warm breath rushed against my ear.

"Then I... I would say... I would say..." nothing at all because my brain was sending out blips and couldn't string a sentence together. I'd been in love with Jake since I knew what love was.

My heart burst. "I feel the same way," I broke out a big smile, "You should keep studying."

"For us?" he whispered into my ear.

"For us," I confirmed, letting him steer me back towards the bed. Loving that man was the most foolish thing this woman could do.

Chapter 22

My hand cramped as I gripped the racket harder. I returned Shelley's volley, and we went back and forth till finally a ball bounced right passed me. And I just had it.

"So close," she said, coming up to the net, "Are we finished here?"

I approached, tossing the ball over to her, "Yeah. I can't take any more humiliation."

Shelley had a wicked backhand. I was more here because she couldn't play alone.

"If we hit the sauna will he be joining us?" she nodded at the large man standing at the edge of the court, keeping a trained eye on us.

"He'll stand outside. Like he did at the locker room."

She frowned.

Couldn't blame her. It was annoying being tailed, but necessary. Dad's office was representing someone accused of killing his accountant and his accountant's dog. Innocent before proven guilty of course, but whenever their clients involved someone with a continuous violent past, we had to be extra cautious. This one made threats that if he wasn't acquitted, Dad would pay. We weren't sure if that meant only money-wise.

I hated when those sorts of clients were taken on. Not only did my freedom get taken away, with curfews and bodyguards, but publicity surrounded our homes. The bodyguard's job was to protect me from getting physically attacked, but also to prevent too many photographers getting my photo for the nightly news.

This case was all over the media. The presumed guilty party was buying into the local football team. He was also a big donor to all the local schools and politicians.

Bodyguard was going to be on my heels for a while.

"He'll be gone soon," I lied.

"But this is Spring Break! And you have to be home before eleven. And you can't stay over. Does your family know how much they are interrupting our Shelley and Marigold Take on The World for One Week plans?"

I laughed, "I'm sure they do. And I'm sure they've lost tons of sleep over it."

"They better," she eyed the bodyguard, "Least he's cuter than the last one. Okay. Sauna time. I will not feel guilty for making him wait on us."

"He's getting paid."

"Did the guy really kill the dog?"

"Presumably, the accused denies it though."

Shelley shivered, "Only a monster goes that far. Maybe I'm sorry for guilting you about the protection following you everywhere."

"Maybe it's okay. I know it's lame."

"What's lame?" an all too familiar voice called over.

I groaned.

I couldn't be protected from everything.

"Jake, how horrible to see you," I said.

"Yeah... you look, you look awful," Shelley added, both wishing she had said nothing.

The man didn't look awful at all. He looked like one of those male cologne ads, out here in a polo and white shorts and a racket.

Jake squinted, "Yeah... Shells, do you mind if Marigold and I have a moment?"

Ever loyal, she shot me a look, inquiring what she should say.

"We have a sauna time booked. What is it, Jake?" I said, pretending to be bored with his presence.

"Can't we talk? We haven't spoken since Christmas."

"There's a reason for that. You never called. Jake, I think we're done. I didn't think you'd ever turn into the sort of man who'd say all the swoony, charming words for a quick lay. I've spent the last few months getting over being used-by you- a person who I've cared for my whole life. I am done caring, because you never did."

"Oh snap," Shelley said, she covered her mouth, "Sorry. I'm trying to be supportive. Go away, Jake. There's no room for you here. On the tennis court."

"Marigold," he sighed.

"Fine. Fine let's go talk," I relented. Why did he still have those expressive brown eyes? It wasn't fair. "Shelley, I'll meet you outside the sauna in a minute."

If I didn't get rid of her, she'd be telling him there wasn't enough space in Dallas for the two of them.

She huffed, but left, promising to get us the big, fluffy towels.

Jake eyed the bodyguard, "Amy has one too. Her edition wears blue."

I didn't laugh.

He noticed. I was always an easy laugh.

"Marigold, I'm so, so sorry. You aren't, never ever, a quick lay. I meant what you said. You're like my future wife. My childhood sweetheart. Home."

"You didn't call."

"I didn't call," he admitted and exhaled, running his hands through his hair, "I didn't call. I got scared. Really scared. I mean, we're in college and our lives are planned out. Even each other. Don't you get scared?"

"Of being left? Of being used? Yes. I always felt there was a future with you. That I was safe with you, but," I shrugged, "You took that safety away. Being honest, I don't think I trust you anymore."

He sighed. "What can I do? What can I do Marigold?"

I stared him dead in the eye, "Do you love me?"

"I... I think so? I'm supposed to?" he squeaked. "We're only in college. What is love?"

I nodded. "Then leave me alone till you know. Either way. Then we'll talk."

"Marigold..." he tried that loving head tilt and puppy dog eyes on me.

"No. Leave me alone, Jake till you know. That's your second chance. Second and last. Use it wisely. Grow up."

He opened his mouth to retort, but nothing came out.

"That's right, don't talk to me till you're a man."

I waved my bodyguard over, "We're done here. Escort me to the Sauna, please."

"You okay?" Shelley asked, as we settled in the private sauna.

"No. He's giving me the old family-plan excuse. Like he can't think for himself," I huffed.

"Men suck. I mean look at you. They wanted you to go into law and be part of the family business. But that would suck, I bet you'd have a bodyguard every day. Only a good thing if he's hot," she laughed, wiping her brow, "I digress. Look at you. Studying interior design. Becoming your own person. I admire that. And you will find yourself a rare non-sucky man that does too."

"Thanks," I sighed, "Do you think I should be more forgiving? Like… I have my brother so he carries on the mantle. So does Amy, because Jake's the mantle carrier. That's stress I can't understand. My mom supports me getting out of here."

"Stay strong. Jake has to grow up and learn what he wants in his life. Free of what others want for him. Let him grow up. You'll only get hurt in the muck as he's learning."

"How'd you get so wise, Shells?"

She shrugged with a wink, "It's a secret."

I sighed. I missed him already.

Stupid Jake.

I had been doing just fine.

Chapter 23

"I'm glad you could meet me without my brother being in tow," Amy said.

"Oh, um of course," I huffed. This better be worth the smirk he gave me as he watched as me leave in his corny Safety Day Volunteer workout shirt. Though I had every intention of keeping it. A cute cat with the phrase "Paws on Yellow," was screen-printed across the front.

I wasn't sure how productive this meeting was going to be, but when Amy suggested we go for a walk, there was no saying no after I'd reached out. If I had known it was power walking... My ego told me I was fit enough to keep up with the short-legged woman, but no. Half-a mile at her pace and my ability to talk was impaired, and I was wondering which curb would be a good one to throw myself onto and claim a sprained ankle.

"Are you okay? This is the only time I get to myself. I appreciate you joining me. Away from the kids and all. Sometimes I imagine I just keep walking on and on and never come back."

"Oh, that's-that's dark," I pumped my arms hoping their

momentum would carry me forward, "I thought you were happy."

"I am," she said, "Thoughts like that are natural. Everyone has them. The grass is greener, etcetera, etcetera. It's not-not in reality. I don't think my Dad killed Emma."

"That's," I panted, "A jump in logic."

"Not really. What would replace her? Another wife? Their relationship was still pretty new, like a year. I didn't see him flirt with anyone at the country club. He's not the type of man who enjoys being alone. One of his weaknesses."

Of course she would know his weaknesses... Maybe this calf-torture would be worth it. An Amy opening up, this was rare.

"Then what happened?"

She eyed me, "You know what our fathers do. Did, in your case. You know what they shielded us from. Why I steer clear as much as I can. Being married to a cop protects me. But what protects you, Marigold?"

What our fathers did. I still think I'm shielded from what they did. I knew they were shady defense attorneys, specializing in shifting assets around before they were frozen and keeping guilty criminals out of jail. White-collar crimes, I was always assured. Lied to likely. But more than that, questions about my father's and Paul's careers were always avoided. The less I knew the better.

"You think it's something to do with one of their cases?"

"Your Dad flew in. He has you and Jake running around keeping your noses clean. He's protecting you the best he can."

"So you really think. Hold on," I paused and dropped my hands to my knees and took a few deep breaths as my lungs restocked themselves with air.

"We can go at a slower pace. I'm usually by myself."

"Alone? After Emma's murder?" I straightened up, "Is that wise? You heard about my peeping tom."

She gestured at me, "You're here, aren't you? In a week or two you'll be keeping up."

"Oh. Great," I took another deep breath, "So you really think your Dad is innocent? Not just because he's family?"

Amy rolled her eyes and began walking. Slower at least.

"Dad loves me. Of that I am certain. I'm another one of his weaknesses. I'm surprised one of his scummy clients hasn't kidnapped me for leverage to win a case."

Well now my head darted right and left. That black Explorer was looking a little sketchy. Kidnappers always preferred larger vehicles. I hoped she did not think that because I was a few inches taller than her that I provided any sort of bodyguard service. The curvy weight I carried was all fluff. At best I could be was a dead weight to slow down our kidnapping and give her time to run.

Amy could easily out-pace me, she'd be the survivor. And now I saw her plan. Great.

She waved a skinny arm as she spoke, "Think about it. How many wives has he had? Has he dispatched any via murder? No. Because he's a lawyer who can turn the straight line of the law into a squiggly piece of spaghetti. He's old, too old to suddenly change patterns. Dad's innocent, so as I said earlier-however ya'll need me, I'm there. Even if I'm the one boiling water. Family."

"I mean... That's actually pretty good logic. I want solid proof it wasn't him. I want this nagging doubt gone." It was more than a bit.

I thought of the bruises on my shoulder, rather my mad arm pumping sent a painful reminder, that harming me was out of his pattern.

"Definitive proof. How often does that happen?" she shook her head, "Dad raised a little girl-me- and was nothing but kind and gentle. He practically adopted you into the family, as your Dad did for me. I'd defend your father, too. But don't get me wrong. We find proof he killed Emma and I'll gut him myself."

I jerked back into a pause, "What! What happened to this is family?"

She stood still with her hands on her hips, "Well I mean, how dare he? Kill a woman after raising one? Knowing the number one danger to a woman are the men around who are closest to her? How. Dare. He. No. I'd take that revenge on for Emma. For every woman."

"I'd help," I said, proud of my old friend.

"I'll need it. Killed my defense lawyer," she laughed.

I joined in. That sort of laugh where a bit humor just felt good and restorative for the soul. We walked on in silence, a little faster, farther from her brick house and manicured neighborhood.

"What if we just kept walking?" Amy asked, so low I could hardly hear her.

Chapter 24

I think I liked him because he was a walking contradiction. I mean, in strides a man with that confident swag and strut, leather jacket and too tight jeans. Fresh off a black and red motorcycle. He oozed confidence. Half-leaning against the bar to face me, towering over as I sat on the stool (trying not to focus on how that white shirt clung to his fit chest).

Scott White emanated the bad boy, don't tell your mother about this one feel. He was the ride you told only your friends about.

He took off his pilot sun shades, hung them on his collar, and gave me a wink.

As for how this first date was going, I was already ready to take him home. He was perfect, too. Just what I needed- just another man to hurt me. But at least I knew it this time.

Those flexing biceps under that tight sleeve told me so. But maybe he'd get to throw me down on the bed first.

And then he ordered a Cherry Coke. One for me, too.

For a moment I thought I'd stumbled upon one of those scenarios where a kid makes a wish on a magic fountain to be a grown-up and that was how Scott came to be, but then he looked me up and down. His eyes tracing from my crossed legs and smirking at my short skirt and skating along my breasts to my lips. His expression was pure sex. This man knew things, could probably teach me things, and make me forget I'd ever met a man named Theo.

I wanted to grab his shirt-front, yank him towards me, and beg him to make me forget.

Yet there was no sexy comment, or hey babe, he only sat, his legs wide, encompassing mine between his, and said, "You look really pretty tonight." And took a sip of his cola.

Having me think, huh, I could take him home to meet my mother.

To recap, in the first three minutes he had me wanting to crawl into bed with him and introduce him to my family.

I took a sip of Coke and thanked him. For the drink, the wink, and the compliments, and for whatever came next. Tonight was in his hands, the bra matched the panties; I was ready for anything.

Normally after grabbing a drink, I'd expect him to lead us to another bar or club.

"Mini-golf. Are you game? It's right around the corner."

Well. That I was not ready for.

He looked down at my stiletto-ed feet, "They do shoe rentals. I called ahead and checked."

Call ahead. Checked. He cared?

My heart was in my throat.

"Mini golf sounds great. Lead the way," I smiled up at him as he took my hand and pulled me off the bar stool.

"Put it on my tab," he winked at the bartender and replaced the sunglasses over his eyes, "Let's go,"

Five minutes into the date, and I'd follow him wherever.

Thirty-five minutes and his hands were on my hips. His thumbs took their lazy time tracing over the top ridges of my jeans.

"If you shimmy, loosen your hips," he coached, his chin on my shoulder and his whispery breath tickling my ear.

"I'm sure that will help."

"It can't hurt, I've never seen anyone so bad at this," he straightened up, backing away, leaving behind warm, invisible handprints on my body, "Watch me."

Scott putted a near hole in one as it approached the hole, near the large stupid cut out of a cat's face. A light tap, and in the cat's mouth it went. "Now you."

"If I get this in, you're treating us to some pickle chips. I'm hungry. If you win, I'll get us the onion rings."

"Deal."

We sat down at the picnic table across from the snack booth, munching on a large basket of onion rings and colas. He insisted on paying. First date rules.

Day fell into evening. Appetizers into juicy cheeseburgers. That slight awkwardness into full laughter and dimples creasing his cheeks. I'd learned he was a doctor-or a dentist, rather. And when I got insecure and covered my mouth, he nuzzled my hand away and said I was beautiful. That my smile was a large part of that.

"... And I don't keep tabs on people's teeth," he reassured,

"Though yours are lovely. When I'm off the clock, I mean it."

"Okay... But how could you pick a career where you spend so much time in people's mouths?"

Scott groaned, "There's so much innuendo in that I don't know what to do here. First date rules."

I laughed, "You seem to have a lot of rules."

"I want to get it right," he paused, "With you, that seems to be important."

I gulped. I was in trouble here.

This was the sort of man futures were built off of.

"So tell me, again, why can't you see me tomorrow? You're making me wait five days for a second date." He said with a cute pout.

Just my luck, I actually had a good reason. This guy-that smile- he was getting under my skin, letting me think for a minute that were still good men out there. That they all would not break my heart. He was waking me up from my sleepy stupor I'd been trapped in since Theo.

Ugh. Theo.

No, I wasn't cured, but this was date one, and it was like he was opening the door and pointing out the sunlight saying, "See? Let's go out there."

"Family visiting. Well, family friend. My dad's business partner and his son. I promised them dinner and showing them Pittsburg's many sites."

He raised a brow, "And his son? Is this a set up? Should I be jealous?"

"Not at all. They tried to set us up twice, it never worked. And they're going straight back to Dallas."

"Why do I feel jealous?" he reached out and took my hand from across the table, "I'll just have to keep competing. Let him know you're seeing someone."

"And if he asks if it's serious?" I edged in, bravely.

"Tell him it might be. You're pretty bad at golf-it's going to take you a while to get you there."

We locked eyes. Holding each other's gaze. A shiver ran through my body as I thought of his hand tracing my hip.

"Please don't tell me you have any rules about taking a girl home on the first date."

That wink! Those dimples!

I couldn't wait to have those lips on mine and those hands on me one more time.

"Now why'd you think I'd have a silly rule like that?" He put down more than enough cash to cover our bills and led the way out to the parking lot.

"You planned this. No one in our generation carries that much cash." Still, I followed.

He laughed and gave my hand a squeeze, so we were holding hands now, "Yes, I planned the most thorough of seductions," he paused and smiled at my laugh, "Okay, there was a little hope, but as you can see, not much." Scott pointed at his motorcycle, "It was such a nice day out I took this instead of the car."

My heart gave a thunk. It was of course, crazy sexy and the motorcycle fulfilled his bad-boy aurora. And the idea of wrapping my legs around him and holding on tight was... appealing.

"Your expression..." he observed, "I only brought one helmet, it's yours of course. Or we can Uber, since I imagine that's how you got here."

"Oh, no, no, no it's okay," I shook myself, melting again at his *concern, "I've never been on one. They seem cool, but, also, well, scary."*

"Ah. Well, I'll go slow. And I live, like two miles from here. No highways. A short, super safe, first ride."

Scoffing, I took the proffered helmet and plopped it on my head, "And you didn't have this planned, Mister, 'I live super close.'"

"Just a happy fact. Now," Scott frowned as he stood in front of me and adjusted the helmet to better fit, "There. It's pointless if it's too big. Safety first. You look adorable."

He took a step back to admire his handiwork.

Glad he thought so, I felt like a bobblehead. But nerves aside, it was electric as he stood so close, right in front of me.

As he gazed into my eyes, he kissed my hand, "Now all you have to do is hold on tight. Ready?" he nodded towards the bike. But it felt like more... Like our night was only beginning. Our story was just now starting.

"Ready," I confirmed.

"Good. Cause I've got you."

Three hours and forty-five minutes into the date, my arms were wrapped around his torso, the wind blowing through my hair, and my lips kissing the back of his neck.

Three hours and forty-six minutes in the date, a pickup truck ran a red light.

Chapter 25

There was lots of beeping. Bright lights when I wanted to sleep. I felt the ebb of a headache, and a wave of nausea, and I shut my eyes right back closed. My brain thanked me and returned to an equilibrium. But the beast of pain had awoken. I didn't want to focus on that, so I peeped my eyes open again.

"Welcome back, can you hear me?" the floating voice belonged to the blurring image of a nurse who had a really, really long nose and circular glasses. I blinked again, focusing on the nose and all the shapes, colors, and lines of the room clicked back into a crisp image. I was in a hospital room, hooked up to an IV. A quick full body survey told me nothing was broken or missing. Just ache. Like a bruised potato, rather than mashed.

"Mmm," I affirmed, I wanted to nod, but the headache was too intense.

"I'm Elle, can you tell me why you're here and your name?"

"Marigold Bryant. Ummm..." I blinked hard for a moment, wondering why I was here. I was eating, on a date, then on a motorcycle- the shadowy figure of a man formed in my mind. And then the shadows

blew away. Scott!

"I was in an accident. My head, that's why it hurts. Where is Scott? How is he?"

"Good!" Elle smiled, "One thing at a time," she picked up the clip board from the edge of my bed and gave it a quick skim before talking to me, "You've been knocked out for three hours. A major concussion. We did some scans, but you've come out clean. After hitting your head on pavement-you're a lucky girl. Lucky that helmet saved your life and your reading level. Your legs and arms are a bit scraped up, but we treated them. Three stitches in your leg, and two in your arm. Other than that, you may experience some bruising. Our chief concern is your concussion. We'll keep you here to monitor that. Likely you just have some whiplash, a bit of dulled impact, but there's no swelling or bleeding according to your doctor and the scans. We will have to keep you for another 48 hours and do another round of scans. You had some nausea and vomiting. And your pupils were dilated. The doctor will come by soon now that you're up for more screening questions."

"Oh..." it was a lot to take in. I felt the achiness set in, the bit of nausea that remained in control if I stayed very still.

"Ice chips are on their way," she smiled, "And I'm afraid we have to keep you awake for 24 hrs now."

"Coma risk?"

"Always a concern," she nodded at the empty plastic chairs, "Your family stepped outside. We called the ICE numbers in your phone. Your father? He said Paul and Jake were in town and visiting you and could look after you. I'd say they have-haven't left your side except for when I sent them on errands to get out of my way. You've got good friends, Marigold. I recommend leaning on them."

I was touched they ran right to my side, even a little surprised they were already in town.

"I do. They're great. This was not the way to begin their trip. Can I check on Scott? The guy driving the bike?"

"Right... Yes. Let me do a few diagnostics first, okay?"

I nodded. Regretted that instantly.

"When will the headache go away?"

"Likely two to three days. But it should start fading soon. I'll discuss with your doctor your pain med regiment, okay? Make sure you are more comfortable."

"Oh, I'd like that."

She smiled and swiftly went through checking all my vitals, even listening to my lungs.

"All normal numbers. You'll be out of here in no time."

"So I can visit Scott?" hope flooded my voice, "I have to tease him about this being the worst first date ever. Worst-best really. I know he's probably kicking himself with guilt right now. I have to let him know it was the truck's fault, not his. Scott hit the brakes hard- the truck did too though, but it wasn't enough. It was all too late."

"I'm glad your memory's flushed out more."

Huh. I guess it was now, and I wasn't entirely grateful for the replay feature in my mind. Not grateful for the audio quality, either. The screeching, the shouts, sirens. Glass. It was like the tape got messed up. The last thing I could see was the truck coming at us. I heard Scott yelling for me to hold on.

Then the brakes.

Glass.

So much sound I couldn't make sense of it all, and then... nothing.

Till waking up here.

I told the nurse as much.

"Mild head trauma. Your memory didn't have time to get stored properly, and you probably squeezed your eyes shut. That helmet saved your life," the nurse paused, "Hun, there was only one helmet, correct?"

Why was she asking that?

Dread flooded my system. It was like when I stubbed my toe and it didn't yet hurt, but I knew that pain was coming my way.

This was that.

Those in-between seconds.

"One helmet," I agreed, "He gave me his."

She took my hand, "He didn't make it sweetie. It happened so fast, there was no suffering."

"Oh."

Of course. That's why she checked my vitals first.

The delay in telling me.

"Oh…" I said again. There were more words out there I should say, but I couldn't find them.

"Don't stress yourself. You're still in recovery."

"How?" I managed, "Same as me?" I pointed to my head.

"From what the police and doctors briefed me… You were both thrown from the bike. Hitting your heads. Your friends are outside now. They know what happened. Should I let them in? They have ice chips and a lovely bouquet of flowers."

"His family? Scott's?"

"Yes," she sighed, "They're here as well."

"Can I see them? They should know he saved my life."

"I'll see if they are up to it. Let's let yours in first though, okay?"

"Yes, right. Of course."

Scott. I exhaled, feeling cold and chilly, like a ghost myself.

I couldn't believe... We were out eating burgers. Going to his house. He was so alive. So warm. His parents had to know how kind and good he was. Probably too good for me.

And while my head felt like it was split in two and that nausea was surging back, I was so lucky. So lucky that he was so good he gave me that helmet and tightened it. His parents had to know.

I didn't know him for long, but maybe there were still good men out there.

Maybe one less now.

My cheeks were damp with tears. I tried to hold them back, crying hurt. The congestion it caused hurt.

Paul and Jake stepped in, hovering around the door. I tried to give them an "I'm fine" smile, but my tears canceled that out.

He died. And I hardly got to know him. We'd only spent a few hours together. I should be only a little jarred, but ultimately okay. I wasn't, though. I wasn't okay at all. I was a spilled box of puzzle pieces.

I had to mourn a man whose kindness saved my life. If he had worn the helmet instead... Or if he never had one at all... Instead, he'd tightened it on me-making sure I secure and safe, my needs before his. Husband material. I had to mourn another lost future. Ours.

"Thank you," I wiped tears off my cheek, "Thank you for coming so fast."

My words invited them deeper in. Each kissed my cheek, squeezed my hand, and sat in a plastic chair, as if they had asked someone how to properly enter a hotel room. They sat the flowers in their pink crystal vase on the windowsill.

"We ordered balloons, but we've beat them here," Paul said, crossing his legs, trying to get comfortable.

"Oh, thank you."

"I'm staying the night here, already got permission. You will not be alone in a hospital room on my watch," Jake said.

"No, Jake... it's so uncomfortable, no..." but my protest died on my lips.

Jake propped his feet up at the edge of my bed and tucked his hands behind his head, stretching out, "I'm the picture of comfort, and if I get stiff, you've got the morphine hook up, right?"

I managed a small smile, "Right."

"I'm afraid I'll be going back to a hotel, but you're in excellent hands. Old back I'm afraid. Your parents are ready to fly down the second you let them see a tear. I told them we've got you-but- it's up to you."

"It's stitches and a mild concussion. I... I'm fine. I'm only here for observation."

"You're here because your good health insurance. In my day, you'd already be sent home."

"Regardless," Jake interjected, "I'll stay in town till you're healed."

Paul nodded, "Good. That'll make everyone feel better."

"That's a lot to ask... Not necessary at all."

The headache was coming back. Probably from talking.

I was lucky they were here. By the time my parents could possibly arrive, I'd be discharged. Though right now, I only wanted a good, old-fashioned mom-hug. Maybe then I'd feel less cold. Less shaken.

"Meanwhile, Jake here could convince you to come back to Dallas? We miss you. What's in Pittsburg?"

"Dad, not now," Jake grumbled, running his hand over his face, frustrated, as if they had discussed when to bring this up many times.

It was more of who wasn't in Pittsburg. Theo. Meg. Their love infiltrating all my safe spots. Seeing them at my bar, at parties, the grocery store, it was too much. I lost the town in the breakup. They owned Dallas. How was I supposed to live in a place where I'd run into Megan and her engagement ring when I was merely grocery shopping? Or in a Korshak dressing room- shopping to cheer myself up? I couldn't!

But what was now in Pittsburg? Nothing.

I didn't have friends here. Just work.

I tried to build a life here.

And all I did was end up in a hospital and get a man killed.

Where was that morphine? That headache was kicking back.

"Not now," I agreed.

Dallas, though, sounded better and better. After I finished out my work contract... How could I even think of rebuilding here after killing a man?

"Is that... Is that her?"

The shrill voice came from a woman, filling the doorway. Causing the hall light to bleed in like an eclipse. She was thin and wiry and reminded me of a scarecrow. But maybe my mind wasn't quite right, yet. A female scarecrow in overalls and blonde hair that stood up at all angles. A feint scar ran down her face. Her eyes bloodshot. Long, thin, fingers gripped the doorway, if she let go, would she fall over or be blown away? The visitor was more baggy clothes than woman.

"Is that her? Is that her?" *This time she pointed at me with a chipped purple painted fingernail. The mother.*

I only stared back. What was I supposed to say?

Was I the woman her son was last with? The lone survivor? Yes. I was that "her."

But the way she said "her", there was frenzy and hate and panic behind that pronoun, and I was not ready to claim such a label laying down.

His mother. They had the same eyes-except hers were now wild with grief. If she leapt into the air and jumped on me, I would not be surprised, or angry. There was no way she could be in her right mind, she shouldn't be. I was selfish to wish to talk to her earlier. And now I was glad Jake was here to possibly pull her off me.

"You killed him," she whispered, "You killed him. My son!" *That last part was a scream.*

"That's enough, now," Paul said, jumping between us, "It was a car accident."

"She killed... She killed..."

"Your son was the one driving, was he not?"

I could only see Paul. He towered over her. I could, however, hear the cold, dead silence, feel her anger radiating.

"I'll make you pay. I'll make her pay for every year she lives. Death will follow you. I will follow you!"

"No. Get out."

"I'll remember you. Remember the name Violet!"

I watched as Paul pushed her out and he closed the door behind her, holding it shut, just in case.

"Why do I feel like I just pricked my finger on a spinning wheel?" *I tried to make a joke, but it fell flat. If there was any joy in this room where humor could live... she had drawn it out.*

"Don't listen to her. She's crazy with grief," Jake said as he came over to hold my hand, "I've got you."

"That's right, son. That's right," Paul affirmed, still holding the door closed, "You're safe with us."

I shivered. Her words rang in my years. Her threat tattooing across me. Violet.

Was I safe? Were they? Did the crazy lady know something I didn't? Did death follow me?

Richard unlatched his seatbelt to talk to me.

Scott took off his helmet and gave me a ride.

Who was next?

"Hey, hey, Marigold, don't cry," Jake soothed, "I won't let you out of my sight."

Maybe you should.

Chapter 26

The funeral was well attended. I couldn't say this was because of Emma's popularity, but more so out of community curiosity and collective guilt. Plus, if one attended the funeral of a murder victim, were your odds of the same fate slightly reduced by some karma agreement?

Row one was family. Paul's side on the left, tear free, solemn and... cognizant of being heavily watched. Paul kept his head down, his hands tightly clasped together. My father next to him, thumbing through the provided Bible, both looking to avoid any conversation, avoiding eye contact. A few open seats where us ladies would land. Amy was already seated. She wore a simple black shift dress and pearls. Her children sat in between her and John. He was out of uniform-a strong signal to the world that he was off duty and his only responsibly was digging through his wife's tote looking for the Goldfish snacks. I couldn't totally read Amy, but who could, she was a closed book. I watched as she smoothed down her son's wayward hair and whispered down some words to him, a few of her pages revealed herself. She truly loved her children, her family.

On the other side of the aisle was more family. *Her* family. Two sisters, one in a black business suit with long blonde hair tied back in a sleek ponytail, the other in a frillier black lace dress that belonged more in a night club than a church, with dark, red died hair. Both with pink, puffy eyes, and black clutches filled with Kleenexes. They had been a trio, the three sisters, Emma the youngest. Their parents already passed on, and now there were two. My heart lurched for them, so I looked away. Their grief made death so… final. Real. They were the ones today suffering the loss, the rest of us were at most surprised. Curious. Shocked.

A little upset, but that was it.

I shifted my focus to row two, where friends sat. Paul's friends, I'd forgotten their names already. Some familiar faces were mixed in.

Shelley, arm-in-arm with Everett walked up towards the church. They would land in row two behind me. Everett too was out of uniform and looking very sharp in a dark suit. Of course, Shelley looked stunning. She wore a black jumpsuit with a tiny bow at her bust, leaving her tanned shoulders bare and her long hair flipping in a very modern 70s style.

She tugged on my arm as she soon as she passed through the church doors and asked, "Are you two official now?"

I often wondered if Shelley and I would pass the Bechdel test. I try to; every time we hang out, I bring up a non-boy related topic.

"Good to see you, Shelley, Thanks for showing up at the funeral," Jake said, stepping in and giving her a hug, "Everett, welcome," he nodded at the detective. Things felt icy but remained civil.

"You're manning the front door with him-greeting guests. What am I supposed to think? It's like putting it on a newsletter."

"I'm being a good…" my words trailed off, I looked up at Jake to save me, but he only smirked.

"I'm looking forward to you performing other wifely duties later," he teased.

"Internally, I'm gagging."

He dropped his voice, "We can work on that."

Shelley betrayed me with a giggle. I silenced her with a cutting glare. One aimed at both of them.

"I hate you. And I will see you later," I huffed to Jake. I did not want to be door-greeting guests with him. Shells was right. That was above my paygrade. Even though it felt natural.

"Yes," Shells reinforced, "Have a good funeral." She now linked arms with me and led us away, Everett following behind.

"I'll uh, get us seats while you two catch up," He said.

"I saved you two seats in the second row with a black jacket," I informed him.

"A black jacket at a funeral. I'll be sure to find it," he muttered.

As soon as we were out of earshot, Shells started laughing. Luckily, we'd spun around and were outside on the church steps and her happiness wasn't echoing around. From our vantage we could see the center front door, and everyone trickle in as we remained on the edge of the large front porch. Here she could be as loud and gossipy as she wished to be.

"Enjoy the funeral? What was that? I'm so weird around Jake. It's not going to stop."

"He's weird around you too," I admitted, "It's like two opposite sides of my life don't click."

She frowned with a little nose wiggle, "Maybe it's because I never know if I should hate him or love him, for your sake. So I push him away till your mind is made up. Will it ever be made up? Should I make it for you? I *will* do that. Best friend services allow that."

I looked up at the tall, handsome figure, greeting guests, clasping hands, taking on the role of patriarch so well. Paul greeting people would have been too awkward. It concerned me how easily it was for Jake to slip into his role; I did not want him to become like his father. His own worst fear. A fear I couldn't say wouldn't happen.

"I don't know. I hope so, we fall in step together so well. But there's…" my voice fell off. Shelley knew of how he always broke my heart. And that warning from my mother to stay away from Jake. How could I ignore that?

"He's handsome and rich. Girls have formed lives around less."

"Unhappy girls. He broke my heart," I countered.

"A long time ago."

"Aren't we supposed to learn from the past?"

"Learn and let go. It's a balancing act," she sighed, "Then I'll just be awkward around him till you know your heart."

"Please. I love seeing him being completely thrown off. And what about Everett?"

She winked, "I like him. A lot. He's different."

"Different, Shelley? This is new."

Instead of letting me dive into that, Shelley dear was saved by if described in another way my head on would be on a pike, a young woman who could pass as my sister, came running towards me.

"I came straight here! We dropped my bags off at the hotel," she threw herself into my hug, never ceasing talking, "And to think from flying in, to checking into my hotel, I have ten minutes to spare. Oh, it's so good to see you."

"Glad you made it, Mom."

She squeezed me harder and laughed when Shelley joined in on the hug.

"My girls."

My brother slunk passed us with a nod. He had his Air Pods in. He had been the one to pick Mom up from the airport and shuttle her around. As Jake's best friend, he was obligated to be here. Otherwise, he'd be... Sulking elsewhere. He was a mystery I often ignored. Row three had space for him somewhere. It was funny how different my brother and Amy turned out from us. At least Amy had a family and whole fleshed out life. My brother had a Spotify playlist.

Well, maybe he had a secret life. Maybe Jake knew. I'd ask one day, if I remembered.

"Let's take our seats, otherwise I'm tempted to stay out here and catch up."

"Dad's already inside holding down the fort."

Her face went cloudy, "And Paul?" Mom asked.

"Seems like the grieving groom surrounded by family and loved ones."

Her mouth set in a firm line, "I don't miss this city."

Shelley and I exchanged a nervous glance, glad that Mom hadn't caught me greeting guests with Jake.

My eyes were dry till the pant-suited sister spoke. She could hardly get the words out. I was in Kleenexes by the time the second sister said her words. She spoke about losing her best friend. How Emma wanted to be a ballerina, then as she grew up, a teacher to help students that were slower at learning, as she had once been. Another tissue got wadded up at that-it was depressing to think of poor Emma as a kid with hopes and dreams. Kid Emma did not know what her fate would be. She paused her speech, shaking her head, the tears drying and anger taking over, "Emma was taken from us too soon. And the murderer is still out there, we can't pretend that he's not. And I won't pretend that I won't take justice into my own hands once we find out for sure who it was." Her eyes glared down at Paul. He didn't even have the decency to shift in his seat.

"Sis..." Lauren said, standing up in the pew, "You wrote a nice speech last night. Go on."

Rose beheld her sister with a studying glance and the rage faded from her ridged form. She softened and closed her eyes, taking a moment. "Right. Not the wisest to make death threats in front of a crowd," she exhaled and continued.

"... My sister loved the outdoors; she'd spend her time under the large tree in our front yard with a pile of books next to her. She was a slow reader, but she was so determined. So stubborn. She'd look over at me and say, 'Rose, it's something to conquer. I can do it.' When she would-"

She did not get to finish her eulogy.

A scream ripped across the church.

Echoing.

The eulogy stopped. Eyes snapped around for the source.

A hush fell over. That familiar heavy breathing... ragged, with a wheeze at the end.

"I'll kill you! I'll kill you! You took everything from me!"

The sniffing and tears stopped. Every eye, dry and wet cast upon the woman in the center of the aisle.

Dressed in a long, black gown, a veil shadowing her face. She stood tall and reedy. A large, black tote bag at her feet, spilling open. One of her long, branch-like arms extended out, gripping a silver gun, pointing straight at a woman in the fourth row.

4th row was country club friends.

The gun aimed at Meg.

This was insane…

The scarecrow woman. Scott's mom, Violet.

I gulped. Why was she aiming at Meg?

At innocent, perfect Meg? She was in a tea-length black silk dress, her blonde hair tucked back in a bun. Light aquamarine stones encircled her neck, she carried herself like the perfect country-club step-ford wife. Theo stood next to her, side by side. The matching husband with a pocket square in light blue. He loved her just enough to stand with her, and face the mad woman, but not quite enough to stand in front.

"What-what is this?" Theo stuttered.

My hero. I rolled my eyes.

"There's been a mistake. I don't know you," Meg said, sounding calmer than one should. As she spoke, Everett crouch-walked to the aisle, kneeling behind the edge of a pew and taking aim at Violet.

"Drop it. I'm the police. Drop it and let's go outside and talk," he demanded.

"This woman. She's a monster. Death follows her. It follows her everywhere. She killed my son," Violet said, her voice cracking along the way.

"I-I've never killed anyone I promise… Please." Now Meg sounded panicky.

Of course.

Of course.

Theo had a type. On a good day I'd look like Meg. The last time Violet saw me was at a distance, when my head was wrapped with a bandage, and I was hospital pale. Her son probably said he was going on a date with a girl who was getting over a jerk named Theo.

She thought Meg was me.

Ohimigoodness. Ohmygoodness.

I sent Jake a panicked look, "Jake," I hissed.

"Don't you dare." He'd realized as well.

"Jake, Jake I have to. I-" my words were shut off by his hand clasping over my mouth.

Everyone's focus was towards the aisle.

I tried to speak again, but his hand muffled my yell, spinning me so that my face crashed into his chest, and he held me still, despite my struggle. I could only look up and glare.

Meg was innocent!

How could I let her get hurt in my name?

"I'm so sorry," he whispered, "I love you. I'm so sorry."

I squirmed more.

"You killed him!" Violet White roared.

I bit his hand, but he held in his grunt and only whispered "I'm sorry, I'm sorry. God forgive me."

"Ma'am," Theo pleaded.

A shot rang out.

And then another.

Chapter 27

Jake held onto me, gripping me around the middle, so I wouldn't go pitching forward and into the scene. At least he removed his hand so I could speak.

"Stay back," he whispered, as if I could move freely.

I lurched forward, having twisted to face the scene, but his arm tightened. There wasn't anything I could do, however, if I got to the aisle.

Everett didn't mess around-a perp with a gun in hand, he couldn't. He took the kill shot. Violet lay in the aisle, a bullet hole between her eyes. Looking at her, on the ground, my main thought was I could finally use my phone again. The harassing phone calls were officially over. As horrible as it sounded, I felt lighter. The stuffy air of the church tasted a little fresher. I was free. Free of the guilt and pain I caused this woman.

That lightness lasted only a second.

Till brick, stone, pieces of sky fell upon me. Crushing. Casting out any air.

That I never reported Violet.

Never had her investigated or charged for harassment.

My negligence let her be free to come inside the church and...

God forgive me.

Theo laid out Meg across the center aisle, her body limp and boneless. Bloody. She'd been hit in the chest. People, I hoped maybe a doctor, or a nurse included crowded in, keeping pressure on her wound. They surrounded until I could no longer see, even up on my tiptoes or standing on the kneeler.

There was nothing I could do. The crowd was directed to back away. I listened. My guilt could not clot a wound.

As soon as I stepped down, basically level again with Jake's shoulder, I couldn't see a thing. Other than Everett, who was now away from the crowd (it looked like John was now coordinating). Everett looked in Meg's direction, then up at that large funeral picture with flowers below of Emma, and then at me.

And I at him.

He squinted.

And I knew we shared thoughts and came to the same conclusion. Meg, Emma, and I looked a lot alike. Same slim build and average height with blond hair, at slightly different lengths and looks- but none of us had a big defining feature to separate us from the crowd. No giant noses or scars or big bushy eyebrows. We all fell into that category of pretty, but generic. Emma had made up for it with loud colors and prints. Meg went with being classy and refined to try and cancel out genericness with elegance. I, however, claimed and basked in my general mediocre-ness. But to an outsider, to someone with access to only verbal descriptions... To someone crazed enough not to do her homework... We were the same.

My knees went weak.

I watched as medics threw open the doors and flooded in, rushing towards the bodies with stretchers.

A stretcher meant for me.

Two women died in my place.

Was that possible?

"You look a little green," Everett said, suddenly closer than he had been.

I gripped the edge of the pew.

"I imagine those harassing phone calls will be stopping. As will the late-night stalking," he stated.

Of course. That had been her. Of course, Shelley would have told him.

A warm hand landed on my shoulder and gave it a squeeze.

"Everett," Jake greeted. Warned. Tread gently, his tone read.

Jake. That's right, I forgot he was there. Currently, I felt it was just me and all the dead blonde women and the detective staring at all three of us.

"Jake," he nodded, "I'll need some last statements if you could escort Marigold down to the station. Considering today, I think our case with your father is all wrapped up."

"You mean..."

"I'm going to recommend the charges against your father be dropped. All the evidence is pointing towards Ms. Violet. She was hunting down Marigold, and not being quite sure who she was, decided to take out every young woman that could match her description. Holding onto any clue about the woman her son was interested in. Wiping them all out to be sure of her revenge."

"That's..." Jake looked at me, watching as I turned greener, "Not great. But, um, I'm glad it's over." He turned to see where his father was, but our families were gone, either with the crowd or outside, "I'll tell him."

"It's not all over. On good faith, only, don't let him leave town yet."

"Of course," Jake said, squeezing my shoulder again, trying to keep me rooted.

"That's great," my voice sounded breathy, "That's great. But she killed Meg," I sat down on the pew and started laying down, feeling dizzy, the world losing its focus. "And she killed Emma. Because she thought they were me. She would have killed me. Should have killed just me."

"What are you doing?" Jake asked, sounding concerned and far away.

"I need a minute. I can't seem to breathe anymore."

Guilt getting its choke-hold.

I closed my eyes. Wishing the darkness would whisk me away.

But it didn't. Because I didn't deserve peace.

"I need a minute," I said again, ducking my head between my knees. Trying to find some calm.

It should have been me.

Chapter 28

"It should have been me," I said, finally sitting up in the pew once I sensed everyone had been filed out.

Jake flinched. "Don't say that."

"Are you okay?" he asked.

"Yeah."

No. Haven't been okay for a while, and I couldn't look him in the face; I didn't know whether to be grateful or angry. Or that I was guilty I was grateful.

"Fresh air should help."

"Yeah, let's get outta here," I added, trying to lie to both of us that I was indeed, doing fine. The dizziness was fading.

But my first step was wobbly, and my hand latched onto his arm for balance. "Maybe give me a minute."

"I think getting outta here will help."

He swept me into his arms. If there was ever a heart melting phrase, it was that.

He carried me down the church aisle, assumedly towards the outdoors and fresh air he kept insisting I get.

I closed my eyes, so he wouldn't put me down. I buried my face deeper into his chest, enjoying the sensation of his caring concern.

Yes, I was mad at him, but in his arms I could not think straight.

"I know you're awake," he whispered.

I squeezed my eyes shut harder.

"Are you avoiding me? Are you okay? Are you mad?"

My eyes opened to see him staring down, his expression filled with love and concern.

"I'm... okay that is. Not avoiding you, because clearly..." I gestured to him still carrying me, "I think I got overwhelmed. But can we tell anyone else my blood sugar got low?"

"I'm sorry," he said, as carried me towards his car. "But I couldn't lose you. It's my responsibility to protect you. So that's what I did. Theo should have stepped in front of her. That's the man you've been grieving over? That's no man at all," he shifted me, grunting, giving me a little bounce as I was re-settled, "You and Meg deserve better than him. I'm sorry. But I would not let you sacrifice yourself. You'd be killing me, too. So maybe I'm selfish. Maybe I was protecting myself just as much."

I sent a hand up to pat his cheek, my heart flooding with love at his rambling words. The anger dissipated from my system. He had no choice but to save me, and if that didn't make my legs go all gooey. Good thing he was still carrying me, or he would have noticed another wobble in my step.

"Do you ever stop talking?" I teased.

"No. Not when I'm delaying you getting mad at me. You have every right to be. But I wanted you to know my side. And I know I might not have done the right thing, but I don't regret it. I'm sorry."

"Mmm... Your side is well registered." How could I be angry at a man willing to save my life?

I kissed him.

For a second, I thought he'd drop me. But then his grip got tighter, and he slung me around so that instead of being cradled, my legs were wrapped around his waist and my arms around his neck. I felt like a sexy spider monkey holding on for dear life as he kissed me back, melting my icy heart down till I was a knot of loosed, and dazed limbs.

He felt right. Like my other half. And I burrowed in till our bodies were inseparable.

"Marigold," he breathed into my neck, as he sealed his word with a kiss. "What now? Don't ask me to go backwards."

"You scare me, Jake," I was breathless. Elaborating was something I could not do.

"You terrify me," he said, staring into my eyes. So close he was out of focus.

"You're going to hurt me."

"Never."

"Always."

Pain flashed across his face, and he let me down, my feet hitting the ground with a feather light touch. My arms still locked around his neck. I could not let him go. Jake was a man I could never fully let go.

"Well," he breathed, "We take it slow. Till I can earn your trust. But let's be done failing each other."

"Slow," I agreed, leaning in for another kiss.

This time it was short, and sweet, but every bit full of love. I was in trouble here. My hands swept down from his neck to his shoulders, tracing their surety and strength. Don't fail me, I wanted to whisper.

His swept through my hair, pulling me closer, for another kiss.

"Well, not surprised," an unwelcome voice interrupted. Paul, sounding amused.

We jumped apart but noticed Jake's hand remained placed at the small of my back.

Alongside Paul were Mom and Dad, looking terse. My brother rolling his eyes. Amy tending to her kids, but she was chuckling at us. Shelley stood next to them all, beaming.

"Jake and Marigold back together! Excellent!" she cheered, ever the supportive best friend. Thank goodness she was overly tall and beautiful that no one could mistake her for me, as she was a fellow blonde. "At last! And it only took a shoot-out at the O.K. Corral."

"You're killing me, Shells."

I wanted to hide. We had forgotten we were in an open, crowded parking lot.

Even though his hand was tracing gentle circles on my back, Jake said, "We're not back together."

It was the right thing to say, this fledgling, whatever we were did not need to be crushed by the weight of all their expectations and expressions. Our history, it was like a sourdough starter, and we were trying to see if we could turn it into a properly baked bread. We didn't need hungry people pecking at us and surrounding with questions.

"Yeah, well. I'm taking Detective Daddy home and not lying about it," she shrugged, "If I can find him in all this mess."

Her words pulled me back into reality. A mess indeed.

How had Jake and I not noticed? The wail of the ambulance stung my ears. Two fire trucks honking. Three more cop cars with their sirens and lights flaring.

"How is she?" I asked the group-really, it was the most important question today.

"I saw a medic trying to stop the blood loss," Dad said as he gestured to his chest, "But I don't know."

That comment tore into Mom, and she threw herself on me, "That could have been you!"

"But it wasn't. I'm fine." My voice muffled by the intense squish of her hug. Though her hug was everything I'd needed. For a long time. That familiar Dior perfume of hers forming a bubble around us. Us against the world. Even if she didn't know everything going on, her hug soothed any anxieties.

"I'm not letting you go."

I hugged her harder, laughing, "As long as you need."

"It seems wrong to celebrate, but I'm glad the killer is caught. Justice is had. Emma would be happy it's all wrapped up. Should we cancel the reception? It seems wrong to have one and wrong to not," Paul said, "We're serving that awful spiked lemonade Emma loved as a tribute. This should still be about her, right?"

Huh.

I pecked Mom on the cheek as she finally pulled away. Her expression was one of lemons, "You can't throw a party. A young woman is fighting for her life."

"It's a funeral reception, it's already... awkward and sad," Amy cut in, "And I think people need to talk about what happened. Everyone could use a drink. Sending them home seems callous."

"Atta girl," Paul beamed.

"Just try not to dance, Dad," she rolled her eyes and shoved her kids forward to towards the reception hall that was across the parking lot, "I'll get John to steer everyone in for refreshments. Family, which includes us, should gather outside the church and continue the service outside. I'll find the pastor. Shelley, can you take the kids to the reception hall? No need for them to join us."

Paul's look of disappointment of having to carry on the service flashed across his face, but he recovered, "Of course. Of course. Let's gather only close family and continue. For Emma."

"Are you ready for this," Jake whispered into my ear.

I squeezed his forearm in response.

Ready for funeral part two and a solemn party.

And two murders because of me.

Sure.

Chapter 29

The funeral was weird. Only a smattering of people went in for part two. The police closed off the church to only police access, so we finished the service at the grave site. Paul's eulogy was properly emotional and a little canned. I saw his eyes tear up, but he was a talented actor. I should have listened harder, paid attention… But my mind was swimming.

Paul was innocent?

Against all odds.

The news was hard to digest. Like some fibrous fact that would not go down. And if he was innocent… Then this was all because of me. The funeral today was because of me. Because I hopped on a bike with an attractive man and used his helmet.

Maybe Violet was always slightly unhinged. I wouldn't know. No guy on the first date would be "hey, my mom, she's like really, really crazy and has a gun…" But they must have been close; they were close enough that Scott told her about me. My stomach fluttered, little butterflies that were flattered that Scott had been equally excited about our date. Telling everyone he knew about this girl, she's different. Sons don't tell their mothers about first dates if they were cast-off one-night stands. Only the special ones.

I'm sorry Emma. I'm sorry I got you dragged into my mess. You deserved a long, and happy life, I said silently, hoping that somehow, she'd hear me.

"You, okay?" Jake whispered into my ear, his breath tickling my neck.

He'd stood beside me the entire time, an arm around my waist, letting me borrow his strength for the ceremony.

I nodded.

"It's over. Let's get that drink," he said, steering me away from the site. "It's over."

I let him lead me away, but his words, while they should have brought peace, they only rattled me. This was *not* over.

Something was missing.

"We need to visit Meg at the hospital," I said urgently.

"After the reception," Jake frowned, "Are you sure? Are you sure you don't just want to go home and lay down?"

"She's at the hospital because of me."

Because of you, too, I wanted to add.

He sighed. My expression read of the words I could not say.

"Okay... But after."

I nodded, I knew what he meant, family duties first. She'd be in surgery anyways.

"Agreed, I need that drink."

"My Dad's innocent?" he whispered, shaking his head, "Imagine that."

Like many gatherings, before alcohol soaked its way in, men were in one circle, while the women formed their own cliques. With only red wine and too sweet vodka lemonade, paired with dulcet elevator tunes, only timid whispers could flow. I caught snatches of gossip guessing who that crazy woman was. Guesses on how Meg faired.

How much conversation was allowed? How much levity? Was I supposed to stand and cry over my plate of hors d'oeuvres?

I hid my awkwardness by standing with Shelley and filling my mouth with mini quiches. Luckily, Everett was outside talking to the other cops, and I didn't have to add having to socialize with him.

"Are you sure you should drink alcohol?" Shelley asked, watching as I accepted lemonade from the server. She chose red wine. "You fainted. What's up with that?"

People were gossiping about that, too. Another reason for holding down the corner.

"I think everything caught up to me, you know? I found Emma… And then Megan… And I didn't faint. I was actively trying not to hyperventilate."

"I always thought you were good at handling stress, but ooo-eee watching Jake carry you out of the church like firefighter? Mmm!" She winked, "Going to have to try that one on Everett. Do you think he could lift me?"

"Pretty sure he could lift you."

"He is old," she frowned, "I haven't dated this old yet."

"Maybe start with something small?"

"Like a suitcase?" she mused.

"Are we supposed to be…" I let my words fade out, but she read my frown.

"I know, Marigold. I'm freaked out, too. Who would shoot Meg? Other than you?"

I glared.

"Sorry, bad joke. Did you try the apple cake? I brought that. But other than that, I'm not good with these things. And Everett wouldn't tell me a thing. I have no idea who that crazy woman was. Someone from her past? I'll press him tonight for answers and let you know."

"Maybe so," I lied. Glad no one else was putting the puzzle together. I didn't need more attention on me.

"But that was her, right?" Shelley dropped her voice, "Holy Smokes... There's no such thing as coincidences. Marigold... You're flinching, she was the crazy lady of the back yard," she grasped my arm, "I knew it wasn't wind. You've never seen things when buzzed. Do you think she was there to kill you? Oh my goodness. Why you? Why Meg? Was she in love with Theo, too?"

She threw her arms around me, nearly squishing the mini quiches, and squeezed, "That is not allowed in our friendship contract, no getting murdered."

"Shh..." I steered her farther away from the crowd and filled her in. She'd guess it out- and loudly if I didn't.

"You're giving me a lot here," Shelley said, stealing the last quiche, "Sorry. Hungry. You think it's all over now? Justice for Emma and Scott's vengeful mother is dead? So, you and the rest of us blondes in town are safe?"

I frowned, "I guess so. That's what the police think... so..." I shrugged.

I didn't know what to think. I was still processing. Everything.

"I think it makes Jake carrying you out more romantic. No wonder you fainted."

"Girls! There you are," my mother interrupted, greeting us both with warm and perfumy hugs, "Shelley, dear, do you mind if I have a moment?"

"Oh, of course. I'll go find Everett. And let me know how visiting Meg goes, okay? That's going to be difficult on multiple levels."

"Thanks, Shells, I will."

"Don't go fainting again," she teased to lighten my mood.

"I didn't faint! I just needed a moment."

How embarrassing.

Mom waited a beat till Shelley was out of eavesdropping range. She held me tight, in an ironclad embrace as we waited.

"Your father wanted to stay and be here, too. This hug'll have to cover for two. The team's going with Paul after this," she finally let me go, "They're sneaking out of the reception to close everything out."

"Classy. Sneaking out of your dead wife's funeral."

"It's best, as the adrenaline is flowing."

"You mean, so the police don't have time to think?"

Mom bit her lip, "Something like that. But it has to be true, right? One killer makes more sense than two running around Highland Park."

"Do you think…"

"I think we need to think this is all wrapped up. With a bow," Mom ruffled my hair. "Imagine… that could be you in the hospital. That she wanted to kill you. A mother's grief…" her voice broke, or there would have been more lamentations, "You look so pretty today, too. I love you in that black midi dress. It's a good length on you."

I let her hug me again. She called me pretty.

"And we weren't there for you in Pittsburg!"

"Because I was fine. Jake was there, too."

"Thank goodness for Jake. I don't know what goes on between you two. But as a friend or something more- hold on to that one. He saved your life today."

"Yes, yes, Mom."

All hail the mighty, perfect Jake, his praises scratched my nerves. He was far from perfect.

"And you'll come to Florida?"

"Yes, Mom."

She pursed her lips, knowing when her daughter was shutting her out, "I'm flying home tonight. You know I don't like it here. Your dad will stay a couple of extra days if you need anything."

And she hugged me again. It barely registered the last one ended.

Whispering in my ear, she said, "Get out of here."

As she stepped back, she said much louder, "Such a tragedy. Poor Paul. And Emma. Still, Dear, always good to see you."

She blew me a kiss and sauntered onto the next circle to make her goodbyes.

I gulped. Wishing I was a child that could grasp her hand and have her take me away.

After a few more calming mini quiches as I stood alone in my corner, Jake appeared and placed his hand on the small of my back. I tried to ignore the warmth he radiated down my spine. Of course he stayed.

"Got a call. Meg's in surgery. Looks like there's plenty of hope. Want to get out of here?"

I looked over at Amy who was stoically comforting the two grieving sisters; I should be there, helping. But I wasn't talented at that sort of thing. I'd say something wrong and cause more tears.

"Yeah. Let's go."

Guilt was eating at me to check on Meg. Even if it meant seeing Theo. Anger and resentment seemed so trivial once someone got shot.

Shot in my place.

Chapter 30

Theo stopped me at the reception desk before I could address the nurse behind the counter.

"Why are you here?" his voice sounded hard, mad, but his eyes were red, weary. Glistening with unfallen tears, as if he had already cried and was currently only in the eye of the storm, "They won't let anyone back there yet. She's in surgery."

"Theo, Jake's parking the car," I said, as if he needed to know that more than the question he asked.

"Marigold, the police told me."

"Told you?" That stumped me, "Told you what?"

Told you?

How much?

Theo, for once in a very long time looked like a regular person. A little weary, stubble dotting his cheeks, wrinkled clothes with bits of blood. He was human. Tired. Not the Ken doll my mind always transformed him into.

"You look ready to fall over. Can we sit?" I grabbed his arm and sat him down on the sofa. You could tell the waiting room was made for long stays, "Do you need any food? We can send Jake out for something." I adjusted the throw pillows around us to settle in.

"Food?" he looked bewildered, like food was a foreign concept.

"Mmm..." I agreed, and texted Jake to bring us sandwiches and sodas, "You need something."

"Why are you here?" he asked again, "Being nice to me? Why aren't you telling me this is karma?"

Theo may have been talking to me, but his eyes were glued on the door where a surgeon might appear.

"It can take hours for an update, Theo," I set my hand on his forearm, "You might need to relax. As much as you can. So you can be there for her."

His shoulders released some tension, and his posture relaxed a miniscule amount, still though, his eyes remained fixed.

This was love. Love in action. It was undeniable. They weren't a society arranged marriage, some fling, or of empire building. Their soon to be marriage was a love bond. And that was humbling. Maybe Theo realized that now as well; next time, he'd step in front of her.

Megan wasn't some dumb, easy replacement that I wanted her to be.

She wasn't an upgrade.

But a whole other, deeply loved person with her own story.

Who was unfortunate enough to get entangled into mine. Again.

"You really love her," I said.

He sighed, "I really love her."

Humbling.

He rubbed his hands together, down his thighs, trying to release all that worry building up inside.

"Meg'll be okay. She seems like a fighter."

"You don't know that."

"I'll pray that. And I know that when she's out, you'll help her in recovery, every step of the way."

"Every step," he finally looked at me, a few tears already escaping, "Why are you here?"

"Doesn't everyone want their ex in the ICU waiting room?"

He snorted, the most un-Theo-like response I'd ever heard.

"Because I used to love you. You used to love me, not at this level, but it was something. I'm honoring our past selves by being here. It's the right thing to do," and I bit my lip, "The police told you? The woman who barged in?"

"It was something. Something good. I'm sorry, Marigold. You- *we-* deserved better than me cheating on you. I deserve every bit of scorn thrown my way. I do *not* deserve you sitting here, getting me through this."

I gulped. He hadn't heard the last part of my statement. I wasn't in a hurry to repeat it.

"Do you remember that birthday?" I asked, "When Dad was in the hospital with Pneumonia? And you came over and kept me company? Just to be sure I was okay? I'm here for that guy. And thank you… for saying that."

"You seem different."

"I think I accidentally grew up."

"Happens to the best of us," he teased, and I saw a tiny smile. "Coming here was very grown up," he nodded, "And the police told me Meg was shot because some crazy lady had it in for you. Got you two mixed up. That your last boyfriend died. I am so sorry you had to go through all that. I don't blame you for this. I blame her wholly."

I took a breath, talking about Scott still hurt, "We'd only met a few times. Not really a boyfriend. I keep trying to remind myself of that. I can't keep thinking we were meant for something more."

"I'm glad for both you and Meg's sakes that she's, ah, out of the picture."

"I'm sorry my crazy life bled into yours and Meg's. I had to tell you that in person. Meg was so nice to me when I met her. She doesn't deserve this at all. It should have been me."

"The woman was deranged," he grasped my hand, "It should have been no one. All around, it's a tragic story."

"Except Meg will be okay."

He watched the door again, "Meg will be okay." After another tear, he tried to rally, "So does this mean if I see you and Jake at the country club, you'll sit at our table and eat brunch with us?"

"Not yet," I admitted, "But I'll say hey and won't make it awkward."

"We're friends, then?"

"Mmm..." I pressed my lips together. "There's gotta be some punishment for cheating on me. For ending a good thing so abruptly. Let's be ER buddies. If something big goes down, we're there for each other."

"Fair. Very fair. I accept ER buddy."

We shook on it. I forgot how we always used to shake on things.

"But so you know... I always felt during our relationship that you always were waiting on Jake to come around. Like I was a stopping point, a time filler till he was ready."

I paled.

"So it's true?"

I hid my face.

Maybe partially. But Theo crushed me. I *had* loved him, which was why we could never be friends. We never were.

"Subconsciously?" I squeaked, "When we were together, I truly loved you... But yes, Jake's always held a part of my heart."

Theo nodded, "Past is the past."

I wished it was that simple.

Theo and I were never meant to be.

"If Jake rolled up with sodas and sandwiches?"

"I'd accept them. But he's not my favorite guy. And her family is almost here," he pointed at the wall-clock, "My family, too."

I stood, "I'll get them from him and have a nurse run it up to you. Sounds like I better get going. Night and day, keep me informed, okay? Clearly, I'm not good with families, so I need to scoot. Especially your family. Apologize to your Mom for me, okay? I should have never bleached her roses. I was mad at you, and drunk, and you always brought me those roses. It was never about her-just you."

He laughed, "Will do. Whoo she was furious, yeah, you'd better go. I'll keep you updated, though."

Theo hugged me tight. It was warm, genuine, and sad, as I sensed even then he was still watching the doors for the surgeon. True love.

"Goodbye, Marigold."

"Goodbye, Theo."

And I meant it. He no longer lived rent free in my mind.

Chapter 31

Jake threw my bags down in the doorway and paused in the apartment's small, tiled entry.

"You live here? For how long?"

He eyed the dishes piling up at the sink, the emptied alcohol bottles surrounding them, waiting for someone better than me to recycle them. My butt firmly planted itself on the scratchy grey sofa and my feet kicked a few soda cans off the coffee table as they propped themselves up. No one warns you when an accident happens. No one says, "Better tidy your place in case the next of kin must deal with your mess, or worse a nosy friend." At least being dead, one wouldn't feel shame. My cheeks reddened, if I had known, I would have cleaned. I would have hidden my life from him like a proper young woman.

Laundry heaped on the other side of the sofa, bras spilling over and onto the floor. Sealed bags of trash sat near the door. I hoped he wasn't going to open the fridge. He'd find it to be empty except for beer, ketchup, and hummus.

His eyes tracked to the blank walls and knick-nak less furniture. It was one of those fully furnished apartments, and I'd failed to make my mark on it yet, well... other than the empty Chinese food container on the end table. Ironic for an interior designer to have a shell of an apartment.

Jake grabbed a trash bag and began to clean, sweeping into it every container and bottle.

I wanted to help... but... it felt like it was too late, like this invasion of privacy was happening and I was going to have to watch. At least it wasn't that bad. The floor was completely clean other than a few bits of laundry.

"It's only been a few months, since I've moved up here."

"Yeah, you've done a lot with the place," he tossed the to-go box in the trash.

I shrugged, "I guess I don't think of it as home."

Jake straightened up and looked at me, "Oh, where is home to you?"

I bit my lip. I didn't want to cry, not when I felt like I was always on the edge of crying. But it was Jake, and that warm expression in his honey-colored eyes was full of love, and not mockery. Jake was a constant in my life. Whether that was good or bad. Even after we'd say goodbye a million times, he was always there for me. My yo-yo man. Jake deserved the truth.

"I haven't had a home for a while. When Theo kicked me out, my parents had already moved to Florida. Shelley would have kicked me out if I hadn't moved here. I was only supposed to be at her place temporarily *anyway. She's psychotic, that one."*

"Oh?"

"Yeah, she had a treadmill in the middle of her living room. And she'd walk on it, eating ice cream right out of the tub, watching television, like it was a normal thing to do. She's a hard woman to live with. I was never at home there. After Theo, Dallas seized to be home."

He scooped up the floored bras and tossed them on top of the couch laundry pile, raising his eyebrows at the lacy ones, but avoided comment, and only said, "Not like you to let a mere man run you out of town," he paused, "Do you want water or anything? Do you have soda or is it only beer?"

"Water. Thank you. Not a mere man. The one I planned the entire future with. We were talking marriage, making plans. Everything there reminded me of him. But Pittsburg's not the best either, right? The memories packed their own little bags and came along."

Passing me my glass of water, Jake began solidifying the laundry pile so he could sit next to it.

"What about you, Jake? How've you been?"

"Me?" he shrugged, "Dad finally trusts me to take on cases by myself, so that's something. There's always something in the house to fix. I think that's become my unintentional hobby-handyman. But it's not so bad. It's nice to do something with my hands and not just sitting there reading. What? You're smiling?"

I shrugged, "I dunno. You seem really grown up. A house. Your law career. You're not the same guy anymore."

"A better guy?" he asked, a little bit of shyness sneaking in his expression.

"A much better guy."

"Don't think I haven't noticed you're all grown up now, too. Working out of state-on your own. But your friends all miss you. I miss you. Dallas is more than one man. We have a ton of happy memories." He plopped himself next to me on the couch and gave my sneakered foot a bop. "Come home. Come live with me till you get on your feet. Let me get you out of here. Make up for being a jerk all those years."

"Hello bag of worms, let's not open you now."

"Then, listen, my stepmom had the guest room above the garage remodeled, it's like a full apartment. Stay there. I'll convince her. She seems nice."

"Seems? Isn't she your family?"

I turned the idea around in my mind; it wasn't that bad. There was no reason to stay in Pittsburg once the project was finished. It held memories now that were just as bad, Scott's face flashed across my mind.

One date. That's all it was. Though I still felt a stab of grief and enough guilt to drown a Catholic.

Maybe I needed to be near friends.

Maybe friendship outweighed everything I'd have to face.

"And Megan?"

"You will have to meet her, eventually. On your terms. We can avoid Theo for a while."

"I have missed Shelley."

He frowned.

"You're here, right now! I can't miss you right now. But I did."

"Better."

"You know what?" I felt oddly excited, "Okay. Once my reno project is over, it's time to make my return. I won't be run outta town. Because.... Because..." I was losing steam.

"You own that city! It's yours. It's home."

Home. I smiled at that word. It filled me with a warmth I hadn't felt in a while.

"I'm so excited I'm going to start packing you up and do those dishes," Jake said, wrapping me up in a tight hug.

My heart lurched. Why did he still feel like home?

"I hate you," I said to rid myself of those familiar butterflies.

To heal, I was going to have to go off men for a while. In order to honor Scott... Scott... I'd received a notice from the doctor, it was a notice from the family, for the sake of the mother, that I avoid the funeral. She was experiencing some metal issues.

Well, who wouldn't? I stayed away, respectfully, sent flowers anonymously. I wasn't family, only a date. Only the date that got him killed.

But maybe if there was something nice, something else, I could do for his family before I left town for good. I drew in a shaky breath, eyed my sad apartment. Dallas. Yes. A new start was what I needed.

Friendship. Family. That was the cure.

"Yeah, well, I hate you, too. Now drink your water. Hydration is important," Jake said, suddenly between the two of us, he was the grown up.

I was grateful.
Sad.
And lonely.
A little concussed.
Truly, a dangerous combination when combined with stupidity.

There was a man on my couch. One with warm brown eyes and dimpled cheeks. One that looked at me and saw a full human. Sometimes he loved me. Sometimes he didn't. But he came all this way for me and stayed when I needed him most.

Then there was the other man. The one that was preparing to love me, to treat me with love and kindness and a little mischievousness, but he was dead. Scott was dead. The more I closed my eyes, the more I saw him. I'd known him for such a short time period... and yet I felt like I had to mourn him properly, for a year. Wear black. Buy a bench and give it a plaque. That wasn't healthy, though.

My leg slunk out of bed. And then the other.

This wasn't healthy either.

But maybe it could speed up the healing? Maybe it would make me feel better? Erase away the last few days? Connect me with my past again and who I was. Jake was always a constant in my life.

"Jake," I whispered, leaning over him as he slept peacefully on my couch. The couch came with the apartment and his legs were hanging over the side, there was no way he'd be in a deep sleep. "Jake you can't be comfortable."

This was a stupid idea. It beat staring at the ceiling, thinking of Scott.

He grumbled something.

"Jake!" I poked his naked shoulder. "Wake up."

This time he did, bleary eyed and struggled up into a sitting position.

"Jake, I was thinking."

But he didn't hear me, "Are you okay? Do you need something? Does your head hurt?" He wasn't looking at me either, as he was rubbing his face with his hands, trying to wipe away all the sleep. For a second, as he was trying to wake, and I assured him I was fine, I debated backing down and saying I needed some water. I wasn't that wise however, not at three am.

"Why don't you try and sleep in my room, you'll be more comfortable."

"Huh?" he squinted up at me, finally awake, "You woke me up to move me, so I could sleep?"

He was either stubborn, dense, or smarter than me.

Maybe he never thought seduction would come his way from a woman wearing faded orange pajama pants and an arbor day t-shirt.

Goodness, he looked cute all sleepy and confused, looking up at me, from under those long lashes, for an answer to clue him in on what I was doing.

"Yeah."

"I'm... I'm good?"

He would not get the answer on his own.

In one deft motion, I slid onto his lap, leaned in, and kissed him.

Out of reflex or love, I didn't know, but returned the kiss, so I pressed his chest back with the palm of my hand and had him on his back and me on top before his head-brain could start thinking for itself.

I was brilliant, soon I'd be too distracted, too tired to have nightmares. I brandished his face with kisses as his eager hands swept over me.

Till he stopped. A hand squeezing my shoulder.

"Marigold, what are we doing?"

Nothing good. Distracting me. Thanking you.

"Thanking you."

That was the wrong one to choose. He pushed my shoulders backwards and sat up. Looking me right in the eyes. It was the most honest connection we'd had in the last few moments. I flinched.

"Marigold, we don't 'thank' each other like this."

"I... I wanted to be close to you. I couldn't sleep." I slid away, to sit on the edge of the couch, and not him.

He frowned, "That's not... You came in hot, you..."

"Maybe I needed a distraction?"

"We should be more than a distraction to one another by now."

"Really?" shame and embarrassment flooded through me turning, my cheeks scarlet, "My on again and off-again boyfriend who gets close to me and dumps me, like it's this cyclical thing? Talk about using. I thought you were here again to pick me up till you tired of me. I'm just doing the offering now, to avoid the dance later. Saves us both time."

I did not take rejection well. And this man had broken up with me more times than I wanted to remember. Like I wasn't good enough for him.

He took a deep breath, "You've hit your head. Gone through a trauma, and now you are lashing out. I'm going to let this go. Go back to bed. So will I. And we forget this in the morning. You see why this can't happen, right? You were just in the hospital. Not in your right mind. I'd be taking advantage."

"With full permission. No attachments. Just make me feel something other than what I'm feeling."

He sighed.

"Isn't this what you came to Pittsburg for, really?" I pressed.

Jake covered his face with his hands, "I can't believe... Yeah, you know what?" he dropped his hands, "Yeah, I was sick and tired of seeing you with a loser like Theo and weeping over him, and then I hear about another rando named Scott. So yeah, I came back to remind you of home and that I was waiting for you. To remind you it didn't work with Theo because you were still in love with me the whole time."

I gasped.

Well done. He'd made me feel something different, pure undiluted anger.

"That is... That's so wrong," I huffed. Not convincing myself, nor him. But I stood up and put my hands on my hips to look even more convincing.

Then he stood, hands on hips, showing off his sculpted arms, his stupid-wide-confidence stance and grey sweatpants. Like he didn't plan this.

"Yeah. So you were still in love with me. Still are," he said.

I glared, shaking my now hurting head, "You are such a jerk."

He took a step forward, fire in his eyes, "I've never changed how I've felt," he smirked at my eye roll, "Fine. You win. Where do you want your distraction? Your bedroom or on the couch?"

I took a step closer. Whipped off my top and watched his eyes dilate as he took in the view.

"Nah," and I spun around, closing the bedroom door behind me with a slam.

Let him know what he was missing.

Jake wasn't there when I woke up in the morning.

Which was fine. It was totally fine. It wasn't like I was planning on making "I'm sorry eggs and biscuits." I could eat those alone. If I made them.

Did I really try to... Just after... I thunk my head down on the counter. Which of course nearly caused stars because I was still feeling gross from the day before.

At the very least, Jake may have run away, but he still cared. My pain pills sat on the kitchen counter with a note that simply read "Take with food. Six to four hours apart. The guesthouse is still yours. Love, Jake."

Filling a glass of water, I choked down those capsules, praying they removed shame and embarrassment as well. I crumpled up his note and threw it in the trash. There was no way I could face him again after that. I had to keep my distance from Jake to think clearly.

I finished the eggs and biscuits, stretching my aching body as I did so. The apartment was so clean, I had to maintain it now, before it returned too quickly to its former chaos.

A bit of egg fell on the crumpled note in the waste bin as I scraped my plate. His "Love" stared back at me.

My cheeks burned thinking of his rejection. How my pride tried to cheapen our relationship.

My brain never wanted to see his again.

But my heart couldn't resist the siren call of Dallas.

It was home, after all.

Still, I covered up that "Love" with another glob of egg. It didn't have to sit there staring at me all day.

Chapter 32

"I can't believe he dumped you. And the day after a funeral," I said, clicking my seat belt in place, "You are beautiful and wonderful and give me another ten to fifteen years of dating men and I might just come around."

After a funeral and a shooting, normal girl problems were welcome. I was glad to help Shells out and cheer her up.

"I don't deserve you," Shelley steered us onto the tollway and relaxed once she secured a space in the fast lane, "Thanks for dropping everything, I knew you would."

"You deserve everything! Don't let one Santa impersonator tear you down, there's a million more. What's the plan? Are we going to the Galleria? Picking up a new outfit or a handbag?"

Shelley chuckled, so I continued, "We could get some shoes, scope out some jewelry. Where are we going?"

Traffic was going at a fast clip. Soon we'd be cruising up to Addison or Plano. I never liked the tollway, you couldn't see far ahead of you thanks to hills and curves, nor could you enjoy your surroundings. High walls shielded the residential neighborhoods that flanked the highway. It was like driving through a concrete funnel. At least her cozy Mercedes made it more enjoyable with its crème leather and wood trim. Poe would decimate this car.

"North. I just want to drive, feel a little bit in control of my life for once."

"Oklahoma, okay, here we come. I'm down."

She fell silent, so I switched the radio on, hoping some divorced Adele or angry Taylor Swift would come through for us.

"It's KXA Pop! Pop top 40. Sixty minutes commercial freee..."

And the musical notes of a sad Adele filled our ears. Perfect. I was a horrible DJ and had to rely on the professionals. Luckily, she didn't seem that bad anymore. Her mouth was still in a tight, grim line and her body was ridged. This was an angry break up. They must have fought. Everett wasn't the most mellow of men... I could see them clashing. Anger was better than a melt down or a true weepy heartbreak.

A weekend of drinking and shopping and keeping her from going all Carrie Underwood and keying his car, she'd be okay again. And maybe me too. A distraction. Jake was with our fathers at the station giving Paul's final statement. It was done.

Maybe Oklahoma was smart. The retribution of damaging a cop car was not something I wanted her to experience.

"Should I call ahead? Book a room at a casino? We've never made it out to Chickasaw Nation."

After our Vegas debacle we vowed to never go to a casino again, but we were older and wiser now. 401 Locos were now illegal and reformulated.

She frowned, "No gambling. No... I'll think of something in a minute," and she twisted her face into a wry smile, "We've gone through life together haven't we? Ballet when our moms forced us. Soccer then softball then tennis... I knew whatever new thing my mom would make me take on that you'd be right there, and it would be okay. High School. College. I was hoping for weddings and pregnancies. Could you imagine our kids? Being besties, too?"

A tear dropped down her cheek.

What was this? I thought Everett was a fun escapade, that it wasn't true love.

"Our luck they'd hate each other," I tried for a smile, "Mine would be a tom boy and yours a delicate pink princess."

"We've been through everything together," she sighed, "I love you; you know that."

"I love you, too... What is going on? Should I drive?"

Now I was getting worried that she'd drive us off the road in some attention-getting ploy. Have Everett come running to our rescue, and he'd realize he was wrong and get back with her purely out of guilt. Together till the next fight.

But the way Shells was talking. She wasn't herself. She was an onward and upward sort of woman. Occasionally a little rage-y. Rage was fine if we were on our bikes and ready to take on the neighborhood bully. Or in a bar, poised, tipsy, and ready for trouble. Or buying a bucket of bleach. Rage was not good at eighty miles-per-hour.

"The Galleria's not too far back..." I began.

"No."

"Oh..."

Now my concern was sky high. I turned down the radio to speak calmly to her, "Shells? I've indulged this long enough. Get off at the next exit and pull over. I'm driving. We can keep going, but this isn't safe."

"Not yet," she sniffed, "I'm trying to make this last... as long as possible. Before everything falls apart." Another series of tears.

Okay, now I was terrified.

I stared at her.

She looked... wilted.

This wasn't an Everett thing. This was bigger.

"We've done everything together," she whispered, "We tell each other *everything*."

"Whatever this is. I'm here for you."

My panic level rose.

Was she going to drive us off an edge or something? Purposely crash us into a tree? My brow broke out in a sweat, because I did not know what to do. I did not know her in this moment. Not this version of her. My mind was kind enough to flash images of Richard's bloody face across my mind.

The brakes screeching as Scott pitched forward.

They were all right. Death follows me. Maybe it was time for him to finally catch up.

I tightened my seatbelt as I dug around in my memories.

Was there something that I missed? I'd been so wrapped up, so busy. On important things, yes, but I'd missed whatever led up to this. I'd missed the silent call for help from my best friend.

It was my fault. As the best friend, whatever was wrong here, I'd been too late. Too gone.

"Shells... I'm here. Pull over, talk to me," I said with my heart in my throat. I failed her.

"I tried to delay it," she shrugged, "But okay. I'm sorry and I still love you and I pray that you still love me after. Just know that I'm in a corner-in survival mode-and there's really no other options, okay?"

Well, that threw me into a soup of confusion.

"You're not going to kills us?" I squeaked out, realizing I had shrunk down into the seat, my hands gripping the belt, as if that would save me.

Shelley rolled her eyes, "How well do you know me? I just got a perm! No!"

I shrugged, still not letting go of the handle above the window, because what else could I do? At least she wasn't going to intentionally kill us- so that was a positive. The fact that she could still refer to Legally Blonde was a good thing.

Yet, given our speed, unintentionally still seemed like an option.

"I can see why car accidents make you uneasy. But with Scott it was a motorcycle," she winced at my obvious flinch at his name, "Still, Love? I'm sorry. And then Richard, too, so long ago. But I've got you. I will not get us in a wreck. It's better, in fact, that you're not driving."

I blinked.

She was right.

I played her words through my mind.

Time slowed. Our speed didn't, the exit to the Sam Rayburn Tollway zipped by-we were heading to Frisco now. Though our destination no longer mattered.

"I... I never told you about Richard," I stuttered.

Never told anyone. The memory was sealed away, locked buried, and burned. Never even spoken about to those that were there. It was labeled in my brain as "here be monsters," so privately, I never went there. Her words were like a shovel in the dirt, hitting something with clashing bang.

I never spoke a word about what really happened in Austin to her. Secret found. Somehow.

"And I'm not mad at you for not telling me. I get it; it's too big, and we were teenagers," Shelley said, "Though I wish I knew. It explains why you were so moody when you got back. Why you and Jake broke up. Everyone thought ya'll would be the high school sweetheart king and queen. But... but I get why you didn't tell me. Gosh. Marigold, what you've been carrying around. I am so sorry all that happened."

She looked concerned, yet my heart was still thudding away in my chest.

"How do you know?"

Somewhere during her speech she had pulled into the slow lane and exited. We were pulled into a gas station. Still and motionless, no longer at risk of crashing, but I felt like I was still on this ride.

Shelley clicked her seat belt off and turned towards me. I did the same. Having a restraint on didn't seem smart, but I was pretty sure the child locks were on. To test my theory, however, meant I was getting scared of my best friend. And that she'd know.

"Paul. We've been sleeping together till recently. For about six months."

I exhaled, "Whaaat?" I felt like a punctured balloon, deflating and wandering back to earth.

Never would I have guessed that. He was so much *older*. He was like a second father to me... I squirmed, wanting out of this car. My friends should have been safe from his womanizing eyes. Guilt hit me in the gut, because this meant every time I brought her around... Oh, my stomach twisted. Shelley was an attractive woman by any standards, and I'd been naive enough to think she was safe. Paul betrayed me, us, in the worst of ways.

"At first I thought it was a one-time thing. But we connected. It was real," she frowned, "At least I thought it was. He was going to leave her for me."

"Ohhh Shells..."

What an original lie. My heart dropped for her.

"He was!" her eyes brimmed with fresh tears, "He loved me, too. But it all fell apart. She was getting suspicious. Everything just went so wrong."

I could see that; Shelley was never subtle.

"One night, in bed, I asked him for assurances that he really loved me. That we had a future," she hiccupped, fully crying now. Mascara running down her cheeks. I wanted to reach out to hug her-it was hard not to, but I felt like that would stop the story. Remaining in place, I merely handed her a tissue from my purse.

"Well," she blew her nose, "That's when he told me. Said I was like family to you, so I should know anyhow. And having something on him so incriminating would be the glue that held us together. Paul said secrets were stronger than blood. Stronger than marriage vows."

I groaned. A perverted twist on romance from the womanizer-not surprised.

"It was romantic, at the time. All whispered under the covers. Like we were the only people in the world."

All I saw was an older man taking advantage of my friend. Like a layer of paint peeling off, all my sympathy, fondness, last little bits of doubt were all stripped away as I watched tears stain her cheeks. My anger flared as her eyes turned red along with the top of her nose. Paul was dead to me. He was never the man I thought he was-no, he was the man we were all scared he actually was.

We'd all been in denial.

We knew.

And lied to ourselves.

He was the 'same old story' killing his wife to get with the mistress. How'd he think that play out long term? His current wife was already a pariah in our society circle.

It wasn't planned. The murder.

It was done in passion, during a fight.

"So what happened that night?" my voice cracked, I didn't want to ask.

"That's why I had to get you alone, to tell you. To tell you I know about Richard. I can share my secret, now that I know yours."

Shelley at least had the decency to look nervous.

"I'm familiar with blackmail," my voice was flat, cold. Disappointed.

"More like mutually assured destruction."

"So, you have been hanging out with Paul. That's his favorite."

"Which is why I'm backed into this corner," she reached behind her, pulling out a Target bag and dropped it in my lap, "Open it."

In my hand I held the knitted fabric of a light blue denim Polo shirt. Accented with dried blood stains, as if someone flicked a paint brush over the cloth canvas as an afterthought. No pattern, no care-just there.

Evidence. I gulped.

"So he did it," my voice came out as a whisper.

"No, Marigold, I did it."

Chapter 33

Oh.

My mouth dropped to say something, clearly, I should say something. But my brain recycled that audio clip. "I did it." She said it so surely, so matter-of-factly, looking me straight in the eye, that I believed her. If Shelley said she did something, or was going to do it, then believe her- it was going to happen. Or in this case, it did happen.

Our trust ran deep. The sincerity flickering in her eye canceled out every "but she couldn't have" thought.

Our trust ran deep. As she pointed out, though not deep enough for me to tell her about Richard. Not deep enough for her to tell me about her affair. Of her, here's to hoping, first murder.

"Oh," I said filling in the silence. Still not sure what to say.

"You're not running?"

That was an option?

I cracked the door open, thankful for the rush of fresh air, for that it was unlockable.

Instead of flinging the door open wider and making a run for it, I closed it again and faced her. Our trust ran deep enough.

Heck-curiosity ran deeper than anything.

"Tell me about it." This time, my voice was sure.

Stress melted off her face, she almost looked like the Shelley I knew from ten minutes before, "I was hoping you'd say that... Thank you for staying."

"Talk," I demanded.

" Okay-okay," she gestured surrender, "The day started normal. It was all party prep for me. Got my perm and my nails done. Picked up a new dress. I was so excited to see you. Scared, too. I knew I'd eventually have to tell you about Paul. But I didn't know how long I could wait or how to tell you. I was a hot mess, literally," she smiled, but I only frowned, this was about a murder, so she continued on, "Paul swore me to secrecy, but I think he knew-with you-that it would be different. And once I told you, we'd both lose you. And you're like family! The night before you got here, I told him we had to end it and keep the secret to our graves. Or he had to divorce his wife and choose me. Only then would telling you make any sense. That way you knew what we had was real, and I had a solid future."

My arrival was the catalyst. Great. They could have all co-existed a little longer, a train wreck inevitable, but maybe all could have survived the collision.

"So," I swallowed, "The shirt?"

"The shirt... I did not foresee..." she pinched the bridge of her nose and squeezed her eyes shut, "Yeah, that was a mistake of epic proportions. I was so sure he was going to choose her-they were married-that I bought him that denim shirt as a gift. A goodbye, no hard feelings gift. He wore a denim shirt on our first date. Well," she shrugged, "He loved the gesture. Told me that night he'd tell her it was over."

"And then the party-you were there-at your party," I frowned.

She gave me a wistful smile, "He texted me to come over, that it all was falling apart. And so, I slipped away…"

"You left your party to kill her," I exhaled, "So you could be with Paul… She wasn't going to leave him."

"I killed her, but I didn't go there to. That you have to believe."

"A crime of passion. Temporary insanity," I suggested, trying to channel what Jake would say, "We're a crew of good lawyers. You know we have your back; we'll refer you to someone. Turn yourself in." Helping Shelley was my duty after introducing her to Paul. After missing her silent calls for help.

"Yeah…" her voice shook, "It's more than that."

More than murder? Maybe I should have exited the car when I had the chance.

My best friend murdered someone in a fit of passion… It was an idea as slippery as oil, my mind could not fully grasp

. I still loved her, because we always would love each other. Did that mean I still had to do the right thing? Was it really on me to turn her into the police and end this. Get some justice for Emma-look out for her, as no one else would, and give Shelley the best lawyers money could buy?

I gulped. I couldn't be the one responsible for sending Shelley to prison for the rest of her life.

But now I had the power to bring peace to Jake. I had the truth.

My stomach flipped. This really was not what I thought my Dallas life would be. Wasn't my plan to hide out a bit more? Find an interior design job and get an apartment? Do some shopping? That's all I wanted.

But death followed me.

Justice wasn't going to be simple either.

Mutually assured destruction.

I couldn't turn her in.

Her secret was now mine because she was armed with the Austin knowledge. She could drag my entire family down. I wanted to resent her for that, but I'd have threatened the same. Survival was not pretty. Nor for the weak. And we were survivors.

She sat there, calmly, watching me, letting me digest the news and gather my thoughts.

Wasn't it Shelley and Marigold against the world? She could have run and disappeared. And instead, she trusted me to do the morally grey thing for her.

I sighed, defeated, "Ok, so what's your plan? You clearly have one."

"That's it?" she squinted, "You're not calling me a monster? You're not... I don't know, freaking out? Crying? I killed a woman!"

"I... I'm not sure I'm fully processing," I admitted, "It doesn't seem real. These things never do, till later. Everything will hit me later. Right now, it's all very abstract."

"Well, okay..." she pinged me a video file to my phone, "My statement. More evidence. You can share that later with the police. With whomever. In 72 hours."

And then she told me her plan.

Her utterly ridiculous plan.

Chapter 34

The freakout happened two hours later. At a bed-and-breakfast slightly more north. I couldn't believe I was agreeing to this. Her plan was a faux kidnapping. The victim? Me. Why? So she could borrow money, say goodbye, all while me not being an accomplice.

"It won't hurt," she said as she knelt before me, sticking duct tape to my arm. "But we need evidence, right? If someone asked, you can honestly say I duct taped you to the chair and took your money."

"This is dumb."

"Maybe. But I've never done a faux kidnapping."

"Any real ones?" Had to ask.

"Har-har. On the count of three. Just pretend it's a waxing. One- Two. Just like the time we did each other's upper lip."

I yelped on three as she ripped off the arm hair around my wrists. Good thing I was blonde or I'd look very patchy. "You are a killer," I teased. Kinda.

She glared, "Too soon."

But then she smiled, "And now your ankles."

I rolled up my pant leg. Good thing I shaved. And a good thing for Shells, I was a tiny bit scared still. This way, according to her, there would be hair on the duct tape, making it look like I had freed myself, without ever actually having to be really kidnapped. Shelley probably read one article on DNA evidence while dating Everett. Lucky me.

" Okay, one-two-threee. Excellent," she said ripping the duct tape and leaving it near the chair in the center of the room, "As soon as I'm at the airport I'll call Jake to come get you, okay? So... I'm going to need your cell phone. Just to be one hundred percent sure you don't call the cops. I need to make my flight. I'll get it back to you."

"I trust you, Shells," I passed it over. Truth or a lie, I didn't know.

"And I'll pay you back every penny."

That was the plan. Getting my bank account information so she could buy a few airline tickets and withdraw enough cash to live. She'd already drained and stowed away hers.

She was fleeing to England. Staying apparently at a Parliamentarian's flat in London. She'd once met him when she did her study abroad, and then some summer vacations, and some winter one's too. He'd keep her safe from extradition.

The woman had a plan. Had to give her that.

"You're looking kind of sweaty. You're freaking out. Take these. Two Benadryl and you'll be out like a light. I'm sorry all my Xanax is packed. And when you wake up, Jakey will be here to pick you up. Okay? Hey, and then you two can toast me for the little extra push ya'll needed. I'm tired of the whole 'let's take it slow' stuff. Invite me to the wedding."

Yeah... Yeah I was getting a little sweaty because the pain made this very real. I was helping my best friend get away with a murder that I had been trying to solve. It was hysterical laughter or sweat. I chose sweat around the unhinged friend.

At least Shelley was a kind kidnapper. She gave me a chocolate protein bar so I wouldn't be hungry. The brand I liked, too.

I swallowed down the small pink pills, agreeing that I'd rather sleep through the next couple of hours than sitting and staring at the wall, over-thinking.

"And I'll leave the TV on…" she clicked through a few channels, "Perfect Gilmore Girls we love that show."

I nodded. Couldn't argue with that.

Shelley fluttered through the room, checking the AC temperature, turning lights off, but flicking on the lamps near the bed, all for my comfort. Finally, she stopped fretting and stood in front of me, running her hands down her sides nervously, as if to wipe down her own sweaty palms.

"I can't stay here, Marigold. I'm dead if I stay," she threw herself on me in a hug, "Visit, okay? London's great. When you're ready. You'll know how to find me."

I nodded. Returned the hug.

"I'm sorry I ruined everything. Really, really sorry," she said again, as she stepped away. "What did we always say? Marigold and Shelley against the world?"

"Marigold and Shelley against the world," I repeated, a vow that I would give her the full 72 hours she needed.

What else could I do?

"Right," a tear glistened in her eyes.

And it was reflected back in mine.

Goodbye.

She muttered a few things about being sorry again as she wiped tears from her cheeks, and backed out of the door, locking it with an automatic, decisive click that sounded louder than any verbal goodbye.

I yawned. Stared at the closed door. Trying not to think how it symbolized the closing of a chapter of my life.

Benadryl and I were fast friends, and I was glad for the tiredness as it numbed my emotions.

Never saw see our friendship ending like that. My theory was that she'd sleep with a boyfriend of mine. Not blackmail me and ditch me in a sketchy hotel room.

But, hey. I was never a fortuneteller.

Chapter 35

I woke up from my nap to pounding on the door. Through the peephole, I saw it was a very frazzled looking Jake. Every hair was out of place, and for him, that was something. For me, I couldn't ignore the leap my heart took while seeing him.

"Jake!" I swung open the door, "To my rescue! I've been kidnapped!"

He stood in the doorway, silent, unsure of how to handle this recuing.

"It was horrible. There were so many episodes of Gilmore Girls I had to watch."

Still not sure how to handle the moment, he held out my phone as I let him in, "Found this in the bushes outside."

Right. I took it. My smiled wavered. I had been going for levity, but that phone, with her confession on it, weighed me down.

"Are you okay?" he asked.

My smile trembled again, "Going to have to stop asking that."

"Need to stop giving me every occasion to."

True.

He kicked at the scraps of duct tape on the floor as he entered and sent me a questioning look.

"I was kidnapped," I shrugged, "Had to look real? This was her first kidnapping, real or not. Next time will be much smoother. Much better thought out."

Jake nodded; he wasn't ready to smile.

Instead, he sighed, "Marigold... I can't believe... You were alone with a killer," his voice droned out as he sat on the edge of the bed. "I never could have guessed. This is all my fault. You're okay... I keep having to tell myself. I was so focused on my own family."

"Jake. It was Shelley. I was never in any real danger. She'd never hurt me."

"You have no idea how worried I was. She left me a long, crazy voicemail saying she kidnapped you and tied you to a chair because you were 'super unhelpful in every way possible' and that she was sick of you thwarting her plans."

I knew. That was part of the plan.

"And then she called me again and again till I actually picked up the phone. I'd ignored the voicemail first like any good millennial," finally he smiled as I sat next to him. He brushed my shoulders off as if I was a dusty statue, "You're safe."

"I think I always was."

Safe, yet confused.

"Jake, this is Shelley. How did you think she was serious, and that this wasn't some weird prank? I mean, you look pale. Technically, I could have Ubered home, but I really didn't want to watch this video alone. And I didn't know my phone was right outside."

"Poe took a poop."

"What?"

"Right as she was calling. Poe likes to eat gold, remember?" Jake asked, as he leaned knees on elbows and hands on cheeks. Closed eyes. Raw exhaustion.

"I really thought you could be hurt. Just give me a second."

My heart thudded in my chest, even though I gave it explicit instructions not to. But facts were facts. When his world was crumbling around him, he came to rescue me.

Was this why Shelley called him? She could trust that he'd be first at the door-no matter what. Leave it to my best friend to have her last act be matchmaking. The entire world already knew it. Our parents, our friends. Even me.

I only never fully accepted it. Till now. We *were* end game, and it was up to me to grow up and say, okay, I'm ready now. I'm done with random men. Done with bad relationships and men that would hurt me.

Maybe it was time to finally pick-the inner feminist in me screamed- but maybe it was time to pick the one willing to save me. Not every girl got a knight. Mine was fitted with dark wash jeans, a light green-button up, and wavy hair that somehow always told me his mood.

My best friend killed someone, and he was now my only anchor in this world.

"Are you really okay?"

"I think so." I wiggled closer next to him, letting our thighs brush.

"Okay... So, as I was saying. Poe pooped, right in my kitchen, and out came a small, gold bracelet with a conc shell engraved 'Shelley.' There's no reason Shelley's bracelet would have been on the floor in their home that's good."

"She was sleeping with Paul."

He sighed. His shoulders slouching, "I was wondering if that was the case."

"She killed Emma. Jealousy. Fit of passion, whatever. She killed Emma." I sounded nervous as I spoke, unsure of putting those words in the universe.

Jake fell silent till finally whispering, "Shelley?"

"Shelley."

A longer incredulous pause followed.

"So, my Dad's still innocent? And Violet was only responsible for shooting Meg? She was a little less rampage-y than we thought?"

"Maybe? Shelley still seemed scared of Paul, but she claimed to kill Emma."

"That doesn't that make me feel any better. Why would Shelley come forward now? Everyone pinned the death on Violet. Technically she was free and clear. Was it guilt?" unconsciously, he took my hand and merely let it rest in his.

"I-I don't know."

"So, is it over?" he asked, "For real this time?"

"I think so?" my voice came out a little high pitched. "I think she sealed it shut for us." I pointed to the shirt on the floor next to the chair, "She left us a video confession, too."

He glanced at the shirt, but did not pick it up, "So, Dad knew the whole time? He was there and was… what taking the fall for her?"

"Because he caused it all. If the truth got out, he'd be in trouble."

"He could have stopped it."

"Not if it was quick. If Shelley was in a fit of rage and he was across the kitchen. Maybe he ran to try but was too late."

"Maybe…" he rubbed his stubbly jaw, "But then he goes and

changes clothes? Leaves her on the ground? His wife?"

"Shelley ran back to the party. He had an hour to call 911 before I got back, and he didn't."

"Paul may not have been the one to stab her, yet he was certainly okay with it. I think I feel ill. I liked the whole Violet theory much better," Jake said, getting up to pace the room, "He was okay with the murder of his wife? Can you imagine the coldness? The sickness that lurks inside that man? If your wife is killed, you sink to your knees and bawl your eyes out and call 911. Then you go all mad and tear up whomever did it."

It was a problematic plot device in too many movies, of the woman dying so that the man suddenly had purpose. If only men showed that much love and devotion when their women were still alive. But I understood what Jake was saying. Paul was relieved his wife had been murdered. Saved him the effort later.

Jake's eyes brimmed with pain, and it tore me to pieces. Maybe he was seeing what I saw whenever I closed my own. Me instead of Emma. Instead of Meg. Which in that church, it easily could have been.

I was so grateful Jake did the wrong thing.

At least we were not too late. We could save each other. I was ready to slay any demons in his path to get that happy spark back in his eyes.

"Unless it was your lovely, young mistress," I said, keeping my plans to myself.

"Maybe he was in shock? If it really wasn't Violet, there aren't any other suspects. He didn't have time to plan anything out."

"For once he wasn't the master manipulator," I bit my lip, "I wonder how much my Dad knows. He just told me to stick with you and not make any waves."

"He knows," we said at the same time. No one earned benefit of the doubt anymore.

"So my Dad's basically a murderer," Jake said.

"And mine covers it all up."

We shared a look-one that said this was sickest form of déjà vu.

"And once again, we do nothing," he sighed.

"Nothing but stay silent."

"And watch the master manipulators play."

"How many times do you think this has happened? Something like this?" I asked. I remembered how good an actor Paul was, how he had blamed me straight away, shaking me.

"Are you saying?"

"We keep investigating my Dad's past relationships? The ones we know about? And see if there are others? For what end? We threaten him- he threatens us. And all this extra knowledge just makes Thanksgiving a little more awkward?" he stopped his pacing and collapsed next to me once again, "I don't see know knowledge helps us anymore, Marigold. We have a confession, proof he was an accomplice-but we know a talented lawyer will make mincemeat of that. I don't see what else. Violet's murdering rampage creates all the reasonable doubt the defense needs."

I didn't respond. I was too lost in my own thoughts.

And Shelley! How could have Paul have done that to her? He knew things wouldn't end well. How could he have told her the Austin secret? Did he think I already told her? His gift of secrets meant nothing.

I mean, I was surprised I hadn't told Shelley.

I only ever wanted to keep it so buried that it would never drift into my consciousness unless summoned. There was no need to burden her with such knowledge. Not telling her was a form of protection.

How could Paul have not left Shelley alone?

I didn't blame her. She had a weakness-any handsome well-to-do man represented love and security to her; She had major daddy issues after her own father walked out when she was in middle school. Paul's love for me should have kept her safe.

But the bruise on my shoulder taught me that his love was highly limited. The bubble of protection-gone-and never was the absolute I expected.

I did not want to be left alone with Paul ever again.

"He ruined Shelley's life," my hands were in fists at my side.

"She took your money," he countered.

"Shells was scared and cornered."

He set a hand on my knee, and looked into my eyes, "She killed a woman. Stabbed her. Watched her life leave her body. Neither of us really knew Shelley if she was capable of that."

I looked away. Trying to blink back tears.

I had to know who Shelley was.

I *had* to.

Because she was a part of me.

The sister I never had.

"Should we watch her confession?" he asked, "Maybe that'll make it feel more real and we can go from there?"

I nodded, wiping my eyes.

Though I didn't want it to feel real.

Chapter 36- *Shelley*-

"The day you got home, Marigold, it changed everything."

I was a horrible friend. I let Theo and Megan in. My mind was elsewhere, and I was dishing out welcomes and smiles like free-after-dinner mints, and in they waltzed. Megan wasn't really the problem. But Theo?

That skunk of a man? I could drive a stake through that vampire. That blood-soul sucking...

I took a deep breath and swallowed down my champagne. Everything was going to be alright.

Marigold would have a blast. I'd distract her.

Distract me.

As Paul was to give Emma the old heave-ho. Which would be

happening right now. He'd tell her, Emma, there's something I have to say. We aren't working out. You don't like it here. You'll be very comfortable with the settlement I'm willing to offer.

And she'd cry, but quickly realize the truth. They weren't meant to be. They had fun, but there wasn't that something special. Emma was young and pretty; she'd bounce back and survive this.

Then part two. Telling my best friend.

I roll-played it in my mind, too many times, and the best scenario was Paul taking her out to lunch, telling her his marriage was frayed. That it had been for a long time, and that yet, another divorce would be in the works soon.

Part three. I'd tell her over drinks. Slowly. The vague I met someone and drop in all his good qualities till she was giddy for me. Then the reveal. Marigold wouldn't be happy for me- not at first, but maybe after a few times of seeing us together. Paul was so sweet with me. So tender. A gentleman. She'd see.

Our generation didn't make men like that anymore. They'd probably ask me to pull out the chair for them.

Mom always re-married older.

She played the game, too well though. Dad left when I was twelve.

Paul's age gap was less extreme. Our kids would know him. At least through high school.

Would Amy and Jake accept our children?

Well, that was another thing. Step four. I wasn't pregnant yet.

I checked on the ice, on the appetizers. Everything had to be perfect. This party would show Marigold how much I loved her. Even the napkins and decor were a deep, rich orange matching her namesake the best the average napkin could. Like I said: Perfect. Because on the off-

chance of her not forgiving me…

At least there was this one last party.

A farewell instead of a hello.

But I couldn't wait till Emma was out of the picture. No more sneaking around. No more back door entrances and hotel rooms. People would call us a May-December romance, but, oh, at least it had the word romance. My fingers tickled the new diamond earrings glittering from my ears. Paul liked to gift diamonds. Soon we could go dancing. Traveling. I could quit my job and become a full-time Mrs.

He'd keep me.

He would.

I was from the same stock. Cultured and bred in Highland Park. I was raised to be a wealthy man's wife. Trained in dinner parties and in charity galas. My grace would elevate his stature and I'd never embarrass him.

Not like Emma.

What was he thinking?

Fun and frills and fuchsia lipstick never lasted.

I hugged myself and took another deep breath. Urging calmness like my yoga master taught. Everything soon would be okay. Marigold would understand; she knew me.

I did not need another Xanax.

But then my phone lit up. It was Paul.

Texting me to get down there now.

From maybe needing a Xanax to needing five in under 60 seconds… My heart was sounding out its beats. I could hear it in my ears.

She wasn't going to leave him. That had to be it.

That had to be…

"…I'm telling you, Marigold. My hands went clammy, my whole body was either going to shut down or it was going to go into overdrive. I snuck out the back door. I wish I never left. I wish so, so hard I never left. I'm so sorry, Love. I am so, so sorry…"

Chapter 37

I hit pause on the screen. Stopping the video in the middle of her tears.

"You okay?" Jake asked, handing me a glass of water. "I know this isn't easy."

When did he get up to get water?

"I'm not okay. I'm about to hear how my best friend murdered someone in a jealous rage. I'd never think she was capable. Never."

Jake's only response was to enfold me into his arms. He exuded warmth and strength, and I greedily absorbed it up. It didn't seem fair. In return he got cold, clamminess, and a bit of teary snot on his shoulder. But this was the deal he made, and I would not end it.

"At some point we need to talk," his voice vibrated against my neck.

I nodded and gripped him against me harder.

"Come on," he gave my back a rub and stopped, all too soon, "Let's get this over with."

"Okay..." my voice was muffled by his shoulder, as I pulled him back towards me.

Shelley's voice filled the room.

When I got there, they were arguing. Paul had given me a key, so I'd wandered in and stood in the foyer listening.

"You have the gall to prance around in the shirt she gave you? As you ask me for peaceful divorce? I'll tell you what, it will not be peaceful. There won't be a divorce."

"If it's money you want..."

"Money? Hah. Do you think that's the only reason I married you? I love you, Paul. I love the life we are creating here. The idea of growing old together. Of having kids together. I want some stability in my crazy life for once. So, what is this? A brief affair? We can do some counseling and get through this."

"I'm not a brief affair," I found myself saying as I stood in the doorway. "I'm sorry. We fell in love. It wasn't planned."

Emma scoffed. She ignored me and began slicing her lemons. Paul had mentioned she always made her trashy lemonade drink in the evening. That he'd try to wind down at night and all he heard was chop-chop-chop as he was reading.

Poor Paul. I'd never be that loud at night. I knew he had to work hard the next day and relax his mind before being able to sleep.

Finally, Emma spoke, "What are you looking for here, girl? Money? A new husband? Imagine how he'd treat you if he left me? Any better? Go home. Go away. You're nothing. There's a million pretty faces, each one more forgettable than the last."

Tears burned my eyes. I blinked them back.

My feet were, however, planted.

Emma dropped the knife on the cutting board after the last lemon was sliced to face me, "Don't just stand there. Go. Now."

A gentle hand landed on my shoulder. Paul. I gazed up at him, craving his approval, that I should stay. For some reassurance that he wanted me- he asked me here. I needed reassurance that I was right, that this was love, that we were different. Like he said we were. I was special.

"You should go."

And I felt my heart fall.

And a bit of indignation rise.

I was not some small child to be dismissed. I was a grown-up woman who was a critical part of this conversation. If I walked out that door, Emma would win. She'd fight for their sham of a marriage and make everyone miserable. There was still a slight chance for Paul and I, and frankly, after the settlement, she would be happy again soon. She could marry for love and not a stack of cash.

The knife was in my hand before I realized.

I didn't think to drop it, because it felt right. If they didn't respect me then... Well, maybe now they would. That bit of a serrated edge gave me power.

"Put that down," Emma said, not scared, just huffy, as if I were a small child and not her equal.

But Paul quirked an eyebrow and smirked.

Of course he liked it.

He liked assertiveness.

"You're the one that needs to leave, Emma. Bow out gracefully. Sign the divorce papers like good little fourth wife. Why did you think you'd be any different? You are not from our world. Neither were his past wives."

"Because, Dear, I have a solid ten-year pre-nup. I get half. Of everything."

Well that nearly made me drop the knife. I recovered and gripped it harder. How? What? How could Paul have signed something like that?

"Paul? Is that true?"

"It is," his expression sheepish.

"How..."

Emma smiled. For the first time it was cold. Cruel. Calculating. Transformative.

"I knew I was playing in the big leagues, Dear. My sister's a bigwig CEO in children's publishing. If he didn't sign the pre-nup on my terms, little Amy's publishing contracts... poof," she gestured a minor explosion.

"I have to admit," Paul said, "That type of energy was hot and I knew she was the one, at the time."

What? I was going to sink. And they were going to drag me down. My knees wobbled as my life around me turned to quicksand.

I knew he liked power... I knew... he wasn't the strongest of moral characters, but I thought his love would extend to me, that I was the special one. But she was me and I was her. And soon there would be someone else. I was risking all my ties here in Dallas for something temporary. It felt like the wind was knocked out of my lungs, like someone had finally rocked me awake. My grip on the knife loosened. The adrenaline drained, and I set it down. I did not know the scared, cornered, jealous version of myself that grabbed it, nor did I like her.

So I said goodbye.

"No," I mumbled towards the floor, feeling more sure that I was once again upon steady ground. No man got to me make me crazy. No man got to treat me like this. "I'm done. Fix your marriage. Or find another mistress. I don't care. I'm out, and for the record," I nodded at Emma, "I am sorry."

And I was.

Shame was a bitter pill, but it was a remedy I was willing to swallow.

I thought I was special. I wasn't.

I wasn't meant for the big leagues. Didn't want to be. Lies and prenups and careers and manipulations... I didn't want any of that. I wanted champagne and travel and shiny things. Maybe love, if that still existed out there.

"Pick up that knife," Paul demanded.

"What? No. I'm going back to my party." Going to spend my energy with those that actually cared for me.

He blocked my exit.

"You make me confront my wife, ruin my marriage, and then walk away?"

I wanted to say something like if I was here in the first place, it was already ruined. That Emma was going to make ya'll work it out. But the time for words had run past. His face was red, spittle spewed out with his words. That veiny thing in his neck bulged.

So this was the monster that we'd all feared. I'd guessed all men had a monster like this inside, something angry, something parasitic. Something some could tame, while others could not.

I wasn't scared.

I was deserving. Of this. Of whatever happened.

"Paul... Paul, now calm down," Emma stuttered, turning pale. She was scared, back to looking like the innocent housewife. Maybe she *was a tad manipulative, but never violent. We were both playing games out of our league.*

Even as a team we couldn't fight this.

He stood over six feet, older, but still trim and muscular. Fury turning his skin red, and I watched as tendons in his arm flexed as he took hold of that knife.

"Paul... Paul... Put that down. We can figure this out in the morning," Emma plead.

I gulped and shuffled backwards. Her pleading did nothing to warm the expression in those cold eyes. I wasn't scared, but subconscious survival skills kicked in and mine was to flee, I kept scooting farther back, slowly, as if a sudden movement would startle him into action.

He stopped me in my tracks. Grabbing me around the waist and yanking me backwards into his chest.

Paul was breathing hard. I could feel it now.

Of course. He was a trapped man. Trapped even more than I.

His hot breath traveled down my neck; I shivered.

He was trapped in his marriage-his own mistake. It had to be infuriating. Even if he loved Emma. She represented his one weakness- the love of his child. I had been his revenge, and now that was over. I couldn't be used anymore to hurt others.

"Paul, put down the knife," Emma said through her tears. She backed up against the counter. The knife aimed at her chest as we approached. My feet were an inch above the floor.

I wiggled harder, to try for a shin-kick, no such luck prevailed, and he had my arms pressed against my side. In response, he only tightened his grip on me.

"Paul," my voice was breathless from being squeezed like

toothpaste, "Stop. You don't want to do this."

"I think I do."

Emma's eyes went wide.

Oh, she didn't think he was capable.

Oh no.

Did she not know the monster in the men that we played with?

"Let go!" *I yelled, squirming harder. To save us both. Emma was innocent, this was all far too over her head.*

We were right in front of her. His feet an inch from hers.

"Paul stop it," *she cried,* "I'll leave, okay? I'll leave. I'll sign whatever. Whatever you want. I don't want to stay here. I don't want your money."

"I was so impressed with your negotiating skills. You knew you had to stand out. Be different. But I think I knew then, how this would end... Still on my terms. I did think it wouldn't be for a few more years."

"Please," *she cried,* "You win."

Smart. Appeal to his pride.

Paul nodded. Was this it? Was he willing to put the knife down?

He stretched out my arm and as he placed the knife in my hand, he curled my fingers around the hilt.

He wanted me to drop the knife for him.

I opened my hand to drop it... but...

A hurricane of force.

A scream.

I blinked.

I was nose to nose, eye to eye with Emma.

Her pupils went wide, rimmed with shock and pain and gurgling noises came from her mouth. A drop of blood trickled.

What? How could? The world was out of focus. I closed my eyes and rewound the last few moments. I could still feel the imprint of his hand on mine... As he had taken over and rammed me bodily into her.

He stabbed her.

No.

We stabbed her.

Paul backed away and stumbled backwards as well, dropping the knife, dropping me. Staring at the purpling on my arm from where his hand had been, I stumbled against the counter, gripping its edges to stay on my feet.

"*I guess we can be together after all,*" *he said. Casually. As if he was talking about an easy divorce and not death. Murder.*

Emma had already slunk to the floor. Blood flowing out from the chest wound. 911 couldn't save her.

"*Stabbing my wife just to have me,*" *he laughed, his complexion settling back to a calm tan,* "*Well that's pretty hot. Don't worry about the cops. I'll protect you.*" *He groaned,* "*Ugh, you look hot with blood on you. Why don't we go upstairs?*"

I stared.

Too petrified to run. He'd turn me to stone.

Cops.

Prints.

Blood.

"*Don't worry, Love, I'll protect you. We are each other's now. Just as you wanted,*" *he placed a light peck on my stone lips,* "*Now, go freshen up and get back to that party. We'll talk later.*"

"I was a robot, Marigold. I cleaned myself up and went back to the *party. I... I started dating Everett to protect myself. I'm sorry. I ruined the pleasant life we all had. I deserve this exile. So please, don't look for me. You know Paul will find me if you do. Keep me safe-stay away. Love you, Marigold. And I'm sorry, Jake. You're annoying, but you are not your dad-at all."*

Jake snapped off the video.

"What do we do now?" he asked.

Nothing.

I fell onto him, and he onto me.

Buried in our hug, we cried.

Chapter 38

I found myself buried into his chest, his arms around me. My eyes closed. We were sealed off from the rest of the world. Together we were enough, we were safe. My tears dried up, but I gripped him tighter.

"Are you okay?" I asked into the wet fabric of his shirt.

"Better than I thought I'd be," he whispered, "As long as you're okay."

I felt a kiss at the top of my head. And my heart flooded with love. That gate, that wall that I kept up around him toppled over. He wiped tears from my eyes and gently held me steady. When his own heart had to be breaking.

"Could you imagine if she just took off?" I pulled back so I could study his face, "She risked everything to let us know the truth. I think to save us as much as herself. Imagine living with that," I shivered.

"I owe her," Jake said closing his eyes and leaning his forehead against mine, after giving it a small kiss, "More than she'll ever know. Knowing the truth, that I can work with. I can move forward."

"Can you?"

"I'd get in that car with you and keep driving north if I could."

"What's stopping you?"

Instead of answering, Jake watched as I wiggled out of our hug and stretched. We'd been sitting on the edge of the bed for a long time. The edge of a precipice that were both scared and ready to tumble over.

"Lack of road snacks," he finally said, but instead of a glint of humor in his eye, it was hunger. Looking at me as if I were that Snickers.

Our lives were falling away around us, but all we needed was each other. We could build off that.

"I'd go. With you," I admitted.

If my walls fell earlier, his were crumbling now, I watched as his expression melt into a warmth that could only come from a free and ready heart.

I felt a little winded.

His hand ran along my cheek, holding me in place, tilting my face up to meet his.

Jake kissed me, roughly, passionately, as if to say I was his, that all our history had led up to this. There was familiarity and love and unfulfilled promises being made right.

Everything lost was to be restored.

"Those words," I whispered against his lips, "Can I have them back? The one's you've been storing for me?"

"I love you."

"I love you, too," I said, pushing us off the precipice.

Chapter 39

"This will not be easy. I have called you here today…"

I put a hand on Jake's shoulder. "She's not the jury, Jake."

"I wish she were," he ran his hand over his face, "How do I tell her?"

"Well, the cupcakes, chocolate bars, mugs of tea and coffee cake might tell her something is up," I nodded down at the breakfast table in his kitchen, "And the bottle of wine? Is that appropriate?"

"So, Amy, our worst fears, well, they are real," he practiced as he set out three wine glasses on the table, "I think so, wine's for everything. 'Dad's a murdering beast.' I like that one," he paused for a breath, "Champagne is a celebration. Beer's relaxing. Hard liquor-ok hard liquor would be good for this, but she's not a fan unless it's in a mixed party drink. Wine. I know she likes wine."

My phone buzzed.

"Hey, hey, look who gets to check messages now?" he teased.

"Shut-up," I held up the screen, "And its good news for once. Meg's out of her second and last surgery. Prognosis good."

"That is good. Not sure about you and your ex being on texting terms…

But Meg on the mend is good."

"You have nothing to worry about. Though we will have to visit and bring flowers whenever they bring her home. I don't think I'll ever get over the guilt," I stopped, not wanting to delve in deeper.

"Add my pile of guilt to the stack. We're going to go broke buying her flowers. And the firm is covering her hospital bills- anonymously."

"A good deed done with a bit of sketchiness. I like it. It's very us."

"Now back to the matter at hand. What do you think?" he held up a bottle of wine and gave it a shimmy.

"White wine?" I wrinkled my nose.

"Red seemed murder-y."

"You've thought of everything. Maybe too much," I said steering him to sit down at the table, "Let's relax. Amy will be okay. Meg is okay. Two big wins."

"That could have been you," he whispered.

"Not with you around," I gave him a peck on the forehead, "Let's focus on how to break the news to your sister."

I thought of our earlier power walking -Amy would be the one to watch out for, making sure she didn't attack her own father for betraying women. To tell the truth, I wasn't sure it was my place to stop her. Her threats were safe with me. My stomach turned at the thought of how many times Paul, what, pretended? To be a caring and loving stand-in father. How many times we put our trust in him. I was lucky he was only a close family friend I couldn't imagine if my own father had…Well, I'd look and feel as miserable as Jake. He was slipping between ready to throw up at any moment, to staring off into space with some disassociated, shocked expression. And now we had to add to the number of people in pain.

"I know Amy will be okay… But… The minute she knows, our

family," he swallowed, looking up at me, holding me in place, by placing a hand over mine, "It'll be gone."

"Mmm, no," I said sitting on his lap, reveling how natural it felt as he wrapped his arms around me. I brushed some hair from his forehead, "Not gone. Different. You have Amy. Your Mom. Me."

"Yeah," he smiled, "Dad didn't kill her. I got lucky there, didn't I?"

I thumped him on the shoulder, "I'm serious. Use this opportunity to be closer to her. With Paul out of the way, I bet she'll be willing to visit more. I know you've been estranged for a while, but it's never because of you."

I gave him a little kiss on the cheek. I wanted to drag him off to his bedroom and show him just how much I loved him. Yet, this was important. Our honeymoon phase would have to wait because this was us, and we were living through a quagmire of bad luck and timing.

And how wrong things were around us, made it feel right that we were together. An umbrella against any storm.

"I think I'll just say 'Amy, let's go to Europe and visit Mom for a bit?'" His voice was filled with mirth, and I wasn't sure if that was a good or bad thing.

"She might know then-just at that."

"And your expression."

"And the vomit bucket."

"I'll put that in the back yard..." I jumped off his lap and set the bucket outside.

"Amy might need that," Jake said, watching me

"Amy?" I asked in disbelief, as if he forgot who his sister was.

"Yeah, no. Never mind."

"Hey," a voice trailed in, as if summoned by her own name. "The front door was unlocked, so I wandered in. What was so important that I had to..."

I froze by the back door.

Her eyes went from Jake to me and back to Jake as soon as she was in eyeshot of us.

"... drive all the way out here. Clearly something's going on." And then she saw the food and the wine. "What's wrong?"

"Remember when Mom and Dad got a divorce? They sat us down over an upside-down pineapple cake on the coffee table?" Jake began, but he stopped when Amy only looked confused and I was rolling my eyes.

"Jake, she doesn't need a speech. Amy, sit. Let me get you some wine." I began pouring us all a glass. We'd need it.

"I never liked pineapple since," Jake continued. "At least I still enjoy cake. That wasn't ruined for me."

"Do you have a head injury?" Amy asked as she accepted a glass from me and frowned. "White?"

"Ask your brother," I shrugged, taking a sip from my own glass, "I'd have chosen a red."

"Oh..." and understanding filled her eyes. She stumbled for a seat and rested heavily on the table, showing more a reaction than I'd ever seen, "I see. More murder-y."

She knew her brother, had to give her that.

He nodded, "I'm sorry, Amy."

And he knew his sister. He did not have to worry for a lack of family.

She exhaled and took a shaky gulp of wine. "Proof?"

"Yes. A video on my phone, a witness testimony," I was not ready to out Shelley.

"A witness? Does Dad know?" Amy asked.

"Yes."

"Is he or she alive?"

Amy knew her father.

"On the run. No plans to return. The video is all we're going to have."

"Which," she set her glass aside, "As we know is not much. Not with what happened at the funeral. Dad's not even a suspect. The case is closed. But... Looking at you two, your expression and the amount of chocolate on this table is not leaving me any room for doubt. So, you're sure. Can I watch it? Something this big, I'm going to need to see the proof myself."

I queued up the video on my phone and passed it to her as Jake opened a chocolate bar and handed it over as well. She took a bite and watched.

"Well..." Amy set the phone down, screen facing the table. "Shelley? I never would have suspected."

"I didn't have a clue." Guilt took its own stab at me as I admitted such.

"You were busy with your own things," Jake jumped in.

He was right. After Theo and Scott, I hadn't been a great friend. Not that it made me a bad person, it was only a fact. I had enough capacity to keep myself together and try to move on and... I left Shells to herself. With hardly any warning, I packed up my bags and told her I was off to Pittsburg, that Dallas wasn't enough for me anymore, and everything reminded me of Theo and I wanted out. She never visited me in the Pitt. I never asked her to. I didn't want her to see me still in the process of healing. All over a man.

I left her alone. Lonely. Practically guiding her into a predatory man's arms. Did they meet at the country club? Was she sitting and chatting with Emma, who was also desperate for friendship? And then he sat down, charming and ordering them drinks.

Shelley was no saint.

And Paul was no one to discourage a sinner.

I bit my lip to keep my guilt from flooding my words, "I... I had a lot going on. We kept in touch, but she never mentioned him-or any guy she was serious about. She hid it."

I couldn't hide the tinge of hurt in my voice.

"They both did," Amy took another bite of chocolate, frowning, "That's disgusting, she's our age. That's..." she shivered, "Did he like check out all our friends when we brought them around? I think I feel like puking." But she kept on eating the bar.

"There's a bucket out back for that," Jake pointed.

"No. Eating is better. But maybe some tea? Tea," she nodded as if that solved all things. "Chamomile."

"I've already got a pot going, let me get you a mug."

I knew my friend.

"I feel like it's wrong I'm focusing on the affair. Like murder, I'm like okay, that tracks given what I know about my father-didn't see it coming- necessarily. But maybe I was hoping for the best? But an affair? That's so unlike him. Never growing up- Thank you, two sugars- Never growing up did we ever catch him sneaking upstairs with someone. If he tired of a woman, he had the decency to divorce her, pay her off, and then move on," she accepted her tea and gave the steam a blow, "Like a gentleman." That last bit held plenty of sarcasm.

"Like trying to be a good father? A stable as a home as possible?" Jake said, "Till we got older..."

"Then he could let that monster out?"

Jake exhaled, even sitting, I could tell he'd stand two inches shorter.

"So what do we do?" I asked, sipping from my mug, "As his kids I feel the vote is entirely yours, and I'll go along for the ride."

"My Dad killed his wife. Using another woman as a tool, a woman he was sleeping with. Like some sick game. Is this the first and last time?" Anne questioned, "How do we feel safe around him anymore? I can tell you the kids will not be near him without John, his gun, and me."

"Do we even accept once?" Jake asked. "Have we already accepted it? Given that we are sitting here, drinking tea and snacking and not running to the police? Have they drilled in loyalty that hard? If any of us do any wrong, is there really not a consequence?"

We let that sit for a moment. The truth stung. We all knew what a good defense lawyer could do. And a great one… with means and no morals… A great defense lawyer could disintegrate the truth.

"Everyone accepts that Violet did it. Emma's family is… gone now. They're moving on. They've found their closure," I said.

"But it's not the truth." Jake insisted.

"Is it less painful to let it be for them? That she was the random victim of a crazy woman? Or the victim of her husband? I don't think either way the sisters liked Paul much. They'll stay away, naturally. They're safe." Amy said, "Why rip off the Band-Aid to apply one again? Nothing will bring Emma back to them. And this way, to them, the killer, Violet was brought to justice."

"Because Paul won't be brought to justice," I clarified.

Jake shrugged, "Shelley's on the run. The only one that can testify the truth to her video. If Paul finds her first…"

I didn't need to clarify. We all knew. If Paul found her, she'd be dead. The video easily buried. We couldn't drag her back to Dallas.

"So we let the story stay?" Amy asked, "Violet did it. And we go on with our lives?"

"I don't think I could ever sleep again. Comfortably." Jake shivered, and I reached out to rub his shoulder-this sparked an eyebrow raise from Amy, who misses nothing. "I think I need to quit my job with him. I can't even call him Dad anymore without feeling bile rise."

"Stay," Amy contradicted, shaking her head vigorously, "He can't suspect we know. Go on a long trip with," she smirked, "Marigold. Get your space and figure out how to handle it. John and I will take the kids to Disney World or the beach, just something far and distract ourselves."

"He gets away with it?" I asked. I couldn't pretend to not hate this decision; I saw it in our eyes, were all hating ourselves.

"Say we tell the truth and play the video. Do you think Paul takes this laying down?" Jake asked, "No. He'll get the video discredited. The jury will already be swayed that it was Violet-by the time the trial happens it'll be common knowledge. We'll have to prove the funeral shooting was unrelated. Are you ready for that, Marigold? That will dredge up Scott, your whole history. Me included. Theo? Paul could twist it right back and say you sicked Violet on Meg. That maybe you killed Scott. And then, with that precedent established? Emma. You were last at the scene, with the body. An original suspect. We go to court... Marigold, for you it won't go well. There will be enough doubt that Paul could be released, and you could end up in custody. Especially with Violet saying that you killed her son."

Oh.

I paled and drank tea as if my life depended on it. It was kind of cruel my horrible dating life was impeding justice for another woman... I was selfish enough to admit that since I was the one still alive; my outcome here mattered more. Slightly more. Right?

"So for me... We pin it on Violet?" I whispered.

Those words made my stomach hurt. I just met Emma, really... I didn't want to be dragged through a trial and charged. That wasn't fair to me.

"Don't forget, for all of us. Your parents, too," Amy said, "Paul could choose to sink the ship. Admit what happened to Richard and screw us all over by saying we helped him hide the body. You'd be disbarred. My publishing career destroyed, who wants children's books from a family like that? I could do Sally the Snail in the Slammer series. Middle grade fiction."

I squinted, "Amy? Did you ever tell John, about that night in Austin?"

She opened a new bar of chocolate, "I did not. I wanted to leave this world behind me. I wanted to protect him from my family. I want my kids protected. So, for me..." she spoke with her mouth full, being surprisingly ungraceful, "It would ruin me. And what a position to put my upstanding cop husband in? He knows we're all sketch, and he politely ignores it, but I think that's all I can ask of him."

"That's fair. But what about Shelley?" I asked, "We leave her out there alone? The only way she's safe to return is if Paul is behind bars."

"She's not one of us," Amy stated, "I mean I don't envy her position, but... she slept with a married man... confronted them. If she was brought to the states, her own trial would drag us all in with possibly the same results. It's best for all of us if she remains on the run. I'm sorry. I know you two were close."

"I'm thinking Shelley's okay. She's like a cat that lands on her feet. She's gotten herself overseas, out of Paul's reach, safer than any of us if she stays away. And Amy's right," he flinched at my frown, "I'm sorry, but she is. Going far and wide with her video in the end helps no one. And she kidnapped you, had the affair, it might be hard to keep her out of jail. Once forensics knows what to look for, they could easily match the evidence to her and if Paul gets involved, you know how'd he'd twist her story. Pinning it on Violet protects Shelley from jail time as well."

"But she's on the run. She was scared and cornered, and Paul could be after her..." I protested.

"I'm not conjecturing lightly, Love. It's for the best," Jake said, taking my hand in his and giving it a squeeze.

"I know... I just..." I took a deep breath. Stunned that there was no way to help her. Because they were right. Helping her would sacrifice all of us and possibly put her in danger as well. There were no heroes in this story. We were products of our upbringing, trained in loyalty and survival. Or maybe we were just trapped. In an endless cycle of cover-ups, and they were right, Shelley was the one that got away. My mom told me to leave long ago.

"So, it's decided?" Jake asked, in lawyer mode, "For clarity. It was Violet, in the public sphere, that's the story. Privately, we cope and stay safe."

"Agreed."

"Agreed," I said, hating myself as the word slid out, sounding more confident than I was.

Jake nodded, "Let's get the hard liquor out then. So, we can toast Paul. Officially a free man."

Sorry Emma.

Sorry Shelley.

We poured our drinks and saved ourselves.

Chapter 40

The next day, I stood on Amy's front door stoop, nursing a slight hangover. I'd spent most of the morning in bed. Jake spent it playing video games. We were both kind of numb and not sure what to do in the aftermath.

Before I pressed the bell, Amy swung open the front door.

"You're five minutes late." Her hands were on her hips.

"For the rest of the world, that's normal. What's not, is suggesting power walking again so soon." Especially after last night.

"But you're here?"

"I figured you needed to talk. But it's a long drive, so you have another...

She shoved open the door to reveal another professional power walker in black Lulu Lemon and her blond hair pulled back in a sleek pony. I knew her. This time instead of wearing running mascara and tears, she wore a look of determination with a squint of anger. While this was not a more the merrier situation, the sister of the murdered woman... Well, I guess there should be no one more welcome.

"Lauren, hi," I greeted.

"I have a plan," Amy said, "Since you first asked for help, I've been thinking she should be involved."

I gulped. I was very tired of plans. And didn't we settle things last night?

The spark in eyes was a dead give-a-way this one was no good.

At first, yes, I'd been perturbed that Lauren had been invited along without consulting me. Then that annoyance melted into gratefulness, as Amy had trained me a bit in power walking, otherwise I would have collapsed, and fallen into a neighbor's lawn. There wasn't time or enough air left to be grouchy.

Lauren could walk. If Amy would be honest, she was having to concentrate to keep up, I saw her huffing her breaths.

Which was how we were learning so much about Lauren. She had anger, adrenaline, and fitness, most importantly: air.

"... When I first met him I knew he was no good. Diamond jewelry and lavish gifts so early on? He was buying her. My little sister. She was over the moony-moon about her new older man. 'So sophisticated.' He took her to the DMA and the symphony. Bought her earrings from the giftshops. My sister loved her earrings. She's sell her soul for them." Lauren's arms pumped, "No. That's not something I can say anymore." She fell silent, looking for a response.

"He was always with the gifts. Women like that," Amy said.

"Oof," I managed between gulps of water.

"I tried to protect her. I told her men like that, that they go through their wives like... what's the saying? Like a clean shirt. Just toss-into the laundry."

I thought of the bloody denim shirt and shivered.

"Indeed," I agreed.

She looked back at me and nodded, "I wonder if my best for her was doing the worst. I wanted to make sure she was safe. Amy, I'm so sorry."

"No," Amy said, pumping her arms and stepping over a puddle with renewed energy, "I admire it. And there's the park up ahead. Ladies, we need to sit and talk."

That park bench was as satisfying as a water mirage in the desert.

And it was with a lack of oxygen in my brain, that I agreed to another terrible plan.

Chapter 41

Jake was still on the couch playing video games with Poe nestling next to him. He cut off the screen the moment I got home.

"How was Amy?" he asked, watching with amusement as I limped towards the kitchen.

"Your sister is insane. I can't feel my feet anymore. Why didn't you tell me how fit she was?"

"So you'd go. Better you than me. Can you imagine if my calf game got stronger?"

I rolled my eyes and chugged down a cold water from the fridge. Jake might have never skipped leg day, but I did not need to feed the ego.

"I'm going to go lay under a fan for a bit and take a shower. But then I've got some errands to run for your sister," I said.

"Back in time for dinner?" he asked, hanging over the back of the couch.

"That's the plan." I froze at this oddly domestic scene. This wasn't us. We didn't get to be like this, "Did you walk Poe?"

Poe answered for him with a happy yip.

For now, between Jake and I, this murder mystery was wrapped. His Dad declared innocent. The stalking from Violet was over. There was no reason for me to be here.

"And... And I guess I need to look online for an apartment," I added, shy at taking advantage of his hospitality.

"No... Um. Take your time. Find the right place. A place that takes dogs."

Ha. He was scratching under Poe's ears.

"Yeah. Thanks."

My stomach flipped, missing Shelley and her acumen at hunting down real estate.

"I wasn't here the whole time you were gone. On the couch. I, ah, was at Paul's hotel room. He wanted to talk about next steps."

"Oh?" That was a surprise. "What are the next steps?"

I limped closer, holding onto the back of the couch for support. This sounded like a long conversation.

He shook his head, "Go have a rest. Dinner later, right? We'll talk then."

I frowned at what it could be but agreed. My mind was still swimming with Amy's plan, and it couldn't hold much more. I was already drowning.

The doorbell rang. The scariest sound to an introvert. I drained the rest of my water, setting it down with a thunk, stalling for time. Maybe they'd go away.

It rang again.

I shot Jake a look, "Expecting anyone?"

"Nope. Want me to get it?" he asked.

"No. You're down. I'm up."

It couldn't be Violet. She was dead.

Meg was in the hospital. Out of the ICU at least.

Paul was… Where was he? Performing some victory dance in the woods? What did men do to celebrate a successful dispatching of their late wife? Plan a fishing trip? Go to Ikea?

Theo. It could be Theo.

Just saw Amy.

Shelley… I already missed her. I did not know what Dallas life would be without her. That pit of sadness back in my stomach told me all that was between us was forgiven; I only wanted her here, on the other side of that door.

Not Shelley. The world was not that kind.

Maybe Dad.

I swung open the door, fulling expecting it to be Dad or Theo, but no, it was Everett. This time that funny stomach feeling reminded me of Amy and her illegal ideas… Could Everett read our thoughts?

Of course not. That was guilt giving me the jitters.

"Everett, what brings you by?"

I could feel Jake's ears twitch up and the video game mute.

"I'll… I'll just be a moment. It's nothing official. I want to apologize for thinking the intruder was wind, and that Jake, about your dad. I'm sorry. He clearly loved his wife. We get it wrong sometimes."

Jake waved a thumbs up from the couch.

"Do you want to come in Everett? Would you like coffee or something?"

"I'll just step inside. It's hot."

That was an understatement. It looked like the man was melting.

I swung open the door wider and invited him in. Despite his protesting, he ended up with a glass of water and some cookies at the breakfast table.

"So you know?" he bit into a cookie, "That's why you're being so kind."

"A bit," I said, settling next to him, "What happened?"

"We got back from the funeral. That whole ordeal. It really messed Shelley up. She was pacing the living room, and it took two shots of whiskey till she was willing to sit down. And then she looked at me with those blazin' blue eyes... Said it was over. That the funeral put her life in perspective, and we didn't have any time to waste. I was, apparently, a waste of her time," his shoulder slumped.

"Oh, Everett. You were not a waste of time. Shelley's not the most stable with men. You can't take it as a reflection of you."

This was the truth. How many of her exes did I end up counseling?

I'd already figured out Shelley had been lying about their breakup; it was a ruse to get me in the car. Silly, really, all she had to do was ask if I wanted to go on an iced coffee run. But I supposed she had to explain the tears and the urgency.

Poor Everett. On some level, she really did like him.

"Thank you, Marigold. I'm glad this is all over for you, too. You seem like a nice person who ends up at the wrong places. Be careful."

I laughed, "An astute observation. I'm certainly trying to be."

His own smile stopped, replaced by creases of worry, "She won't answer my calls. Um... Well, I know she hasn't been home. I just want to talk to her and make everything okay."

"You stalking her, Everett?" I teased, knowing that wasn't the case at all.

"No-no, not at all. I mean, I get it. You see a girl like her... Well, I feel lucky for the time we had together. I'm not wealthy, I knew she'd be onto bigger and better things soon enough, that I was a stopover. An experiment. I'm more concerned about her safety. Can I confide in you-as her best friend?"

"Um... Of course," I said.

I felt awful not being able to give him any more closure or let him know Shelley must have liked him. For her sake, though, I couldn't have him go looking for her location.

"I think she was using me as protection. She woke up in a dream one night, yelling for Paul to get off of her. All this murder stuff, it got to her. Death. I get why she'd break up with me and run out, but she can't be okay. I figured if I can't help her anymore, you could."

Everett was a good man, through and through. Another time, another place, I wondered if they could have actually ended up together. Shelley must have realized this, and broke her own heart running away. She probably didn't feel like a good enough person for him.

"I appreciate it. You're right, of course," I half-lied, "Shelley said she felt safe with you. She didn't like the idea of a killer out there. She felt like any of us could have been Emma, and maybe she was right," I said, noting my childhood acting classes were kicking in, "I know she liked you and enjoyed your company. But I also know she did not see it as long term. She's, spending time with family friends right now to clear her head. Privately. I am sorry."

He stood, "Thank you. I'll stop reaching out now that I know she's okay."

I pat him on the shoulder and guided him out, "If any of my single friends confess a thing for hot cops, I'll let you know."

He laughed, stepping outside, "Please do. But I'm taking some time for myself as well. My brother owns a ranch in Montana. Heading up there for a spell."

"Big sky country. Good luck."

"Good luck to you too, Marigold. I think you'll need it."

Did I ever.

I shut the door behind him, locking it.

But maybe luck was already heading my way. The nosy detective was leaving town.

Chapter 42

For our plan to work, the timing had to be right. There was still plenty of time for me to chicken out, and that internal debate on whether or not to go through with it raged inside. I swallowed some Tums as I hauled a box down the grand staircase.

Amy had me running errands for her since she lived so far out of town. Uh-huh. Sure.

She wasn't quite ready to face her dad, or her childhood home. Nor was I. But I'd already seen the kitchen since the murder, that Band-Aid had already been ripped off, and now I was getting more comfortable with the inside of the house again. Would I want to live there? No. Between our families, that big house on Lovers Lane did not have a future. Selling it and moving on was the smartest course of action for Paul to take.

My feet skidded to a halt as they hit the last step, and the items of the box clanged together. Their cacophony announcing my presence and echoing through the halls. I held my breath.

I'd stopped because I heard muttering from the kitchen. Something clanged, and a chair squeaked.

"Hello? Someone there?" Paul called out.

The right answer would be to respond with a, "No," and run out the front door. Because the front door was *right there*. That's what Smart Marigold should have done.

Dumb Marigold, however, was at the helm, and I found my feet heading towards his voice in the kitchen. He might have killed his wife there, but he couldn't keep stabbing people in the same room. It would look suspicious, and his whole game was staying out of prison. The kitchen was probably the safest room in the house.

So with Dumb Marigold driving, I rounded the corner and into the kitchen.

I didn't think he'd be here. I thought he'd be out on a golf course, or tanning or at the country club eating steak and bragging about his victory and telling stories about that poor girl Meg. At least she would be okay.

But I really didn't think he'd be here.

I shouldn't be here. I should have ran out that front door. But I wanted to know, with one hundred percent certainty, if I was making the right decision to carry out Amy's plan. If I could actually do that to him. Guilty or not. It was certainly a test of my mettle, and throwing me into morally grey soup.

And I hated myself for wishing Jake came with me. He wanted to, but I said... no... for some-odd reason. For trying to be independent. For trying to protect him. That's why he didn't get to know Amy's plan. Jake would try and stop us, or possibly do something even more stupid-but stupid and alone.

Paul saw me and smiled, he was a handsome man, like his son. I couldn't see that resemblance anymore. I could only see he wore a mask of charm.

"Marigold. It's good to see you. I just got here. Thought I'd look around."

"Your car wasn't in the driveway," I said, fully entering the kitchen.

"Driver dropped me off."

"Oh, of course. I don't know why I missed that. Am I bothering you?"

"It's always good to see you."

Paul took a step closer. Each step a full, separate movement. By measure, I stepped back, trying to keep the distance between us equidistant.

"I didn't think you'd be here," I stated, my voice didn't betray me, it only sounded mildly surprised than appropriately horrified. I never wanted to be alone with him again.

"Amy said she was prepping the house to sell. She thinks that's what I want."

"Isn't it?" I asked.

He rubbed his chin, "To be honest, I'm not sure. Despite the last… There are a lot of wonderful memories here. Raised a family. Built an empire. It's my home. Selling it seems like losing. Like running away from one bad memory."

"More than a bad memory. Your wife was murdered." By you. I held that last part in.

He stepped closer, "And her murderer was brought to justice. We'll grieve for a bit, but that is a chapter closed. We'll re-do the kitchen and move on." He dragged his fingertips across the granite counter, "But leave? This home is my fortress. I'm not looking forward to telling Amy it's not for sale; she's already been talking with a realtor. Getting you involved, I see."

I gulped, keeping the box of sentimental knick-knacks in my arms between us.

"Amy's a force," I gave the box a small shift, "She has me cleaning out personalized clutter. Apparently, realtors are picky about a cleanly staged home."

"You seem nervous," Paul frowned, "I told you earlier. I harbor no ill will. You'll always be a daughter to me. The actions of a crazed woman are no reflection of you. I know you didn't plan to have your drama interrupt the funeral. You don't have to apologize."

"A-Apologize?" I stuttered back. That was the farthest thing from my mind.

To think he was trying to cast blame my way!

As if I didn't already feel awful about Megan.

"You sound nervous," he observed again, as if proud by his effect on me.

"Nervous?" I tittered, "Never."

Was he noticing my shaking voice? The back peddling? The sweat glistening off my forehead?

"I knew you'd be here," he said, "I knew that you had to come back eventually."

"Oh?" Now that came out as a definite squeak. I cleared my throat. Was this the point I should cut and run and appear to be the mentally unstable daughter of a friend that I really was? That really seemed to be the thing to do here.

Was it?

Taking off and running away with my box? Leave the box? I'd be faster. Would that…

He took a step forward. "Ah… I see. You know."

"I know?" My voice cracked, "I know?" The second time sounded much more on the level. "I know, what?"

"I was wondering. I was hoping keeping you close; So that I'd know when you'd know."

"Paul, I'm just helping tidy up. Getting the sentimental things out before people are touring in and out. If you want to cancel the sale, it's Amy you've got to talk to. I get the sentimentality. She already boxed up and left with some valuables, has she given you the storage unit or the…"

"Shelley told you… Finally. About our affair," he interrupted my rambling.

I froze.

So *that* had been my exit earlier. Great.

Now I only had the hope of running faster than the old man and yelling bloody murder in the front lawn. Neighbors always liked a show; I'd give them one. Loud and public so there would be nothing but jail time for him. I was pretty sure I could outrun him, getting past him in order to run, now that was where my plan folded.

"Put the box down, Marigold."

Did Emma have time to try? Or was she bad at missing her exit cues as well?

I put down the box.

Wait, why did I listen? It was reflex from a childhood when the directions were: wash up for dinner. Answer me. Take out the trash.

Authoritative and directive. In the past for our best interest. Now as a gamble to stay alive.

"Sit," he nodded towards the breakfast table. That wooden one all families in the 90s owned: circular with wooden spoked seats. The same table where we'd have after-school snacks and do our homework.

I sat. This was his game.

He came closer to sit, but instead, he stopped in front of me, towering over.

I looked up. Ready to flinch. Expecting a slap. My eyes tracing his every movement, trying to predict his next-

Defying every expectation, he traced a finger down my cheek.

My body was too in shock to react.

"Make no mistake, Marigold. Only *like* a daughter. Not actual family."

My spine tingled with repulsion. Though I held it straight and steady. Instead of cowering, I held the eye contact, glaring fire into his eyes.

"Not scared of you, Paul. Not scared of you, old man."

Instead of getting angry, Paul smirked and sat across from me, his hands clasped on the table-in my sight. "I've always liked that smart mouth on you. Always made things interesting. But that's enough for now. You're part of my plan, Marigold. Always have been. From day one. You're going to marry my son. Have his little children. No more of those romantic escapades. Marry Jake, you love each other, so that's easy. Frankly, it's what's keeping you alive. My son's love for you. Mine for him."

"What a Brady Bunch," I said, trying to be smart to keep my spirits up, but really, I was very, very scared knowing what happened to the last woman who was in here with him.

"If you marry Jake. Keep him around, at the family firm. He can fully fulfill his role. Your brother's done a remarkable job. But Jake? He keeps threatening to leave."

"He needs a family you can threaten," I whispered, my bravado fading.

Paul shrugged, "Only till he steps up. Becomes the man he was born to be."

I let out a sigh, "So if I marry Jake... You'll let me walk out of here? With everything I know?"

He leaned in on his elbows, so close I could taste his breath, "If you give me Shelley's location."

"Never," my eyes flashed.

Paul smiled. Leaned back, looking self-satisfied, "Exactly. If you marry Jake, then you'll officially be family. Under my protection. Just remember, I want grandchildren."

"And if I don't?" I tried to sound defiant. I was not going to be coerced into marriage. I would not trap Jake into this sick alliance.

"Well..." he spread his hands wide, and I noticed just how big they were and gave in with a tiny shiver of fear. He could definitely kill me.

"Well, you wouldn't be family. I couldn't trust you anymore. And if I can't trust you... We can see how far you run? One last game?"

I stood, knocking the chair down with my speed and clumsiness.

He stood. To full mountain height. Cracking his knuckles for effect, as if he actually wanted to play.

A beat of a moment passed as I swallowed my anger. My defiance. This was unfair; we both knew he won the second we were alone together. At least my mind was made up: I'd help Amy without any remorse.

"The second Jake proposes, I will say yes." I relented, my voice was firm and strong. I wanted to live. I loved Jake. This was a battle not worth fighting.

It felt like the world was snapping together, one last puzzle piece clicking into place. This was the plan. Jake and I were always meant to be.

Which was why Mom was always warning me to stay away.

Sorry Mom.

My self-destructive streak never let me fully run away. I had to stay and see things through.

Paul smiled, his mask looked genuine and unmenacing, truly like someone normal heard he was gaining a daughter-in-law. Only his words didn't match those of a well-adjusted man, "You can't tell Jake of this. Or Amy."

"Of course not."

He stuck out his hand to shake, and I did so. Like two equals. Plotting out the future.

"An engagement gift, then, Marigold. It wasn't your fault."

"What?" my arm fell to my side.

"It was inevitable. I saw you being too close with that man. After Jake and I went up there to convince you to come home, I couldn't have you get attached and stay in Pittsburg."

"You..." Another puzzle piece falling into place.

"That's right," he grinned, "I had his brakes cut. Didn't expect you to get on his bike," Paul laughed, "But it worked out. Scott died. His mother went nuts, and it all threw you back here and in Jake's arms. Everything fell together, better than I'd imagined. Like dominoes."

He killed Scott.

"So, you see, what happens if you go back on your word with me? The consequences? You and those around you are only safe if you stay with my son."

He killed Scott.

I covered my mouth so I wouldn't vomit. This mad man had me trapped like a caged animal.

"It all works out. Even got Emma out of the way. That was my bad- she had me with that prenup. But even I'm not perfect. No more prenups for me, tell you what. I thought I'd have to push her off a cruise ship one day," he laughed, "I guess you know the feeling. Now. Let me help you carry that box to the car like a good Father-in-Law. And I'll have Jake text me when you get home. You will go straight home?"

"Of... of course."

"Atta-girl. Smile, Love. Nothing's changed." He cupped my cheek and gave it a light pat, like an affectionate father would. But here it held a threat "Act the part."

I smiled. The expression not reaching my eyes. If I married Jake, I'd be issued a mask as well.

He led the way outside.

My feet and body followed behind him, my eyes watching as he loaded the car, then waving at me from the garage. Much as he had done that one night so long ago.

Instinct and survival made me wave back and pull down the driveway. Somehow making it to Jake's.

Through the front door. Into the foyer, dropping boxes. As my brain screamed silently for help.

But help from whom?

Chapter 43

Jake was in the kitchen making pizza, leaning over the island, stretching the rolled-out dough across the flat pan. Tomato sauce simmered on the stove and browned ground beef sizzled in the pan.

His head snapped up, "You're early."

I was lucky to be there at all.

Poe looked up at me lazily from his dog bed, too tired to offer a hello bark.

Where did that chew bone come from?

"I guess I am. Not many boxes left to get."

I'd dropped the first box in the foyer. The next on the front porch, and two were still left in my car. Unloading all the boxes, so my chore wouldn't become his, was what I should have done, but I wanted to see his face. My future husband's face. Yes, I still felt that fluttering of love and adoration. I'd still jump on any landmine for him, not giving any thought to myself. My stomach felt things too though, felt things in the way that made it unreceptive to pizza. It felt all the fear it digested on the drive over. It felt what my heart could not yet acknowledge.

Instead, my heart flipped at the simple way he blew his hair from his face or the way his well-defined hands kneaded through the dough. It watched that furrowed brow as he concentrated drizzling over sauce and cheese. My future husband, thumped my stupid heart.

"You okay? Amy didn't have you haul too much? I don't know why she didn't want me to go with ya'll, but I figured I could help with dinner."

Husband-like words. My stomach gurgled.

"I'll need your help to unload later."

Í talked with your father, was what I should have said.

I watched as Jake did the dishes. He made us a really tasty pizza and let me kick up my feet after dinner. He insisted I take a break as he cleaned.

'Twas a shame we were destined to turn into our parents.

This could have been forever.

But at least it was now. Had to savor that. Our last few moments together.

I could have married him, and this view every night would have been mine: Rolled-up sleeves with soapy forearms and a clean kitchen. Another sip of wine passed through my lips to cool my nerves. After all this time, he still made me nervous.

But marriage weaponized as a trap? As a cage? How would that work? The only future I saw was us resenting each other, and then a divorce. By then, he'd have turned into Paul. Me into my mother, before her Florida escape. Constantly looking the other direction from my husband's shady actions and friends. Pretending that having bodyguards during a trial was normal.

Paul already demand grandchildren; it would be his decision. Not ours, and the cycle would continue. How many other Shelleys and Emmas and Richards would have their lives ruined by our families?

The longer I stayed, the more impossible to leave.

Oh, and it wasn't easy now. I'd be leaving my heart behind.

Breaking his.

Jake sashayed towards me with a new bottle of wine and a glass for himself. A hippy, sexy walk, matching a teasing smile. The show ended as he plopped down next to me, grace-free, nearly landing on my thigh.

"You look lost in thought," he said, "Remember the purpose of tonight was to hide from the world."

"I am. I promise."

He frowned, perceptive of my lie, "Are you worried about how good of a cook I am? That I'm planning on opening a food truck that turns into a restaurant, that turns into a national chain? That once my pizza becomes so famous and, it's in the frozen food aisle, that I'll leave you for one of the frozen food heiresses?"

"Relax, Chef. I know you can cook exactly five dishes. One per weekday," I teased.

"And then out on weekends. It's efficient," his voice got a little defensive at the end.

I sat my wine down on the table and snuggled deeper into him, "There's so much to unpack there."

I didn't want to leave.

"It's better than knowing, what, three? I think I've seen you cook spaghetti, chicken, and what was your last one, Julia, darling?" he ruffled my hair.

"Tacos. From the box."

"Oh, no," his fingers now danced across my arm, "A lot of our meals overlap. Combined, we got six."

I nodded, "I think we'll survive then."

My heart skipped a beat. That was a lie.

"I do," I lied again, not yet ready for what I had to do.

I believed we'd survive if I left him.

"Would you say that again?" he asked.

"Say what again?"

"Will you marry me?"

"Wha-ha..." my jaw dropped as he slid onto the floor, onto his knees, and pulled out a green box, as if he had planned the whole conversation.

"Will you marry me?" Jake repeated, and that box snapped open revealing a large marquis shaped diamond surrounded by deep green emeralds. "It was my grandmother's. I tried to spell it out in cheese. It all melted together, though."

Oh no.

My stomach spoke louder than my heart, gushing acid into my throat, reminding me of Paul's threats. If I said yes, I'd be safe, but I didn't feel safe. That wouldn't put out the fire.

I imagined Paul, standing behind him, smiling, holding a dripping, bloody knife.

My heart was there, too though, and it flooded me with love, and it screamed *yes*. I wanted a future with this man.

"You... you seem... I can't read you. This was not the reaction I expected. I..."

"I love you," I squeaked out.

He paled, and scooted back onto the couch, tucking the ring box back into his pocket, and hiding his pained face in his hands, "I love you, but…"

"You're the only man I'd ever consider marrying," I said, wide eyes, trying to demonstrate how much I meant it. But he wasn't looking at me. He was still looking down, between his knees, hiding his face. I wished he'd see my tears.

I wanted to say yes and run off into the night together.

If said yes, I was saying yes to Paul and his plans. Yes to always being fearful.

"Jake… Jake it's not you. I've got to get away. I've got to get away from everything."

"Was it too soon? I talked to Paul, to get the ring, and he said the way you stood with me through everything was admirable, that we were finally ready," he scoffed into his hands, "Why did I think he was right for once? I think I wanted him to be right. Because I'm ready. I love you, Marigold. I'll love you whether you say yes or no."

I groaned. Oh no. Please don't say that. My heart leapt into my throat, choking me.

Is that what happens when you hurt someone so deeply, when you break their heart, that your own expels itself from your body? Leaving a cold shell behind.

Was not having a heart better than a broken one?

"I… I have to go," I said, springing from the couch and running to my room. I had to go. He was everywhere in this house and the walls were closing in.

Jake leaned in the doorway, watching me pack. I was a tornado, shoving odds and ends and bits of clothing into my suitcases. Organization could be found later.

"I don't understand," he said, "I love you."

"And I love you," but I still rolled up a summer dress and shoved it into my bag.

"Then... then explain. Something's got you extra rattled."

"I can't."

If I explained, he'd convince me to stay. Some compromise that would eventually unravel over time, and we'd be stuck under Paul's thumb.

"Then don't go."

"If there was any other way... Trust me, I'd stay."

"I..." he gave up on speaking and only threw up his arms, yet he remained watching. Much in the way Theo kept his eyes on that hospital door. That same expression. A loving anguish.

True love.

Still, I shoved my cosmetic bags in. Running away was how I would show my love. By not trapping him into a life of endless mind games and covering up murders. That would be the future his father planned for us. How our marriage would ensnare us.

My safety would constantly be held over his head for him to comply.

"... whatever it is, we'll figure it out, Marigold, together. We make a great team."

"We did, didn't we?"

"Past tense?"

I drank him in, pausing in my panic packing to merely stand and admire.

Jake was a good man. A rare find.

He'd make a woman very happy one day.

In another universe, I saw us standing together in front of a beautiful house. Him looking down at me adoringly, already holding a hand of our child who stood next to a yippy puppy (and Poe, too). Other universe Marigold and Jake had it all. A long life together full of love and happiness. Maybe this Jake, if I stepped away, could. If he was smart and left his father's practice. He could- Paul would have nothing to threaten him with, no family, no responsibilities to hold over his head. Jake could be free; he wouldn't turn into his father. If he stayed? What would happen? Would he witness more death? Be paid to keep overlooking crimes and defending the criminals? Without a choice?

And I loved him too much for that.

I loved him too much to watch his morality erode.

For that spark to fade.

I loved him too much to watch him turn into his father.

To be the cause of it if I stayed! That would kill me.

I shoved more clothes into the suitcase.

My mind continued to race.

Everyone wanted me to escape to Florida, yet if I went there, to seek their protection... Was that how Godfather-like wars broke out? There was no way I could involve my parents in the mess I was creating. Directly, that is. I would tell them the truth about their business partner in some serious way, like a certified letter with instructions to shred upon reading. It would have a link to watch Shelley's confession. Always good to have the power of blackmail over a man like Paul.

"Marigold..."

"Please..." I begged.

"How can you look at me like that after breaking my heart?"

"Because I think you know why I'm leaving."

He met my words with silence, only a grunt. Jake didn't owe me words anymore.

His gaze intensified from across the room, making my knees wobble.

I knew my name would taste like honey on his lips. His glistening warm, brown eyes. Those classically handsome features.

A bit more steam must've emitted from my expression, because I caught a new glimpse of hunger in his.

One last time.

No one would blame us.

I rushed across the room, toxic as ever, grabbing the sides of his face and pulled him down to me.

One last time.

I sucked that honey right off his lips and plunged my tongue in, trying to memorize every bit of him. He matched my frenzy, wrapping his arms around me, yet lifting my body into the air, swiping the suitcases off the bed (undoing a bit of my packing in the process) and throwing me down onto the bed.

He knew, as he slowed our pace with lingering, slow kisses, it was his turn to drink this all in.

One last time.

For the memory.

Chapter 44

Far too used to me on her doorstep, Amy ushered me inside and up the stairs and into the guest bedroom, closing the door behind us, blocking out any curious ears.

"John and the kids are doing homework… Jake called after you left."

I called on the way over, giving Amy the low-down of what happened on Lovers Lane, and with her brother. On ex-Lovers Lane.

Ha. Ha. Ha.

No. I was not ready for that, too soon. I'd just left a man, that after breaking up with him, still helped me load my car. Granted with puppy-dog eyes and long sighs and that jaw-snap, when he'd open his mouth to say something and then close it back tight. Either respecting my boundaries or trying to salvage his pride.

But geez did I know how to mess up a family.

For a moment I paused, imagining such a simple, domestic scene of kids doing homework. Choking back the tears, that Jake and I would never get something so simple. Something most people took for granted.

We were cursed.

"I'm never going to get to learn algebra again," I signed, dropping the suitcases at my feet, where I stood. Most things remained in my car. My worldly goods were tiring of being shuffled around. "Or-re-read Withering heights."

Amy frowned, "That's an odd thing to say. You can always pick up a book, but I don't see how that's relevant here."

"Ignore me."

"Your eyes are red from crying and your hair is stringy and sticking to your cheeks-so, no. And not after that phone call. Jake proposed, and you said *no*?" Only concern, no judgement, was heard in her tone. Good 'ole Amy-all the facts first.

"So much has happened… I think I'm still processing everything. I'm that old printer that's spitting out garbage," I said, brushing the hair from my face. I looked that bad?

"Hold that thought. I'll give you a second to yourself." She held up her palm, gesturing for me to stay put, "I'll be back."

Ten minutes later she came back upstairs with two steaming mugs of tea, Fig Newtons, and we sat against the back of the bed with our legs stretched out in front of us. On the floor, tucked away in a small corner of the world, we hid. In that ten minutes I'd gained a little bit of my composure back, and freshened up in the bathroom. I felt and hopefully looked a little more human. I had to outwardly represent that I'd made the right decision, because the innards wanted to jump right back into that car and say yes.

A life of entrapment. I could do that.

For keeping Jake, I could.

But... While neither of us were the "I wanna have a kid" type, what if we did? Would I have to ask my child to shovel dirt over a dead man's face? Jake once told me it was dirt around the eyes that got him, that he kept waiting for Richard to wake up and brush the muck out. In his dreams he did.

For our future, nonexistent children, I had to say no.

"Thanks for taking me in. I'm sorry if it causes any awkwardness... I promise I'll be out of your hair soon. Look at me," I threw up my arms, "A professional couch surfer. I literally am homeless. All I have is in the back of my car... And in my storage unit. I got one when I moved to the Pitt. I guess I knew I'd make my way back or that Pitt just would not be the place I'd land," I sniffed, "I miss my furniture. And the area rugs. There are a lot of good ones in there."

Amy laughed, "Only a designer would cry about her area rugs."

"But truly. Thank you, I can't thank you enough. I mean you should be out there consoling your brother-not me."

"Maybe later, but you first," she studied me for a second and tucked a strand of hair neatly behind her ears as if she was struck by a bit of shyness, "Marigold, I know everyone sees me as being cold. I... I don't know how to be anything else, or any other way."

I flinched a bit at that. There was truth there.

"But do you remember, after school one day... We were finishing our homework and Dad and Jake were talking? Dad was telling him the school nurse referred me to a doctor. That I was a high-functioning autistic child and that I'd need special help and extra understanding in order to succeed. Which was true, and nice I guess. But then he said the future of the family all rested on him now."

I sucked in a breath, remembering that night. The tears that had gathered in her eyes and the way her hand shook as she tried to draw wobbly little flowers around her math worksheet. Drawing had always been an escape for her.

"You've never treated me differently. That night you finished my homework for me, and let me sit there. You handled it as you handled all problems back then, by telling me men sucked and got us some cookies and Cokes. You'll always have a room in my home. Even if it's because of weird things with Jake. All men suck." She paused, "And trying to spell out 'Marry me' in mozzarella? Good Lord, I'm embarrassed he's my brother. You were right to leave."

I threw myself on her in a big hug, it was the only appropriate response.

"Oh!" she was taken at back but still hugged me.

"I always thought," I pulled back knowing she never liked long hugs, "You didn't pursue helping run the family business because of what happened in Austin. That's why I didn't."

"Partially why. Partially since it was clear Dad would never see me as a full equal to Jake. Jake looked out for me, he said he'd split the business with me 50/50 whenever it was his. But I said no. I was right to… Look who Dad really is? How blind were we? I took your Mom's warning to heart, but not enough, apparently."

"Same."

And I was relived Jake tried to make things right with Amy. He'd always been a loving older brother, even if he didn't fully understand her.

"Thanks for hauling the rest of those boxes out of the house of old stuff. I'm trying to keep John away from everything."

"Oh, of course," I took a sip of tea. Peppermint. Yum. It was soothing. Mellowing out the fact that I had torn my life apart and ran-again.

"I think soon I'll just head my way to Florida. Send for my stuff later."

That was a lie, I wouldn't go to Florida. But keeping Amy safe meant keeping her in the dark.

"Your Mom would like that."

"Mom would love that. Too much."

"And Shelley?"

I raised an eyebrow up at her, "What do you mean?"

"I know you. You sacrifice true love to save my brother. You're not going to leave her out in the cold in a foreign country. You're practically sisters. No way. The data does not add up."

"It doesn't, does it? But it has to look like it. Make sure Paul or anyone he hires doesn't follow me. I'm not too worried about her. I feel like everyone underestimates Shells, goodness, even I did, but she's clever. She's the only one of us able to escape Paul."

"What are you going to do?"

"I'll go visit the city she's in. Start spending from the account she took from. She'll be watching it; if she wants to reunite, then it's up to her. I want to let her know I forgive her. That I understand how trapped she was," I frowned, "Now your turn."

"Excuse me?" she hid her expression in her mug as she drank.

"Amy. I know you're hiding something. I can sense it. You're drumming your fingers on your knees."

The drumming stopped instantly.

"Drat."

"You're pregnant."

I laughed as her mouth formed a surprised "O."

"Amy, you made me get all the heavy boxes. You didn't drink any alcohol when we played you the confession. Peppermint tea? That's for nausea and all you drank last time you were pregnant."

"Well... I... Yes. And here I thought I was all secretive."

I scoffed, "Most telling you let Emma's sister in on our plan. You'd know I'd need help. Help you couldn't provide."

"Seriously, Marigold? Pregnant PI over here," she huffed.

"I'm my parent's daughter," I frowned, "We need to move up the timeline. If Jake lets it known about our broken engagement... I need to be on a highway to the Sunshine State ASAP."

Amy nodded and ran her hand over her flat stomach, "I'll invite Dad and Jake to dinner tomorrow to tell them our grand news. Reservations for 7:30. You know what to do."

I gulped. I did.

There's no rest for the broken-hearted.

Chapter 45

If I ever asked for adventure, well, I didn't mean this.

My hair was tied back into a tight bun and tucked under a black baseball cap. A black T-shirt and grey jeans (I didn't own black jeans and there wasn't time to go by Nordstroms) finished the look: night prowler. Crouched low in Lauren's car, a car we hoped no one would recognize, a silver Infinity, nothing that would stand out around here, we waited. She was equally dressed in black and handed me a mask-just in case.

We figured there wouldn't be any cameras. Why would a guilty man have an extensive camera network? If there wasn't any video feed from Emma's murder, there wouldn't be any feed after. So we parked only one driveway over- a known blackout area. Anywhere else we'd be up against pesky Ring cameras. Lovers Lane was in the nice area of town, it was an old road and a principal thoroughfare loaded with traffic; our car wouldn't be noticed.

"I can't believe we're actually doing this," Lauren said as we watched Paul jump into John and Amy's SUV, "There they go. It's seven-fifteen. We have two hours at the minimum."

They were off to a family dinner at Terra.

I was super jealous of Amy's role. Terra was on the third floor at NorthPark Mall, where I got my Italian food fix. And I could really go for noodles right now. Noodles instead of... this.

Jake would join them. I tried not to think about how that wasn't a table I'd be welcome at. Amy gathered them all with her "I've got a big announcement" Which was conveniently true, if not already guessed. If they had, it definitely helped explain why the dinner was so important and time sensitive.

"We have more than enough time," I said.

Lauren gave a curt nod, "Let's go."

We were operating in total isolation. We could not tell Amy our status, or vice versa, we'd left our phones with Lauren's younger sister in their hotel room. She was our alibi, a girl's night of new friends brought together by loss. It wasn't much of a stretch; I'd hope to keep in contact. I admired their strength. Lauren's sister, Rose, didn't know the whole truth. She didn't know why her sister and her sister's new friends needed alibis, and despite her questioning us, she gave in. Rose was a younger sister who was used to being in the dark. Lauren was trying to step up as the elder and lead. Especially in this time of grief.

Lauren wanted revenge. Something physical to avenge Emma. A body for a body. It took some talking down for her to settle on this plan.

Amy and I wanted to send a message: That he couldn't get away with anything. That justice would be had in some way.

Thus, we were taking away his empire.

By burning the palace down.

I tucked Amy's curling iron in the back of my jeans. By luck she had a new one, never used, a duplicate that lived in the back of a bathroom cabinet.

We scurried up the driveway to the garage, running around to the back door. I had the key from my brief visit. We were in. It was a large three-car garage with a boat. Next to that boat were three red plastic gasoline gallon tanks. There had already been a full one for the boat, I added the others when I came in last time to collect their heirlooms.

I shivered.

One gallon for upstairs.

One for downstairs.

One for the garage.

"Okay," Lauren whispered as we crouched by the tanks.

Being near real gasoline made our plan suddenly seem really dangerous. But we thought it through. We thought through every dangerous scenario and planned for it.

That was enough.

I gulped and wiped my brow, and smiled, pretending not to be nervous. Suddenly wishing we practiced somewhere, in a field with a small shed.

"Safety check. Goggles for smoke," I said as I pulled out goggles from my messenger bag. We both slid them around our faces "And masks and gloves."

We suited up.

"Okay," she said again, "Let's go over the plan."

I nodded, "Okay. Together we gasoline the first level of the garage. I'll then go upstairs in the main house. Plug in the curling iron.

Turn it on. And then pour the gas all over the floor. I'll meet you at the back stairwell. By then you'll have only done the front part of the first level. You'll light the candle in the living room on the coffee table. Only do the back half once I'm downstairs. No gas in the kitchen. Too explosive."

The plan counted on the fumes from the gasoline getting to that candle, giving us an anxious ten minutes to get out. More time than needed.

"Roger. We'll run out the back patio, leave the gasoline jugs by the grill and run to the car."

We had a couple of gallons of water in the car to douse ourselves with if needed, if any of the gasoline got on us.

Lauren produced two lighters and two candles. I'd light a candle upstairs, on the bathroom vanity near the curling iron.

She'd light one downstairs.

And then hopefully… a fire.

Amy already did the hard part for us. Paying off the arson investigator to ignore the amount of gasoline at the site and blame the fire on lit candles or a curling iron. A tragic accident. It helped that her husband was a local cop, so she knew everyone in town. Amy was always one step ahead.

"Don't forget, Lauren," I added, "We book it to the car, and we are outta here. No looking back. Amy'll drop him off at home and she'll report in. Got that? By then it should be up in flames."

She frowned, "I know. I feel that's leaving it up to chance. What if it doesn't catch?"

"It's a timber box filled with gas. It'll catch."

"Okay…"

I took a deep breath, wishing she was Amy. I needed her confidence.

This plan was solid and foolproof, right?

I took another deep breath.

Alright.

"Let's burn down a house," I said.

Chapter 46

My brow was already dripping with sweat as I raced up the back stairwell. Not from exertion, but from my conscience. Setting someone's home on fire clearly was not the right thing to do. It was the exact opposite. It was street justice. Intimidation. It wasn't me, and that guilt went from being a thought and condensed into sweat pouring off my forehead.

I could stop at any time.

That was a lie.

I stalled out for a quick second, fiddling with the backs of my two-carat diamond earrings.

The garage was already coated in gasoline. Lauren started the downstairs. If I didn't do my part, the house might not catch fast enough. People might go in and try and stop it. We didn't want anyone to get hurt.

It had to be scorched earth.

I plugged in the curling iron; we'd partially have that blamed for the cause of the fire. Part homage to Emma's curly hair. I dragged a towel towards the device. Hoped that investigators would think that in Paul's grief he never moved or cleaned up her items from the night she died. The curling iron left on, for all those days.

What a tragedy. Truly lucky no one was home.

Paul couldn't deny it, he was the grieving widower.

Ironically, this was Amy's idea. The cleverest of us all. It was her house-it had to be her idea.

But the sweet, cherished memories of her childhood home were tarnished with blood. How could one ever sit in the kitchen again and make Christmas cookies? Eat a Thanksgiving meal in that dining room?

Paul would rebuild, eventually, though it would take time. Time for us all to get our lives in order. Would he come for us in revenge? The safe answer was yes. Which was why tonight I'd jump in my car and drive off into the night.

This was my goodbye, pouring gasoline across Jake's bedroom. Down the hallway to Amy's green sponge panted room. We'd played dolls in there. Shut Jake out, yelling "Girls only!" as he tried to annoy us with wiggling toes under the door.

This was goodbye. There was no coming back for me. Jake was wrong. We couldn't be end game and my heart felt spliced into two. Torching his room gave me no closure. There wasn't any anger this time around between us. Finally. That's how I knew it was the end.

Anger always snapped us back together, something unresolved always pulled us back together like magnets.

I left him Poe.

Hopefully the yappy dog would help in his healing.

Disappearing and starting over. That's how I would heal. No men.

No close friends. I was cursed, death followed me. The curse even had a name: Paul. I would give it nothing to threaten.

I splashed the last bit of gas in the master bedroom.

"For you, Scott. You're not forgotten."

Giving the upstairs a last look, I headed down, letting the empty can trickle drops on the stairs.

"For you Emma," I said, as I reached the first floor and peeked into the kitchen, where I heard rustling, "You finished, Lauren? We need to get out of here."

We really did. With the N95 mask, my nostrils were already feeling the sting of gasoline. I'd been on again and off again holding my breath, pretending that helped me inhale fewer fumes.

She stood in the center of the kitchen, as the island, running her fingers along the cool granite, "She's really gone," Lauren said, her eyes hazy with tears, "I keep thinking she's going to walk through the door and laugh and be like 'just hiding. I'm here. I'm alive.' What... a... joke."

"Lauren," I said from the hall, "This place is about to blow, there's a candle down here surrounded by gasoline. We can talk in the car." I was giving her two seconds. I would not go deeper into the house to pull her out.

"If we do this, if I set it on fire, she can't walk through that door."

"Lauren, look at me. She can't come back. We've already done this. The fuse is lit, and we don't know how long we have."

"I... I..."

"Forget this. Get out of here. We don't have time for a freak out."

I had one last thing to do. From my messenger bag I pulled out that bloody denim shirt and set it on top of the dirty laundry pile. We were done. Yes, I had taken pictures, but nobody wanted to hold on to proper evidence. It was too risky, so it came back home, left to whatever fate it'd receive. Frankly, it felt like a ton of rocks being unloaded from my bag.

And I must have been lightheaded because I took a deep breath... and ran to the kitchen, linked an arm through Lauren's and ran us down the hall and outside. We dropped the gasoline jugs by the grill, ripped off our masks, and flew to the car.

Gasoline burned my fingertips and my nostrils, and I felt like my head was being hit by a hammer... but we made it. We were safe. I rinsed myself off with our water reserves and she took hers, but the jug held loosely in her hand.

"You saved me."

"No one else gets to die in that kitchen."

"I freaked out," she said coming to and rinsing herself, "That's not something I do. I don't freak out."

"It was your sister. I get it."

We shouldn't have asked her to help. That was on us. It should have been Amy or Jake. Or I should have done it alone.

"But I could have gotten you killed, too. Not just me. I can't believe..."

"I'm driving, get in," I said, still in mission mode, "We need to leave."

"Yes, yes, of course. I'm still blabbing..." At least she'd doused herself while talking.

Before her bottom hit the seat and the door fully closed, I'd eased us out of our parking spot. Driving with one hand, drinking some water with the other, I pulled us onto Lovers Lane, pretending everything was normal. It wasn't normal, and it wasn't okay. But it was over. And that was worth something.

"Thank you, for… for everything," Lauren said between her own gulps of water.

Despite our rinsing, all I could smell was gasoline.

I laughed, "Bryant Home Burning Services, ten out of ten."

It wasn't funny.

Yet she laughed. I didn't stop laughing, and soon we were hysterical, racing down I-75, eyes watering.

"So-so," her voice was breathy from laughing, but she was trying to calm and be serious, "What if they get home and it's not, you know… And they go into the kitchen and stood where I was?"

"Amy's taking Jake home first, and if it's not aflame, then she'll make an excuse that she forgot something at his place," I squinted at her, "I thought you didn't care? I thought in fact you wanted to kill him."

"Abstractly! I don't think I could murder anyone. Or hurt anyone. I'd freeze. Like I did," she scoffed, "I spent my whole life cultivating this cold, stoic persona. Ha. It's clearly an act."

"That's a good thing, Lauren," I said, "Lean into your Emma-like side. Your sister's going to need that."

She nodded thoughtfully, "What about you? After today? Do you think you could kill anyone?"

"No. This was different," I said, but my heart thumped. I'm not sure I believed myself. How death seemed to follow me. It seemed like one day I'd have to be strong enough to kill in self-defense. I think I could. Hoped I could. Better than me being the victim.

I kept those thoughts to myself. We spent the rest of the drive in silence.

At their hotel we said goodbye, I reminded them to get out of town, and we promised to stay in touch. We would, for a bit, but then our efforts would fade because we all had to move on.

"Thank you," Lauren said again, hugging me, "Thank you for getting me out of that kitchen."

"We'll do better next time," I waved and jumped in my car, grateful it didn't smell of gasoline.

Chapter 47

They were right; criminals always return to the scene of crime. An unworldly pull I could not resist tugged at me, possessed my car, and had me pull in a few homes down. It was risky, but I was still in black, and my sneakered feet crept closer. I hid in the low-rise bushes in the yard of the Smithe-Owen home. Their house was always dark and shadowed, an under-lit Tudor that made my trespassing a cinch. The Smithe-Owens spent their summers in Boston, so no one would look out their window and see me crouching between the leaves, blending in with the branches.

I should have gone home and showered and left town immediately; that was all still on the docket, but one thing was left. Tasting victory. Hearing from Amy how it went was too distant; her plan was to send a vague text when it was over.

Vagueness wouldn't work for me. Not now.

Not after his threats. After him trying to control me.

Forcing me to break up with the man I loved in order to be free.

This wasn't simply about revenge for Emma and Scott and Shelley anymore. This was about taking back my life, too. Nothing could bring back Emma. No revenge or jail stay could bring her back. But maybe we could make sure it wouldn't happen again.

Some sort of justice could be had.

I wanted to witness his pain. After he betrayed all our trust, I didn't feel guilty for the thought. There were times for forgiveness, and this was not it.

I had to get out of Dallas before this became who I was. This could only be a temporary switch flicked on. Once I got out, I'd be myself again. Everything that happened within the 635 loop would remain in the past. Another event to never be spoken of; boxed away and taped up. Till then, I'd crouch in the bushes, my eyes fixed on that three-story colonial home.

My breath hitched as something yellow bloomed from behind the windows. Bright and beautiful and Marigold in color, flames danced across the first floor. Traveling room to room. Licking up the walls and swallowing the ceilings. Busting out the windows and climbing like a vine up towards the second floor.

I could hear it now. Crackling and popping.

The chatter of people, coming out onto their front patios and running inside to call for help. Soon the fire department and the cops would arrive.

But I never knew my exit cue.

The white Land Rover arrived. Right on time. To see flames kiss the roof and embrace those dormer windows.

Paul and Jake jumped from the car. They ran to edge of the drive and stood in horror, hands in their hair and waving around. A heated discussion. I wished I could hear it. Jake ran back to Amy and the car.

Paul though, he stayed behind. On that edge of the drive. Watching. Bending over to his knees and sucking in air. Shaking his head. He stood, and spun around in a circle looking for answers, but there were none. Only the crackling of the flames answered him back. Defeated, he sunk to his knees in the grass, hands over his face, shoulders shaking. Crying.

And it was done.

I felt oddly at peace.

Time for that shower and getting out of town. The fire department would be here soon.

Once I got back in my car, I checked my messages (it was so relieving to not have a hundred missed breathy messages).

One text from Amy: **Dinner was great, but I'll call later. You won't believe it. Jake and Dad are with me, everyone is okay.**

I texted back: **?? Hope everything is ok.**

Lights off, I retreated.

Chapter 48

"Are you mad? Are you a raving lunatic who doesn't care about your own life? Are you absolutely insane?"

Jakes' words started spewing the second he slammed his car door shut and started stalking toward me.

He knew. Amy must have clued him in. Of course, she would, I only hoped the download would have happened once I'd hit freeway.

I'd manage to jump in the shower, take a shot of whisky, and drag my luggage and road trip snacks into the car before he got to Amy's driveway. Unfortunately, I'd taken a long soak under all that hot water and did not have time to drive off into the sunset. We'd already broken up and essentially said our goodbyes, I didn't know why he had to come here and make things harder. He could have simply called and yelled at me for burning down his family's house. It didn't have to be an in-person thing.

Okay, maybe it did.

I kicked myself for not getting out of town sooner, but I really did have to go back. I couldn't let Amy have all the fun of watching it unfold.

"The neighbors," I hissed, "Don't bother them."

"Mmm, right. I won't," and he stopped right in front of me, toe to toe. "Are you insane?" his voice dropped to a whisper, "You could have been hurt, Marigold. Killed."

That took a moment to register. He wasn't worried about the house. He was worried about me. After I'd broken his heart, ran away, and then burned down his house. The only last item on the crazy-girl checklist was keying his car and smashing the windshield in with a golf club.

"I… I burned down your childhood home," I stuttered, not making sense on why he was wrapping me into a hug. This was not a normal response to something like that.

"Did no one tell you growing up that playing with fire was dangerous? Marigold, why didn't you tell me? You did not need to be the one to…" his voice caught, "I'm supposed to be the one to protect you and… it was a fireball. I don't think a thing could be left," he pulled away, "Please, never do something like that again. If you feel you ever have to, come to me first. You were so lucky."

A fireball, huh?

"Geez," he took another step back, gripping at his hair, "And you're smirking! I don't believe this!"

I mean, that was my first fire, and a very amateur operation.

We'd succeeded.

Yeah, I deserved that smirk. I was a powerful force to be reckoned with.

Who knew?

"I'm not sorry about what we did, Jake. I am sorry that it affected you. Destroying something so important. I am sorry for hurting you like that. You don't deserve it. That's why we got all the sentimental and valuable items out of the house first. I've been sneaking them out. Amy knows where everything is. You've lost less than you think. That house meant a lot to me, too. There were a lot of good memories."

He shook his head, "No," and took my hands in his, "You're not understanding. I care about *you*. Not the house. If I had been there, I'd have helped you light the match." He squeezed my hand, "You did the right thing. Take out the lair. Shrivel his confidence. If we're a team, he knows he's not untouchable."

"Exactly!" I bounced on my feet, so relieved he wasn't furious at me. So relieved he wasn't yelling and filled with hate for what we'd done. That he didn't think any less of me.

"Amy told me," his voice went lower, more serious, and he swung our hands down, "What Paul threatened if you didn't marry me," his face looked pained, "I'm so sorry, the position my father put you in. You were right to leave. Marigold, you're bright, crazy, brave… Get out of here. You deserve so much more." At that he let my hands drop.

And that didn't feel quite right.

The world felt better when we were joined. A team.

"Jake," my words collided into my throat, making them hard for me to get out, "I ended it for you… So that you'd never feel trapped. I want us to be a choice that we both freely make. Paul getting involved it… it crushed us somehow; it made our love *his*. Running away is the only way to be free."

"It would never be a trap with you. I love you, Marigold Bryant."

I wanted that to be true. Seeing him again brought back all the pain of leaving him. Now that we had gotten a smidgen of justice, Paul's grip on me lessened. My plans for the future weren't only wrapped in fear. Watching flames destroy everything he cherished brought a wicked smile to my lips. In those embers came our freedom. With the house, all his plans were destroyed. Even after he re-built, Paul would never be the same, because he'd know that were consequences. That we were watching.

"Then ask me. Ask me again."

Jake didn't need a single moment to think, dropping to his knee and looking up at me, he asked, "Marigold, will you marry me?"

I didn't need a moment either, "Yes!" I tried to say it regularly, but it came out as a cry between a gulp and tears.

He kissed my ring finger as he stood, "A kiss till we pick you out a ring," a new ring, and swallowed me up in a hug.

"You think mighty highly of your kisses," I joked through my tears.

"Well I don't give them out to just anyone."

"Well, now, I've got a question for you," I whispered into his ear.

"Mmm? What's that?" his response tickled the nape of my neck.

"Come away with me." It was more a statement than a question. It was the only way this could work. Disappearing into the night.

"My luggage is in the car," he answered.

"What?" I pulled back, enjoying his laughter, "That was pretty optimistic of you."

Jake shrugged and kissed my ring finger again, "You and me, baby, we were always endgame."

I clapped him on the chest, a sarcastic remark on my tongue, but I swallowed it back when I saw Poe's little face sticking out the car window.

"Oh. Yeah. Poe. I'll leave him in the Kennel in the backyard for

Amy. Her kids will love us."

"She will hate us."

Jake gave me a wicked smile, "All for the better," and then sobered, "Now... If you would give Poe and I a moment? I have to explain I'll be back to visit."

Dog separation anxiety was overriding my engagement.

Yup. This felt right for us.

Once we got our luggage loaded, my little BMW packed tight.

We took a detour on the way out of town.

One last drive through Lovers Lane. Past the large, stately homes and honeysuckle bushes and canopied trees. Past the drives we road our bicycles up and down. Past the embers of one formerly large colonial style home. Grey and charred, like a skeleton waving goodbye.

We didn't slow.

"So... Where to?" Jake asked.

I turned up the radio, smiling at my fiancé.

We were endgame, as he said all along.

"KTX5 Oldies! It's a sweaty 101 degrees outside in Dallas today, so let us play you some-hot-hot-hits."

And answered him.

Not even Amy knew.

Nobody needed to know.

1227

1225

1223

1221

...

Epilogue #1

From: Amysnail@gmailer.com

To: MGoldigger@gmailer.com

Dear Marigold,

Are you supposed to address emails with Dear?

Anyways, things are pretty hot here. Can you believe the entire house burned down? It's crazy sad. I think I embarrassed Dad when I told the Fire Marshall that he left the curling iron plugged in and the candles going, just as his late wife had, to remember her. The poor widower, it's all so sad. They declared the fire a tragic accident. Dad's getting the help he needs, grief counseling mandated by his doctor.

Life goes on. It's lucky landscaping crews watered all the lawns that morning. All the neighboring houses were safe.

In more happy news, John and I learned we are having a little girl. We are naming her Jasmine! After you, kind of-a flower name.

I hope you guys have a long, fun vacation.

Don't come back! Ha-haha. Of course, come back, we miss you (just not soon, we are Orlando bound.)

Lots of Love,

Amy and Jasmine, John, and the other kids

P.S. Thanks for leaving Poe. He is a delight and has already eaten John's high school ring.

Epilogue #2

Milky Ways. Snickers. Gummy Bears- Haribo and the ones with the little A's on their bellies, all found a new home in my basket.

"Here you go," Jake dropped in his selection, Goldfish, Fritos, and Doritos. I handled the sweet, he got the salt. Our future marriage seemed promising.

"And for drinks..." I wandered towards the cooler, but something caught my eye.

A familiar smiley face looking up at me from a stack of newspapers.

"Dallas Socialite Engaged to English Lord." The headline read.

She would.

"She's marrying her Englishman?" Jake asked, taking the basket from me as he filled it with sodas and waters.

I grabbed a couple of copies of the paper. This was going to be cut out and framed.

"She's engaged to Lord Grey Harrington. That's her friend!" I took a breath, "Shells is okay. This announcement, all the way here, in the papers? I bet she orchestrated this to let us know. Do you think we'll be invited? I bet she did this to let *him* know."

I was practically jumping.

Jake chuckled into my hair as he pulled me tightly into a hug, probably to stop the jumping in public.

"We'll make sure our passports are up to date," he said.

Shelley was okay.

She made it overseas, clearly her plan worked.

A politician's wife.

A royal, titled woman.

Paul couldn't touch her.

I squeezed Jake harder.

I'd get to see my best friend again.

Chapter 49- *Rose*

Rose was blonde. Her hair was freshly colored "Sunny Beach Blonde" and hung down mid-back; she was young, too, just how he liked them. Dressed in a short, red dress, sheer black tights, and ruby red lips, she was dressed to kill.

"It's a lovely house. Mid-century modern is seeing a resurgence. You could easily ask one-hundred thousand more."

"I want it off the market as soon as possible. Please, let's sit," Paul said as he directed his realtor to the couch in the sunken living room. He poured them iced tea from a crystal carafe on the coffee table and sat, leaning back comfortably.

"The furniture's included?" the realtor's eyes traced the lines of the leather couch and Eames Chair in the corner.

"I'm reducing my firm's real estate portfolio. Consolidating. Into one grand piece."

"That's usually the opposite of what I'd advise," Rose took a sip of her iced tea, "But okay. I'm looking forward to the commission."

"There's been a lot of corporate re-shuffling. Jameson Law needs a new headquarters."

"You mentioned on the phone the title's in Jameson and Bryant Law LTD's name."

"Will that cause a problem?"

"Not in the least."

"Good," he winked.

A normal woman would have shivered at his lecherous smile. But Rose wasn't normal, at least not today. She wasn't a realtor either. But her business card with the puffy haired glamour shot, and strand of pearls around her neck, made her convincing. It was so nice his regular server, Kevin, was willing to pass along her only business card.

Rose knew he'd call.

She'd expected he'd only be selling the lot on Lovers Lane, but as pleasant surprises went, a meeting at a house in the M-streets made for a lot more privacy.

Instead of acting on her repulsion, she leaned in. Tickled his leg with her stiletto. Making his brain drain of blood, enjoy playing with her prey. See, his house burning down wasn't enough. Rose knew he'd move on and build somewhere else, something grander and intimidating with extra security.

Rose never believed Violet killed her sister. That was too easy.

She even went to the police to tell them to keep investigating Paul, but no one listened. He probably paid off the whole department. She was told that to convict a man like Paul, they'd have to have overwhelming evidence and a written confession.

After which, Rose admittedly had given up, defeated and instead shifted into trying to focus on her own healing. That was until Lauren came back to the hotel that night, shaking and reeking of gasoline. As Rose poured her a lavender bath and a glass of whiskey, Lauren told her about the plan she'd participated in. How she froze in the kitchen and could have died herself. She'd known Lauren was up to something, but she was too trapped in her own grief and failure to care. Lauren had always been the strong one, and she'd failed her sister by not checking in on her. Rose failed both her sisters.

It also grated on her nerves that they'd kept her in the dark. Did they think that she was weak?

Rose tucked her black clutch in her lap and unclicked the clasp.

She knew Lauren was only being protective. Now it was her turn. Burning his house down wasn't enough. Not for Emma, or for (almost) Lauren.

"You're a lovely woman, Rose. I recognize you from somewhere."

"My advertisements have been working."

"No. From somewhere else. I can't place it."

She smiled, big, white teeth flashing.

From your wife's funeral, you fool. Rose thought of the video from Paul's mistress that Lauren showed her.

Her blood boiled.

That was her sister.

"And the land as well, we'll be selling that, too?"

He nodded, still trying to place her.

"There's been too much death on Lovers Lane," and then that flicker of recognition. Anger tightened the lines across his face; he'd been had.

It was time.

Paul's face reddened as he sat up… That veiny thing in the forehead bulged, "Why you little-"

That was her cue.

Sure, true, and confident, Rose pulled her gun from the clutch and shot him through the heart.

Her aim was true. Her draw faster than a twitch of an eyebrow.

An instantaneous death.

He wasn't the mythic monster they'd made him to be.

Just a mortal man.

Slipping on gloves she removed his wallet, took the cash, his gold ring on his finger, and more importantly, her business card. She threw the empty wallet down onto his chest.

"Oh no, Paul, look, you're bleeding," She mocked, "Should get that looked at."

Rose put her tea glass in the clutch, to be smashed and disposed of at home,

Surprisingly still calm, Rose took a deep breath, plopped on her sunglasses, and slid out the back door. The house had a lovely backyard to disappear into.

The End.

ABOUT THE AUTHOR

Crystal Gore is a Lake Jackson native that found herself settling in Dallas, Texas. She has a mission to set stories somewhere other than New York City. Given her last name, she feels even though being a romance writer would be fun, thrillers and mysteries are her calling. Check out: Amazon.com: Crystal Allison Gore: books, biography, latest update for other novels.

Made in the USA
Columbia, SC
11 February 2023